The Conjurer's Riddle

The Conjurer's Riddle

Andrea Cremer

PHILOMEL BOOKS
An Imprint of Penguin Group (USA)

PHILOMEL BOOKS

Published by the Penguin Group
Penguin Group (USA) LLC
375 Hudson Street
New York, NY 10014

USA | Canada | UK | Ireland | Australia | New Zealand | India | South Africa | China
penguin.com   A Penguin Random House Company

Library of Congress Cataloging-in-Publication Data
Cremer, Andrea R.
The conjurer's riddle / Andrea Cremer.   pages cm.—(The inventor's secret ; 2)
[1. Science fiction. 2. Government, Resistance to—Fiction. 3. Voyages and
travels—Fiction. 4. Refugees—Fiction. 5. New Orleans (La.)—History—19th
century—Fiction.] I. Title.
PZ7.C86385Con 2015   [Fic]—dc23   2015000377

Printed in the United States of America.
ISBN 978-0-399-16424-8
1 3 5 7 9 10 8 6 4 2
Edited by Jill Santopolo.   Design by Semadar Megged.
Text set in 11.75-point Sabon MT Std.

In honor of Harriette Pine and Charles J. Olsen III

British
Territory

Disputed
Weste
Territory

Mexican
Territor

Pacific
Ocean

Indian
Territory

Mississippi
Trade
Zone

Amherst Province

Cornwallis Province

Atlantic
Ocean

French
Territory

Arnold Province

Spanish Territory

Disputed British / French
Caribbean

This is the patent age of new inventions
For killing bodies and for saving souls.
All propagated with the best intentions.

Canto I of *Don Juan*, Lord Byron

1.

THE SUN RETREATED at the approach of dusk, but the dimming light did nothing to obscure the thick plumes of smoke that rose unceasing in the distance. Charlotte couldn't see the flames, but her mind found it far too easy to conjure images of fire consuming all that had been her home. Even if the Catacombs hadn't been completely destroyed, oily clouds so dense and unrelenting signaled devastation beyond recovery.

Every step Charlotte took was hard-won. As her small troupe of exiles retreated deeper into the thick forest, her party enclosed by trees, Charlotte wondered if she'd made the right decision. Linnet had offered refuge courtesy of the abundant resources of Lord Ott. If they'd stayed on the *Aphrodite*, they wouldn't have been forced to scuttle the

Pisces in the shallows of the river. Ott would have provided shelter and food while they strategized the wisest course.

But in making those choices, Charlotte would have acted under the assumption that Birch and the young children in the Catacombs were lost. Returning to the Floating City meant abandoning any hope that her friends had survived. Tantamount to those assumptions was that forsaking the Catacombs required Charlotte to reject the carefully structured plans of escape in the instance of a catastrophe. Plans that her brother, Ashley, had required Charlotte to study each day until she could, without error, recite each exit from the caverns and route to the rendezvous point.

Charlotte recalled her meticulous studies with a brief, rueful smile. However prepared she had been to execute this plan in the moment of crisis, her knowledge didn't make traversing the rugged ground along Esopus Creek any easier. The waterway offered a helpful guide, for which Charlotte was grateful given the density of the woodlands, but she knew the farther westward they progressed, the more difficult travel would become.

Remaining on the *Aphrodite* might have been the easier choice, but Charlotte had to see this commitment through—just as Ash would have. And now Charlotte headed up an odd quartet—Pip, the tinker's apprentice and the youngest of their troupe, Scoff, sometime alchemist and proprietor of an unpredictable apothecary, and finally Grave, who was perhaps the strangest of them all.

Glancing over her shoulder, Charlotte made brief eye

contact with Grave. The lantern light made his tawny irises flare. The skin of her arms prickled at the other-worldly sight, but when Grave returned Charlotte's gaze with a slight smile his alterity diminished and all felt right again. Unusual as Grave could be, Charlotte had grown fond of him, trusted him.

Only a short time ago, Charlotte had encountered him in the New York Wildlands. A boy with no memory, whom they came to call Grave. Much of Grave's past remained in the realm of impossibility as far as Charlotte was concerned. She'd had no time to ponder the strange tale an inventor, Hackett Bromley, had spun for them. He'd spoken of the death of his son leading to blood as iron and to bone as steel—how could that be more than the ranting of a madman? Charlotte had only begun to accept Meg's insistence that an unseen world existed beyond that which Charlotte knew, and that Meg—like her mother—could commune with these elusive spirits.

Charlotte's mind could have been lost for hours con-templating the bizarre path that Grave's life, and pur-ported death, had set her upon. But her thoughts strayed elsewhere, provoking her anger and causing her distress. Secrets beyond Grave's had been discovered in the Floating City. Trust betrayed. Hearts broken.

Slipping her hand into her skirt's pocket, Charlotte traced the paper edge of Jack's letter.

I've ended my engagement.

There had been moments when those words made

Charlotte's pulse quicken with hope. But that sweet possibility was fleeting, soon overtaken by a cold fury. Each day of her adventure in the Floating City had revealed so much of Jack—and too much of the way she was drawn to him. On the airship, he hadn't kissed her, but then at his childhood home, he had. And more.

Tell me the truth, Charlotte. Do you love me?

Yes.

No matter how much she wanted to steal that admission back and bury it forever, Charlotte had bared her heart to Jack. In turn, he'd blackened it with his deceit.

Something unseen scuttled across the path ahead of her, low brush rustling as it passed. Charlotte trudged on without hesitation. Any creature of the wilds that posed a threat—bear, wolf—would balk at the size of their group, and Charlotte couldn't afford to waste time worrying over every porcupine or fox that crossed her path. A cool breath of wind caught the hem of her cloak and Charlotte pulled the garment tighter around her body as she gave in to her brooding thoughts.

Jack had ended his engagement, but the awful truth was that he had been betrothed to another. He'd knowingly caught Charlotte's affections in a web of lies. Only Jack's brother, Air Commodore Coe Winter, had the courage to show Charlotte where things truly stood between her and Jack.

Coe's intervention, while revelatory, had thrown Charlotte's mind, and her heart, into confusion rather than clarifying her sense of things. Coe himself added to that muddle of hope and doubt, desire and repugnance. Jack's elder brother had more than suggested he craved an intimate relationship with Charlotte. She simply didn't know if she could banish Jack from her heart, only to make room for Coe.

Charlotte broke from her meandering thoughts when she heard Pip sniffle again.

"Stop it." Charlotte didn't turn around to look at the girl. She smarted at the coldness of her own words, but held fast to her belief in their necessity. They couldn't afford to lose any time. If Pip fell apart, Charlotte worried it would take far too long to convince her to carry on.

Another voice, quiet and soothing and much deeper than Charlotte's, reached her ears. She took some comfort in Scoff's attempt to calm Pip. She'd also taken to glancing back every so often, vigilant of any sign that Scoff might try to dose Pip with one of his concoctions. While Charlotte allowed for the possibility that an elixir held the potential to ease Pip's suffering, the risk that Pip could grow horns or turn blue seemed more likely. Thus, Charlotte's role had become one of surveillance and enforcement. She discovered quickly enough she held no fondness for either.

In the small space of hours that had passed since Charlotte left Linnet to join Pip and Scoff in the *Pisces*, she'd developed sympathy for Ash's often-brusque tone. When she'd thought of herself primarily as Ashley's younger sister, Charlotte had chafed at his sternness and the irritating frequency of his reprimands. Now she understood them more than she liked. With each difficult mile, Charlotte grew more weary, not only from the effort of trudging along this seldom-used, grown-over path through the thick forest, but also because of the constant heightened awareness required to do all she could to give her little troupe safe passage to the rendezvous point.

Every so often, self-pity tried to creep into Charlotte's heart and nestle there, whispering of her faults and all that she lacked compared to Ash's experience and certitude. She chased that fear and despondence away the very moment she began to feel its effects, rendering any emotional encumbrances null with memories of Ashley's charge.

You were made for this, Lottie.

Charlotte could hear Ashley's voice as clearly as if he walked beside her. She could not fail him. Bolstered, she called over her shoulder to Pip and Scoff.

"Courage, poppets. We're nearly there."

Her voice, tinged with cheer, belied the chill in her blood. If they arrived at the meeting point only to find it empty, Charlotte didn't know what her next move would be. The *Pisces* provided minimal supplies—neither Pip nor Scoff had anticipated this journey. Linnet had offered what aid she could, but the four refugees could only carry so much without sacrificing speed in travel due to weighty goods. Charlotte had despaired when she deemed it prudent to abandon Pocky—the gun had never been intended for ranging—but she took some comfort when Linnet promised safekeeping for Charlotte's favorite weapon.

Little time could be spared to wait for the others to appear. Charlotte knew they had food enough to last a few days, but if Rotpots and crowscopes scoured the woods for anyone fleeing the Catacombs, it would be too dangerous to stay in one place for more than a night.

If there still are others who survived that explosion and escaped injury to make it this far. Charlotte shivered at the thought. Other questions, should she think on them too long, would cause much worse than shivers. *What caused the explosion? An accident? An attack?*

Shadows engulfed the last of dusk's murky light, erasing the already muddled boundaries of the path. Charlotte reached into the roomy pocket of her skirt and fished out the torch Linnet had provided. With each turn of the handle's crank, sparks jumped from the fine webbed metal on the interior of the torch's glass-globed head. When the wicks of the beeswax candle within the globe caught fire, Charlotte stopped cranking. The torch offered gentle light, enough to guide her steps, but not so bright as to signal and draw forth enemies.

Pip's snuffling and broken breath no longer accompanied their hushed footfalls. The path rose sharply and despite her impatience, Charlotte forced herself to take more care in her steps. Thick, twisting roots served as poor replacements for true footholds as they climbed to the top of the ridge. When she crested the rise, Charlotte turned to hand off the lantern to Grave, so Scoff could keep his focus on Pip.

Charlotte crouched down and then crawled slowly forward, belly nearly touching the ground. She stopped when she could spy the rocky outcrop below. Now that the lantern was away, Charlotte let her eyes adjust to the lack of light. After a few moments, she could just barely differentiate the mossy gray boulders from the niche they clustered around. She stared at the crevice, watching for any sign of movement. Any glimmer of lantern light. She saw nothing.

Though her stomach tightened like a fist, Charlotte knew hope wasn't lost. If Birch followed protocol, then staying out of sight, staying silent would be his aims. She turned away from the ridge's edge and crawled to her companions.

Pip and Scoff looked at her, tight-lipped but silent. Grave's face didn't reveal any emotion, but he stayed quiet like the others.

"We can go down," Charlotte told them. "It looks safe enough."

"The others?" Pip whispered.

Charlotte reached out and squeezed the girl's fingers. "I don't know yet."

Pip swallowed hard, but she nodded.

"Shutter the lantern." Charlotte waited until all three of them were again cloaked in darkness. "We'll descend along the western slope. Move slowly and with great care; it will be difficult to make out loose stones and uneven ground."

Moving along the lip of the ridge in a crouch so she

could see as much of the ground's features as possible, Charlotte led the way to the far side of the rise that lay above the clustered, overgrown boulders. The western slope proved more forgiving than the steep climb they'd made from the eastward approach, and they made it to the bottom with nary an incident.

"Wait here." Charlotte motioned for the others to tuck themselves behind the first stone they reached. "I'll whistle for you if all is well. If not . . ."

"We know," Scoff told her. "We'll run."

"You too." Charlotte faced Grave. "Stay with them. Keep them safe."

"I will," Grave answered.

"Good." Charlotte's blood rushed through her veins as she crept forward. She kept her back against the rough stone, dagger held low and ready.

Charlotte closed on the hollow, edging along the rock as it began to curve inward. She stopped, mouth dry and breath making her chest rise and fall too quickly. She listened, but couldn't hear anything beyond her own thumping heart . . . except . . .

A soft scrabbling sound came from above and over Charlotte's left shoulder. Very slowly, she turned and set her eyes high on the boulder face. Something small was coming toward her, crawling along the rock. Charlotte had to hold her breath so she wouldn't scream as the thing came closer, its claws clicking and scratching as it moved. What had been a featureless blob began to take form. Large ears compared to a small head and body, and very long limbs. It was very near now; Charlotte could hear metal scuff on stone when its limbs dragged across the boulder's surface.

The scream building in Charlotte's throat died away, to be replaced by a tremulous hope.

Looking at the little beast, which had stopped and seemed to be waiting, Charlotte dared to whisper. "Moses?"

The creature tilted its small head before launching from the boulder into the air above her. The rapid beating of its wings stirred her hair as it sailed past and disappeared into the niche.

Charlotte wrestled with the impulse to give chase. Knowing how reckless such an action could prove, she continued forward at the same, agonizingly slow, pace until new sounds brought her to a halt. Quiet footfalls stopped on the other side of the massive rock that framed one side of the hollow.

"Charlotte?"

A dizzying wave of relief made her rock back on her heels when she recognized Birch's voice.

"Charlotte, is that you?"

"Yes." Charlotte's answer came out as a croak, even as she sheathed her dagger.

Birch's head and shoulders peeked from behind the rock. Moses crawled up the front of Birch's shirt and into its front pocket.

"Merciful Athene." Birch stumbled out of the niche and

took Charlotte's hands, gripping them tightly. "I didn't know if you'd come. There was no way for me to get word to you. To tell you what happened."

A dozen questions wanted to roll off Charlotte's tongue, but there were other things to attend to first. She summoned her trio of companions with a low bird whistle. When Pip saw Birch she ran forward, arms flailing. Moses scrambled onto Birch's shoulder just in time to avoid Pip's crushing hug.

"*Mawligh nunf gubba doo*" came out between Pip's sobs and unintentional mouthfuls of Birch's shirt. "*Tirgle onay pucklegin.*"

Birch patted her green hair and smiled.

Scoff hooked his thumbs through his suspenders, giving Birch a nod. "Good to see you, mate."

Though he sounded calm enough, Charlotte noticed Scoff's muscles quivering. While he'd been consoling Pip, he'd buried his own anxieties. Only now did Charlotte realize how distressed Scoff had been.

Charlotte stepped aside in surprise when Moses took off from Birch's shoulder to swoop at her. But the bat flew past her to settle on Grave's folded arms. He'd approached so quietly Charlotte hadn't even noticed him standing mere inches behind her, and it caused an unsettling hitch in her breath.

"What happened? The Catacombs—" Pip had surfaced and now peered at Birch with wide, glistening eyes.

"It—" Birch started, but Charlotte stopped him.

"Not here." She pointed to the niche. "Out of sight. Quickly."

Birch startled at Charlotte's abrupt tone, but when Scoff and Pip hurried into the nook without pause, Birch fell into line behind them.

"Are you happy?" Grave asked Charlotte, as they walked into the dark opening. Moses had crawled up his head to nestle in his hair.

Charlotte hadn't grown completely accustomed to Grave's odd questions, but they no longer surprised her.

"Yes." She bent her head to the side to work out the crick in her neck. "They could have been hurt. Or worse."

Without prompting, Grave raised the lantern's shutters. "But we're not safe." He said it like an answer to a question she hadn't asked.

Charlotte stopped to look at him. Though the bat in his hair made Grave look a bit ridiculous, his expression and bearing were otherwise solemn.

"I would like to make you safe."

For the second time in a handful of minutes, Charlotte found herself uneasy with regard to Grave. She wasn't afraid of him; she'd never been afraid of the strange boy. Nothing about Grave exuded malice or aggression. But she'd had only glimpses of who or what Grave truly was.

His wasn't any empty declaration. If anyone could keep Charlotte—maybe all of them—safe, it was Grave. He had strength and resilience like no one else.

He can't be killed.

What troubled Charlotte about Grave was her own inde-
cisiveness about his place among them. She didn't object to
his providing defense, but Grave could do more than that.

He's the perfect weapon.

Charlotte's skin prickled with awareness. Grave had
followed her, even before Ash named her leader of their
band of exiles. The dead boy, now alive by mechanics—
and magic, if Meg spoke the truth—swore allegiance to
Charlotte.

And she didn't know what to do with him. When Charlotte expected to return to the Catacombs, her assumption
had been that all of them would fall into a routine not
unlike those they'd followed before the revelations of the
Floating City. The Catacombs would provide safety and
sustenance while she waited for news from Ash . . . and
Jack.

Charlotte winced as Jack's face flashed through her
mind's eye.

"Is that wrong?" Grave asked, frowning at her pained
expression.

"No." She shook her head. "Not at all. Thank you.
We'll talk more about this later."

Grave nodded and handed Charlotte the lantern
when she held out her hand and hooked a finger toward it.

While the half-moon of boulders protected only a hollow in the earth, the back of the hollow gave entrance to

a spacious cave. It wasn't a maze of caverns like the Catacombs, just a single sphere carved from earth and stone. The cave offered room enough for two dozen people to shelter comfortably. Thus, there was no need for the children to be clustered tight together against the far wall. Yet they were. A dozen wretched little creatures hiding in the wilds.

More disturbing than their huddled, shivering bodies was their utter silence. They'd been told how important staying quiet was, that their lives depended on it.

Birch had gone to the little cluster, and a few heads turned toward the new arrivals. Charlotte took in their wide eyes and gasps. One girl gave a joyful shout, then clapped her hands over her mouth in horror and looked as though she'd soon cry.

Recognizing the butter-hued curls of the child, Charlotte went to the girl kneeling beside her. "No worries, Lucy. You've done nothing wrong."

Lucy murmured through her hands. "We're not supposed to be loud. They'll come for us if we're loud."

"It is important to be quiet," Charlotte replied. "But there's no need to make yourself so upset over it."

Lucy's eyes became hopeful and she peered past Charlotte toward the cave entrance. "Where's Meg?"

The question pinched at Charlotte's heart. "Meg has her own task to attend to. She's not with us."

"But she's safe?" Lucy's eyes were tearing up again.

"Yes." Charlotte had no idea if Meg's safety could be

guaranteed in the Floating City—not even in the Temple of Athene—but Lucy didn't need to know any of that.

Charlotte patted Lucy's cheek and stood up when Birch came toward them.

"We should talk," Charlotte said to him, lowering her voice. "But away from the children."

Birch nodded, glancing at the little ones who now crowded around Scoff and Pip.

Charlotte frowned at the pair. "They're going to want to know, too."

"I'm sure," Birch said. "But the young ones get anxious if I stray too far. They need the reassurance that someone watches over them. It's been a trying journey, to say the least."

"If you don't mind telling your tale twice—" Charlotte began, but Grave surprised her by interrupting.

"I can sit with the children."

Charlotte's first instinct was to laugh, but she caught the bubbling sound before it could leave her throat.

Birch frowned at Grave. "Are you sure . . . is that a good idea?" He looked at Charlotte as he finished the question.

"I will keep them safe," Grave answered him. "I don't need to know about the explosion right now. Charlotte can tell me later."

Without waiting for their assent, Grave waded into the cluster of children and sat among them.

At first the little girls and boys shied away, surprised by Grave's sudden appearance. But as Grave continued to sit very still, smiling at them all the while, the braver of the bunch ventured toward him. Wary of the children's investigation, Moses abandoned his roost in Grave's hair and flew back to Birch, settling on the tinker's shoulder.

"You came back with Charlotte and it made Ashley mad." A boy named Rufus squinted at Grave's thatch of dark hair. "But your hair is different."

"Yes, Charlotte did bring me to your home," Grave answered. "And yes, my hair is different—it didn't have a bat in it before."

A doe-eyed girl called Edith began to giggle. The other children's tinkling laughter soon joined hers.

But Rufus squinted at Grave. "The *color* is different. Why?"

"Because I had to hide."

That answer drew all the children closer.

"Why'd you have to hide?" Rufus pressed. While most of his peers had dropped to sitting positions, Rufus remained upright and wary.

Grave hunched down and whispered to the closest children.

"What?" Rufus frowned, but when Grave didn't acknowledge his question, Rufus abandoned the role of skeptic and joined the others sitting around him.

"That's . . . odd." Birch looked to Charlotte for reassurance.

All she could do was shrug. "Everything about Grave is odd."

"Does he even like children?" Birch asked, seeming torn between the desire to intervene and relief that someone else held the attention of his recent charges.

"I have no idea," Charlotte said.

"More important," Birch continued, "do you think he's dangerous? Did you learn anything about him in the city?"

Charlotte hesitated. Wasn't she the one who'd always defended Grave? Who insisted he posed no threat to them? But after all she'd witnessed, could she promise Birch that Grave was harmless?

"Of course he's not dangerous." Pip had made her way from among the children and now addressed Birch in an earnest tone. "He saved me on that boat."

"He did . . ." The reluctance in Charlotte's voice made her uncomfortable. Pip spoke the truth. Grave had stopped a sailor from laying hands on Pip, but his sheer power had frightened her. Standing up for Grave when Ashley held the ultimate responsibility for the strange boy's fate gave Charlotte more bravado in her arguments that Grave should remain with them. Now that all of Grave's actions were subject to her guidance, she weighed her response more carefully.

"Yes, he did," Pip continued, smiling brightly. "He's so brave. Grave is brave . . . ha!"

Scoff followed Pip to join their small conference, and caught the green-haired girl's proclamation.

"He seems all right," Scoff said with a nod. "Bloody strong. I'd wager he could swing the hammer of Hephaestus himself!"

Birch still waited for Charlotte's affirmation.

"It should be fine," she said at last, and drew their group apart from Grave and the children.

Now that the right moment had arrived for Birch to share his story, Charlotte couldn't help but burst from her restraint.

"By Athene, Birch, what happened?"

Birch's eyebrow went up at Charlotte's abrupt change in demeanor, but she didn't care.

"Was it the Empire?" Charlotte asked. "How did they find you? How much was lost?"

"It's all gone." Birch grimaced and shoved his hands in the pockets of his apron. "I made sure nothing would be left."

Charlotte knew she must have heard something wrong. "That doesn't make any sense, Birch."

Birch dropped his gaze to the cave floor, kicking at the soil with the tip of his boot. "I had to."

"Had to do what?" Ruffled by Birch's discomfiture, Pip hooked her arm through his elbow and tugged until he looked at her.

"Had to do what?" Pip asked again, faith evident in her open expression as she gazed up at Birch.

Birch smiled at her and then looked at Charlotte.

"I'm the one who blew up the Catacombs."

2.

PIP UNHOOKED HERSELF from Birch's arm and shoved him so hard, he stumbled a few steps away.

"Why would you say something like that?" Pip's fists were on her hips. "It's not funny. How could you think it would be funny?"

Birch stared at the indignant girl, helpless to reply.

Charlotte squared her shoulders, adopting a stoicism she didn't truly feel. "I don't think he's joking, Pip. Am I right, Birch?"

Birch nodded and Pip began to shake her head, stubborn with disbelief.

"Why?" Charlotte's heart banged in her chest, but she managed to retain her calm facade.

"I thought about just blowing the entry points." Birch fidgeted without ceasing, and spoke as though recalling a bad dream. "But there wasn't enough time. The only option was to overload the generator. I knew that would create a blast large enough to collapse the caverns and bury anything we'd left behind."

Pip sat on the ground, drew her knees to chest and hid her face there. Scoff knelt beside her, putting his arm around her narrow shoulders. He looked up at Birch.

"Obviously you had a reason for doing all this," Scoff said. "But it would help a great deal if you'd tell us that reason."

Birch startled at the question. "The reason? Well, the Empire, of course."

"The Empire found the Catacombs?" The words felt brittle as they left Charlotte's mouth. "When? How did you avoid capture?"

"A warning came." Birch frowned, pulling a scrap of paper from his pocket. He handed it to Charlotte.

A brief message had been scrawled on its surface.

They're coming for you. Get out now.

The note was signed *L*.

"I knew it couldn't be a jest," Birch said. "No one would send such a message—no one would know where to send a message—unless they were part of the Resistance.

Whoever sent it knew we could evacuate, given enough time."

Scoff left Pip's side and peered over Charlotte's shoulder.

"Who's *L*?" Scoff asked. Charlotte didn't protest when he grabbed for the note.

"Lazarus," Charlotte said quietly to no one in particular. "It must be."

"Did you say Lazarus?" Birch looked at Charlotte in puzzlement. "Do we know a Lazarus?"

"Not exactly," Charlotte answered. "Ash and Jack met him . . ."

Charlotte words drifted away as she grasped how little she knew about Lazarus. She'd never taken the time to ask Ashley what meeting with the mysterious figure had been like. The night of that meeting, Coe's trickery had demanded all of her attention—that was the most forgiving assessment, the least being that she had allowed her heartache to consume her, neglecting all else.

Nonetheless, the only other *L* in Charlotte's life was Linnet, and she'd been on the *Aphrodite* at the time of the explosion.

"Lazarus is the leader of a rebel faction within the Empire," Charlotte said, pushing her jumble of thoughts aside.

Scoff scratched at the stubble on his chin. "That's an odd name."

"It's not his real name," Charlotte said. "His identity is a secret."

The conversation proved interesting enough for Pip to lift her head. "A secret?"

"He's a high-ranking officer in the Imperial Army." Charlotte mined her memories for anything else she could share about Lazarus. "When the time is right, Lazarus will incite a coup. Then the Resistance will join forces with Lazarus's and seize power."

"Is that all?" Scoff flashed a lopsided smile at Charlotte.

"That's good news if I've ever heard it." Birch rocked back on his bootheels. "And I've been in dire need of good news."

"I think we all have," Charlotte replied. "I wish I could offer more."

Birch shook his head. "A little is better than none. I'm afraid I've done a poor job of supplying this sad expedition."

He turned and pointed at a heap of misshapen sacks near the children. "We had so little time to prepare, no time really, and the small ones could hardly carry a full load of parts."

"Don't fret about it, Birch," Charlotte said. "What matters is that you were able to escape."

"Yes." Birch squeezed the bridge of his nose between his thumb and index finger. "I suppose that's true."

"Absolutely it is," Scoff said, nodding. "But I have to ask—"

"No." Birch sighed as he shoved his hands into the pockets of his scorch-marked leather apron. "I had to prioritize food and weapons. I couldn't retrieve anything from your lab. Even if I had, all those glass vials and jars of powders . . . I doubt we could have transported it without breaking everything along the way."

Scoff shrugged. "Tragic, but I'll make do. Starting over will be an adventure."

He gave one of Pip's pigtails a tug. "Besides, all I need is my trusty assistant. You're up for more experiments, aren't you?"

Pip brightened for the first time since they'd left the *Aphrodite*. "Of course!"

"We'll all be starting over," Birch said. "But there was no helping it."

Charlotte closed her eyes when she felt a hot sting begin to well up. Their home was gone. Not just abandoned, but destroyed. There would be no return to the Catacombs.

"So the question now is where we'll be starting over?" Scoff asked.

Though she tried to fight them back, a few tears slipped down Charlotte's cheeks. "Yes."

"Have you decided where we should go?" Pip asked Charlotte.

Until now, Charlotte's only thought had been to get to the rendezvous point, but there was no denying the urgency of finding an answer to Scoff's question. This cave served its purpose—it had never been intended to offer shelter for more than a night or two.

Charlotte looked at the cluster of small children. One of the youngest had crawled onto Grave's lap and fallen asleep. Grave sat still, a sentinel over his new charges.

"We have to find a place for them to be cared for," Charlotte said. "They won't be able to make the journey with us."

"What journey?" Birch frowned.

"The mandated evacuation route," Charlotte told him. "To New Orleans."

Pip gasped. "We're going to join the Resistance? Holy Hephaestus." Her eyes went wide with excitement.

Pip's enthusiasm had always been a source of amusement, but Charlotte now found the girl's exclamations and unpredictable, careening moods more irksome than gears badly in need of oiling.

She has yet to reach her fourteenth year, Charlotte reminded herself. *She's only acting the way a child grasping at maturity is like to do, swinging from thoughtful to impulsive without warning. She needs patience and kindness, not reprimands.*

"Can we do that?" Scoff asked, sharing none of Pip's enthusiasm.

"It's what we're meant to do in a situation . . . well, exactly the situation we're in." Charlotte welcomed his brusque tone, hoping Scoff's sobriety might be an example to Pip.

"That's a long trip." Birch glanced at the pile of sacks. "Costly, too. I don't know how far bartering that lot will take us."

Looking at the haphazard bulges and swells that constituted their belongings, Charlotte shared Birch's doubts.
She'd never undertaken a journey such as that she'd just
proposed. What it would cost, the specific threats they
could encounter, how they would be received upon reaching New Orleans—of all these things, these pivotal fac-
tors, Charlotte knew little to nothing.

"Trading will take us as far as it can," Charlotte said.
"And then we'll make do. We shouldn't have to use much
until we get to Moirai, in any case."

Her answer satisfied Scoff, but Birch twitched with nervous reluctance.

"Scoff and Pip." Charlotte gestured toward Grave and
the children. "Give them food and water and tell them to
sleep now, because we can only afford to wait here a few
hours."

Birch offered Charlotte a measure of respect by waiting
for Scoff and Pip to leave before he questioned her, though
he was shifting his weight so frequently from one foot to
another that he was almost hopping.

"You want us to travel at night, then?" Birch spoke
in a tone that Charlotte hoped was anxious, rather than
horrified.

"Ash told me to take charge." No sooner had Charlotte
blurted her defense than she recognized such an exclamation undercut her authority.

Fortunately, Birch ignored her misstep, bobbing his

head in affirmation. "And I think he was right to. We can't stay here, obviously. We must go somewhere. But New Orleans is so far."

"It is." Birch's skittishness was understandable. Charlotte reminded herself to be patient with him. He'd led the children here—forced himself to blow up the Catacombs. The amount of stress he'd been under had to have pushed him near the point of breaking. "But traveling at night will decrease the chance we'll be sighted. We have to take the children to a crèche—it's the safest place for them. The allotted site is Moirai. That's where we go first."

"And New Orleans? You think that's where we're most needed?" Birch appeared less frantic. His trust gave Charlotte space to more comfortably occupy her leadership role. She felt a rush of gratitude toward the tinker for giving her an unintentional, but much-needed, boost of confidence.

"Jack and Ash will arrive there at some point," Charlotte answered. It was getting easier to say Jack's name, to remember him without balking. "Probably even beat us there. We can rendezvous with them, take stock, and find out what the Resistance wants us to do—they must have a reason for sending us there in the evacuation protocol. If we stay out here on our own, finding a new place to hide, attempting to eke out an existence like we had in the Catacombs, we'll founder."

Birch nodded. "New Orleans it is."

"But first we take the children to safety," Charlotte replied.

"Jack and Ash had a Dragonfly to get them to New Orleans." Pip said. "How are we going to make it that far?"

An anxious shiver got hold of Charlotte's limbs and she set to giving her arms a vigorous rub to ward it off. Even though she was following a plan that had been established by her elders, the steps involved were still intimidating. "We stow away on one of the Imperial supply trains heading west," Birch cut in.

"That's the plan?" Pip bobbed up and down on the balls of her feet. "Has anyone done it before?"

"Well . . . not as far as I know," Charlotte admitted. "But this is the Resistance evacuation plan for the Catacombs. We have to trust that it's sound."

"Of course we do." Pip dropped back and beamed at Charlotte, who couldn't return the smile. The logistics of stowing away on an Imperial train were overwhelming. It was one thing to plan a covert journey when you planned to keep far away from the enemy, but catching one of the trains put the exiles directly in the Empire's path. Charlotte had to find a way to believe what she'd just told the others: this plan had to be sound.

A minute *click, click, click* sounded as Moses stretched out a wing. Birch reached up and used one finger to gently scratch between the bat's ears.

"Imperial trains headed west leave from the Foundry, offload rubbish at the Heap, then they'll bring goods from the Floating City to Albany before heading west," he said. Moses climbed onto his hand and then took flight, winging a lap around the cave before shooting out into the night.

Birch watched Moses depart and then said, with a hopeful note that verged on desperate, "We could get to Albany. That's where we intercept the trains, isn't it? I read the plan once, but I didn't exactly commit it to memory."

"It is." Charlotte was glad to offer Birch a piece of information he might take comfort in.

"And the boxcars will be empty. I guess that makes sense," Scoff said. "But can we risk going to a city?"

"Albany isn't much of a city," Birch said. "It's more like buildings full of paperwork and the houses of clerks and ministers who create, replicate, and distribute that paperwork for all its official Imperial purposes. But the city itself isn't in play. Since the goods will have been offloaded, security should be lax at the rail yard. And that's where we'll be."

"Think of it as a run to the Heap," Charlotte said, and with a crooked smile added, "without the rats."

"I suppose we don't have much of a choice," Scoff admitted.

Birch uttered a doleful laugh. "Yes. There's that as well." He laid his hand on Charlotte's shoulder. "Now you get a bit of sleep. I'll wake you when it's time to prepare the children for the next leg of this journey—assuming you want us away by midnight."

"Yes." Charlotte put her hand on top of his and gave his fingers a friendly squeeze.

His calm, assured words unknotted tension that had held Charlotte captive and kept her alert. Exhaustion made her body sag and she let herself sink to the cave floor. She removed her cloak and rolled it so she could tuck it beneath her head.

"There should be a blanket we can spare." Birch's voice was already fading as Charlotte's mind retreated from consciousness.

Soon she existed only in a cavern of dreamless sleep.

A poke, poke, poking into the flesh of Charlotte's upper arm woke her into irritability. She opened her eyes and found Pip crouched beside her. The young girl's finger was extended, ready to jab Charlotte again.

"I'm awake." Charlotte batted Pip's hand away.

"Birch says it's time to go," Pip told her, springing up from her crouch. "He and Scoff are waking the children now."

Charlotte nodded, pushing aside the blanket that had been laid upon her while she slept. Pip watched Charlotte shake out her cloak before pulling it over her shoulders.

"I'm supposed to help you," Pip said, explaining her expectant expression.

Looking across to the gaggle of children, all squinting eyes and sagging shoulders, Charlotte said, "Can you find me a length of rope?"

"Of course!" Pip's pigtails bounced as she trotted to the

corner where Grave was sorting and redistributing their supplies between sacks.

Charlotte rolled up the rough wool blanket at her feet and went to join Grave.

"Has Birch put you to work?" Charlotte asked as Grave moved smaller, tied bundles that clicked and *ching*ed as their metal contents were jostled, from disparate locations to a single sack.

Grave canted his head toward the sack receiving his deposits. "I'm moving the heaviest items to this sack. Birch tried to spread them out when they left the Catacombs."

"Of course he did." Charlotte's forehead crinkled at Grave's words. "Why would he tell you to put them all together?"

"Because I can carry the heavy sack," Grave answered, giving no indication as to his feelings about taking on this new burden. "And those carrying the lighter sacks will tire less quickly."

"Oh." Charlotte cast her gaze toward Birch and Scoff, who were coaxing the smallest children to take sips of water and munch bits of bread before their departure.

Grave's assignment created a stew of mixed emotions in Charlotte. She couldn't deny the logic and pragmatism behind Birch's decision. A part of her was even a bit abashed that she'd failed to reach the same conclusion when they'd abandoned the *Pisces*. What had they left behind that Grave might have carried?

Of course Grave had strength beyond any other in their

party, and from all she'd witnessed, she doubted this heavy load would take any kind of toll on him. But admitting that truth didn't alleviate the discomfort Charlotte encountered when dissecting the thought process that would have led to this action. It was a physical sort of unease, like she'd eaten something that was off and might make her sick. Grave's strength and endurance were assets, of course, but Charlotte couldn't embrace the notion of defining him only by those traits, of using him to their advantage. He was a person, not their pack mule.

Charlotte didn't believe that Birch bore any ill will toward Grave. Birch was a gentle, if eccentric, soul with the awkward mannerisms of one more attuned to mechanics and machinery than navigating the shoals of relationships. The tinker had seen a logical purpose for Grave and he'd acted accordingly. She couldn't fault Birch for that.

"Do you mind?" Charlotte asked Grave. "Carrying the extra weight?"

Grave shrugged. "I want to help."

Charlotte pursed her lips, but nodded. In terms of social niceties, Grave could be just as perplexing as Birch, if not more so. She decided to stow away her misgivings at present.

"Here!"

Pip's exclamation made Charlotte lurch back in surprise, but Pip grinned when she held up a coil of rope. "See?"

"Thank you, Pip." Charlotte found Pip's good humor

to be catching, that and in eyeing the rope Charlotte determined it would be long enough for her intended purpose. "Come along."

Leaving Grave to his task, Charlotte and Pip joined Birch, Scoff, and the children.

"I think we're about ready," Birch said. "Some of the smallest ones might have to be carried from time to time."

"We can take turns at that," Charlotte said, thinking but not adding, *We will not make Grave take up this burden as well.*

Grave might not care for the extra assignment, but Charlotte was becoming more and more convinced that treating Grave as one of them—not as someone . . . or something . . . apart—would be essential to their cause. She couldn't quite pinpoint why, only that at any juncture where Grave's differences were emphasized, Charlotte's hackles went up as though she were a beast menaced by some larger predator.

Scoff was looking at Pip. "What's the rope for?"

Pip opened her mouth to answer, but then realized she had none. She looked to Charlotte.

"Too much light will endanger us," Charlotte supplied. "I think we should have no more than two lanterns if we can manage. One at the front and one at the rear, since the narrow game paths make it necessary for our group to move in single file. The rope is for the children to hold on to as we move in so much darkness."

"Would it be even better to have the children tied onto

the rope?" Scoff asked. "In case one of them should let go?"

"I considered that," Charlotte said. "But in the event that something should happen where we need to run, or to scatter, it would be disastrous for the children to be tied to a single line."

"Good point." Fear creased the corners of Scoff's eyes.

"With Athene's mercy, it won't come to that," Charlotte added quietly.

Birch spared Charlotte an enthusiastic bob of his head before his gaze traveled over the children who were huddled close to one another, taking comfort from the only familiar thing they had—each other.

"Athene's mercy indeed," Birch murmured.

3.

THE MARCH THROUGH the forest took three nights, but to Charlotte their time lurching forward in the dark could easily have been weeks. She, Birch, and Scoff each had turns at the head of the group. Even with her lantern throwing a dull gleam against the shadows, forging the way along the game trail proved harrowing and full of unpleasant surprises. Low branches stretched long, thin fingers that caught at Charlotte's hair and scratched her cheeks. Stones and roots sprung up to trip her and bruise her toes. The worst had been when Charlotte walked into a spider's web, invisible in the darkness. The web wrapped around her face in a fine, sticky net. She spluttered and coughed as she rubbed the spider silk from her face and wished with all her might that the spider was off hunting and not crawling along her shoulder. Without looking for fear of letting out a shriek, Charlotte furiously brushed herself from crown of head to tops of boots to be certain she hadn't gained unwelcome passengers.

Though the terrain gave them no quarter, the children managed the journey as well as Charlotte could have hoped for. They moved through the woods with determination, silent and keeping any frights to themselves. Should one of the youngest falter or whimper, whoever walked alongside the line would swoop in and carry the child until he or she was restored enough to fall in with the trudging troupe once more.

A little before dawn put an end to their third night of travel, they'd settled into the cover of a wooded ridge, one of many along hills that sloped down toward Albany. Given its proximity to New York's Floating City, the contrast between the two Imperial hubs was severe. Albany lacked the constant drone and buzz of airships and the bright chittering and squeaks of the trolleys whizzing along rails. Nothing glittered here, nor did anything shine. From Charlotte's vantage point she could see unassuming buildings squatting in an orderly fashion along streets straight and narrow. Albany seemed a sensible and stern place, concerned with its purpose more than its appearance. Persons in miniature moved between the buildings and along the streets, but they were too far off for Charlotte to discern their activities.

Albany's rail yards sat at the southern edge of the city,

hugging the west bank of the Hudson to best facilitate exchange with shipping traffic. At this hour the yards were quiet, but Charlotte wagered they'd come to life with the rising of the sun. The main rail line sat empty, awaiting its next arrival. Finite tracks branched off from the core rails. These short tracks were occupied by silent engines and boxcars, some out of commission, others awaiting repair. The trains stretched along the tracks like slumbering, coal-black snakes. Charlotte regarded the stillness of the yards with unease. She saw no gates, no sentries walking the perimeter. Their access to the rail yard appeared to be unimpeded, in a disconcerting way. She didn't trust the emptiness of the broad swath of land, criss-crossed with ribbons of iron.

So focused was Charlotte's concentration that she jumped in alarm at the multi-toned blare of an approaching train. She tracked the direction of the sound, but the train was still hidden by thick forest. She could make out the trail of smoke puffing up above the tree line as the engine devoured coal and belched hot breath into the sky. In the yards, uniformed figures, unarmed porters ready to offload the cars laden with refined goods from the Floating City, appeared and swarmed toward one of the empty tracks. Retreating from the ridge, Charlotte slipped into the trees and hurried to rejoin the group.

"There's a train approaching," she said, when she reached the others.

Pip, Scoff, and Birch were slightly apart from the rest

of their company. The children had clustered into a heap nearby, most of them already sunken into the sleep of exhaustion. Grave sat beside them, quiet and watchful.

"We heard the whistle," Birch replied. He was crouched down, tightening the laces on his boots. Moses zoomed in from his nightly flight to settle on Birch's shoulder.

"There won't be much time." Birch scooped up the little bat and tucked him into a shirt pocket before he glanced at their charges. "We'll have to rouse them."

Pip wore a plaintive expression. "But they're so tired. Can't we wait just a few more minutes?"

Birch stood up, sparing Pip a reproachful look. "They can sleep on the train. It's a long ride to Moirai."

Pip kicked at the ground, but didn't argue.

Scoff gave her a playful nudge with his elbow. "Come on, girl. Let's round 'em up."

It was obvious that Pip made an effort not to smile, but in the end she did, and looked quite happy to trail after Scoff.

"I've been watching the yards," Charlotte told Scoff. "And I haven't seen any kind of security. No watchmen. Once the workers have emptied the cars, we should have a small window to sneak into the yard and board the trains."

"There are no guards overseeing the workers?" Birch frowned. "That's odd."

"I know." Charlotte had hoped one of the others might allay her fear, but she could admit that such wishfulness was born of frivolity, not prudence.

Reading the worry on Charlotte's face, Birch said, "With luck we'll mostly avoid the yard. If we can find space at the rear of the train, we can avoid getting too close to the center of things."

Charlotte nodded and felt a painful twinge in her neck, a reminder of how all her sleep of late had been on the ground, in caves and hollows. The boxcars weren't likely to be any more comfortable, but at least they'd get a reprieve from all this walking.

Scoff rejoined them. "We're ready—at least as much as we can be." He scratched his mad thatch of blue hair, casting his gaze back at Pip.

She was gesticulating emphatically. Charlotte assumed Pip was attempting to bolster the children's enthusiasm for this last leg of their journey. The children appeared either bleary-eyed or bewildered. Pip began to cluck her tongue, waving the children forward in a cluster like a mother hen rounding up chicks. Grave followed behind, his face unreadable as ever.

"I'd like you to take charge of the group," Charlotte told Birch. "And I'll scout ahead. If there's a clear path to the boxcars I'll retrieve you and we'll make our dash for the train."

"Be careful," Birch said. "And good luck."

Charlotte offered a wan smile, then moved off into the forest. She'd debated whether or not separating herself from the group was the wisest choice. If Charlotte went off on her own, would the others feel abandoned? Was the mark of a leader always remaining close to her followers, tending to their needs, and keeping watch over them?

After a brief discussion, the group resolved that they would all be best served by playing to each other's strengths. Birch rarely left the Catacombs, preferring his workshop to missions outside their shelter. More often than not, he'd had Pip for company, and he'd also been a patient and enthusiastic teacher to any children who demonstrated interest in his contraptions. Charlotte, Jack, and Ash had been the primary scouts for the Catacombs, and Charlotte felt more at ease on her own, detecting risks, and charting paths for others.

As she threaded her way through the hilltop forest, Charlotte fell into a familiar and oddly comforting pattern of solitary reconnaissance. Her weariness sloughed off as her senses heightened. Charlotte crept forward, her boots falling soft and near silent on the forest floor. Her gaze flicked swiftly from one point to the next. In Charlotte's assessment, they shared the ridge with no one other than chirping forest birds and squirrels rustling among tree branches.

When she reached the southern edge of the rise and deemed it safe, Charlotte hurried to collect the others. The long, shrill call of the train whistle was much closer now, and night's shadows retreated from the rose-gold tinge of dawn's approach. Very little time remained before daylight would scuttle their plans.

The train was pulling into Albany's rail yard by the

time they'd gathered at the point from which they'd need to descend. The sight of the roaring machine made Charlotte's jaw clench. An iron lion composed the body of the steam engine. The beast's jaws were agape and its mane flared back. At the rear of the engine the lion's tail curved up, more like to a scorpion than a feline. The cars trailing the engine had no ornamentation whatsoever, and their dull iron shade served to make the lion appear all the more ferocious, as though the beast could come to life at any moment and leap onto the tracks ahead.

The train slowed, coming to a stop alongside the sidetracked cars that occupied the yard. Charlotte's heart thudded in disappointment when the final boxcars passed beyond the forest line near the river. She'd been hoping to use the dense tree cover as much as possible when boarding the train, but the train's length meant they'd have to traverse at least some of the yard, forcing their group to be much more exposed than Charlotte wanted.

"We're less likely to be noticed if we break into small groups," Charlotte told Birch and Scoff. Pip and Grave hung back, keeping watch over the children. "Each of us can take four children at a time. Pip should go along with you, Birch."

"What about Grave?" Scoff asked, his brow creasing just a bit. "Where will he be?"

"I'd like Grave to come with me and the first group of children," Charlotte said. "He can carry the two smallest, so we can move more quickly."

And if there's trouble in the yard, Grave has the best

chance of fighting it off. Charlotte kept that thought to herself.

"All right," Scoff said. "I'll get Pip and we'll separate the children into groups."

When Scoff stepped away, Charlotte looked at Birch. "Be watchful of what happens when Grave and I reach the boxcars. If we're attacked, don't try to save us; just get the other children out of here."

"Are you sure?" Birch frowned.

Charlotte didn't like what she had to say, but knew it was true. "If we're discovered, the plan has failed. Even if you can help us get away, the Empire will know we were here and it will only be a matter of time before they catch up to us. Better to let a few us of be taken than all of us."

Birch sighed, but gave her a nod before he went to join Pip and Scoff. He passed Grave—and the three children trailing their sometime guardian—who was on his way to join Charlotte.

"These two should be carried." Grave gestured to a chub-cheeked girl who clung to Grave's pant leg with one hand while she sucked the thumb of the other. The second was a boy, who, while older than the girl, had a sallow complexion and spindly limbs that gave him the appearance of frailty. The third child to join them was Rufus, who hooked his thumbs through his suspenders and looked up at Charlotte.

"I'm going to help Grave watch over the littlest ones," Rufus said. He brandished a thick branch.

"And I thank you for that," Charlotte answered, as she kept a smile from twitching its way onto her lips. She wondered if she should tell him to leave the makeshift stick sword behind, but could see no real harm in his having it.

A slightly shorter boy with a mad nest of ginger curls stood just behind Rufus, watching the older boy with adoring eyes.

"Jamie, yes?" Charlotte asked. "You're coming with us as well?"

"He's with me," Rufus answered for him. "He's all right."

"Very good, then." Charlotte smiled at Jamie, who returned her cheer with a gap-toothed grin. She was happy to see that despite his admiration for Rufus, Jamie hadn't found it necessary to find his own battle stick.

Turning her attention to Grave, she said, "I'll lead the way. When I stop, you stop. If I tell you to run, run."

Grave nodded and scooped up the small children, holding one in the crook of each of his arms. The thumb-sucking girl tucked her head against Grave's shoulder, ready to fall asleep. The sickly boy hung on to Grave's arm and shivered with fear, illness, or both.

"Rufus, Jamie, stay close to me," Charlotte told him.

Rufus nodded, gripping his makeshift weapon with both hands. "All right, Jamie?"

"All right," Jamie answered.

The path Charlotte chose took them through the brush-covered slope, offering some cover, if not as much as the forest. She angled toward the last cars on the train, but made certain to remain in the line of sight of her companions still up on the ridge. More and more light spilled over the trees. A jolt of nerves quickened Charlotte's pulse, but she knew she could not rush their progress. In her peripheral vision, she caught Rufus stalking beside her, mimicking her every movement.

They'd reached the decommissioned boxcars and Charlotte still saw no evidence of surveillance or guards in the rail yard. Albany wasn't a military hub, so perhaps the Empire considered it a low-risk site, a place that would never be under threat of attack. If that was the case, all the better for her purpose. At the last set of tracks before the supply train, Charlotte stopped. She peeked around the back of one of the sidetracked cars, searching for guards, maintenance workers, anyone who might spot them.

She saw no one.

In the distance she could just make out the silhouette of the lion's head at the front of the train.

"Quickly," Charlotte whispered.

Staying low, they hurried across the gap between the boxcars. When they were tucked alongside the train, Charlotte again waited for any sign they'd been detected.

All was quiet.

"Grave, put the children down and open this door, as slowly and making as little sound as you can manage."

Charlotte gently shushed the little girl, who had mewled

her protest at being woken. The boy was still trembling, but he made no sound.

The metal door groaned as Grave slid it open. When Charlotte was certain he'd created enough space to accommodate their needs, she grabbed his arm.

"That'll do," she said. "Let's get the children on board."

Grave lifted the small girl and boy into the car. Jamie scrambled up after them.

"Sit against the wall and rest." Charlotte offered a reassuring smile. "The others will be here soon."

She was about to tell Rufus to join the other children, but was surprised to find him still standing beside her.

"Go on, Rufus," Charlotte said.

She glanced up the hillside. Birch and Pip had begun their descent with four more children.

"I think I should stand guard with you." Rufus's pronouncement brought her attention back to him.

Sizing up the boy, Charlotte pointed to the edge of the boxcar. "Can you stand guard here? In the doorway? You'll have a better vantage point."

Rufus looked at her, then at the door. "Yes. That's a good idea. I'll stand there."

"Thank you."

As Rufus took up his post, Charlotte stood beside Grave, her attention split between watching Birch and Pip's progress and scanning the rail yard for imminent threats.

She detected the far-off sounds of Albany coming to life with morning's arrival, but in the immediate vicinity they appeared to be alone.

The second group reached the bottom of the slope and began to cross the yard. Scoff and his tiny flock emerged from the forest at the top of the hill.

Something flickered at the corner of Charlotte's vision. She pivoted quickly, pistol drawn and cocked, but found no evidence that anything was amiss. Still, her skin continued to prickle and an anxious surge kept her on guard.

"Stay here," she told Grave.

Slowly, Charlotte moved down the line of boxcars. A small sound reached her ears, the gentle rasp of something soft brushing against metal. She listened hard, watching all the while for the slightest movement.

The shriek of the train whistle nearly shattered her skull.

"Spear of Athene." Charlotte spat out the curse.

"Charlotte!" Birch's sharp whisper beckoned her. "The train will leave in another minute. We have to get everyone into the car."

Still rattled, Charlotte swore again as she began to turn back to her friends. Then she became still as stone.

She saw its eyes before anything else. Eyes that shone despite the shadows beneath the boxcar. Golden eyes. Alert. Cunning. Fixed upon her.

Charlotte's breath became shallow. She was desperate to know if Scoff had reached the train, but she dared not look away from those eyes.

She was being hunted.

Charlotte began to back toward their car.

Well aware that it had been seen, the beast to whom the eyes belonged crept along the ground beneath empty cars on the opposite track, matching Charlotte's every step. Charlotte had her pistol aimed at the stalker, but had only a poor shot—one that was likely to ricochet off the metal of the car and do her no good at all.

"Charlotte, Scoff's nearly here." Birch's voice was low and urgent. "What are you—by the gods. Stop, Charlotte. Don't move."

Something in Birch's tone filled her blood with cold dread.

"When I say it, you must dive toward me," Birch said, keeping his words steady. "Don't hesitate. Jump low and far as you can."

Fires of the forge, what could he see? Charlotte's arms began to tremble, robbing her of steady aim.

"Now, Charlotte!"

Charlotte threw her body backward in a blind launch toward Birch's voice. Just before she crashed into the dirt, she heard something hit the ground nearby. Then a low snarl followed by a hiss.

Birch grabbed Charlotte's arms, hauling her to her feet. She whirled around.

The catamount was crouched low, its tail lashing the air. The iron collar around its neck marked it as a kept beast of the Empire, a predator intended to keep the rail yard free of pests. Its eyes were still fixed on Charlotte.

But this wasn't the cat that had been stalking her from beneath the cars. This cat had come from behind Charlotte. From above.

"There's another one," Charlotte told Birch.

"I know," Birch answered. "I saw you tracking it with your pistol."

"Do you see it now?"

"No."

Charlotte had her pistol trained on the catamount in sight, but she wanted to avoid firing if she could. The discharge of a gun would carry a long way, and could bring more trouble than catamounts alone.

Without taking her gaze from the cat, Charlotte asked, "Where is Scoff? Close?"

"Coming across the yard now," Birch answered. "I sent Grave to help."

A hard lump formed in Charlotte's throat. *Where is the other cat?*

The train whistle screamed again and Charlotte didn't hesitate. Her finger squeezed the trigger and a moment later the catamount dropped to the ground, a bullet buried in its skull. She hoped the whistle had been enough to cover the sound of the shot.

A great shudder traveled down the line of boxcars. They began to lurch forward. The children inside the car cried out, startled by the sudden movement. Pip knelt beside them, her own face drawn with fear.

"Pip, stay with them!" Charlotte called. "Birch, get in there, too."

Birch hesitated, and she shoved him toward the open door. "Go!"

Charlotte pivoted, her eyes searching for Scoff. Four children were running ahead of him. Grave had almost reached them.

The other catamount darted from beneath the abandoned cars, rushing at the children.

"Grave!" Charlotte bolted toward them. "The catamount! Stop the catamount!"

Without breaking his stride, Grave turned, spotted the cat, and jumped. He hurtled through the air, his body crashing into the cat's. Cat and boy slammed into the ground a fury of limbs, teeth, and claws.

Charlotte reached the children, whose steps had faltered at the cat's ambush.

"Don't stop!" Charlotte urged them on. "Run to the train. Run!"

Scoff grabbed her arm. "What should—"

"Just get them on that car." Charlotte pulled free and kept running toward Grave.

Grave had landed on the catamount's back and now his arms wrapped around the snarling, struggling beast. Charlotte stopped and drew her pistol, hoping to get a clear shot.

The catamount slashed at the air with its claws, but Grave held on. He didn't shout or scream. He made no sound at all. But the cat's fury had become panic. No longer trying to attack, the catamount desperately struggled to free itself from Grave's arms. Charlotte didn't understand what was happening until she heard a terrible series of brittle snaps as the catamount's ribs crumpled beneath the power of Grave's constricting embrace. Only when the great cat went limp did Grave release his hold. He looked at Charlotte.

"Are you hurt?" Charlotte called to him.

Grave shook his head.

"We have to hurry." She waved for him to follow her. "The train is leaving!"

The train rolled slowly forward, but Scoff had to keep pace with the moving car, lifting children up for Birch to pull safely inside. Scoff had just handed off the fourth child when Charlotte heard Pip scream.

Charlotte had no idea where the third catamount had been hiding, but now it charged at Scoff, knocking him to the ground. Scoff threw his arms up, trying to defend himself. Charlotte's lungs burned as she ran toward him. In a few seconds she'd be close enough to shoot the cat.

A figure jumped from the boxcar and rushed toward the cat. For a moment, Charlotte thought it had to be Birch, but then she realized the person was too small to be the tinker.

"Rufus, no!" Charlotte screamed. She lifted her gun, aiming as she ran.

Rufus gave a wild yell as he brought his tree branch down on the catamount's flank. Startled, the cat snarled, pausing in its attack. Rufus struck again. The catamount twisted and lashed out, knocking Rufus back with a single, long swipe of its paw. Rufus rolled along the ground and didn't move again. The cat turned back to Scoff, but Charlotte's bullets struck its neck and its chest before it could attack again.

"Get Rufus," Charlotte gasped out her words to Grave, having little breath to spare.

Charlotte didn't stop until she fell to her hands and knees beside Scoff. His arms were still thrown over his neck and head. Blood flowed from angry slashes on his forearms.

"Scoff!" Charlotte grabbed his shoulder.

Scoff coughed, his breath coming in difficult wheezes as he rolled onto his side. "Charlotte?"

"Merciful Athene," Charlotte's voice cracked. "Are you all right?"

He sat up and coughed again. "I think so. Just couldn't breathe when that thing knocked me down. What was it?"

"Catamount. An Imperial pet of sorts." Charlotte took his hands, helping him to his feet. "We're going to have to run to catch the boxcar. Can you manage?"

Scoff spared her a thin smile. "I guess we'll see."

When they set off to chase down the boxcar, Grave and Rufus were nowhere to be seen. Charlotte prayed that they were safely aboard the car and that Rufus's injuries weren't too severe. The train was moving at a fair clip now, making for a hard run. Scoff kept pace with her and soon they were gaining on the line of boxcars. Charlotte could see the open door coming closer, closer. And then they were alongside the car.

"Go!" Charlotte waved her arm, ordering Scoff to precede her.

Scoff surged forward and threw himself into the car. He rolled away into the shadowed interior.

A thrill of triumph gave Charlotte's legs the strength to put on a new burst of speed. She was ready to jump, but suddenly she stumbled. Something—a rock, a root, a discarded rail spike, it didn't matter what—but something snagged her foot and she was falling.

"No!" Charlotte cried out. But she knew it was over. There would be no catching the train now.

Charlotte cried out again, but this time from sudden pain as she was jerked out of her fall. Her body swung forward and then up. And then, impossibly, she was inside the boxcar, collapsed against Grave whose fingers were locked, vise-like, around her forearm.

"Hephaestus's hammer, Grave!" Charlotte gasped. "I thought I was done for. Thank you." Charlotte wanted to laugh, but she was still trying to catch her breath. "We made it. We all made it."

Grave let go of Charlotte's arm and nodded to Scoff, who stood nearby. Charlotte would have thrown her arms around him in a joyous embrace but for his expression.

"What?"

Scoff didn't answer, just turned his head to look at the far corner of the car.

Birch was there, crouched beside a prostrate form.

"Rufus . . ." Charlotte hurried to Birch's side.

Rufus was pale and unmoving. His eyes were closed.

"Is he—" Shock swallowed up her question when she saw the deep gashes running from the boy's neck to his chest.

"There was no saving him." Birch looked up from where he sat next to Rufus. "He lost too much blood, too quickly."

A flat numbness crept into Charlotte's mind. "The other children?"

"Frightened, of course," Birch told her. His grief and anxiety were mirrored by Moses, who scuttled in and out of the tinker's pocket, making tiny squeaks.

Charlotte followed Birch's glance and saw Pip hovering over the rest of their flock. Many of the children were asleep, too exhausted to stay awake even under the alarming circumstances of their flight. Charlotte's eyes found Jamie. The ginger-haired boy sat slightly apart from the group, tearless but glassy-eyed.

His hero had been slain, his world tilted out of balance, and his innocence broken.

Charlotte knelt beside Rufus's body. Would his death be the toll demanded for this journey, or was this loss only the first of many to come?

Though her limbs ached with weariness, Charlotte knew she would not soon sleep. It would be a long time, she thought, before her mind found enough peace to seek sleep again.

4.

THEY COULDN'T KEEP Rufus in the boxcar, but Charlotte didn't want to discard his body without honoring the boy whose courage saved Scoff's life and cost his own.

At Charlotte's urging, Birch and Pip scrounged through the packs for thin scrap metal, from which they crafted a small copper flower. Pip laid the flower on Rufus's chest, and Charlotte bade their weary, sorrowful band to gather around his body as the boxcar rocked from side to side as it sped along the tracks. Grave shepherded the children into a semicircle around Rufus, and Charlotte took her place standing opposite them.

When the eyes of all her companions fell upon her, Charlotte felt a hitch in her breath. She knew she must speak, but what was the best thing to say? Should she boast of Rufus's bravery—say that his last act proved what an incredible warrior he would have become? Should she decry the Empire, pointing at their ruthlessness and stoking fury at their role in the boy's death? Or perhaps offering words of comfort would prove the most helpful for a group already so frightened and worn at the beginning of their journey?

"I only had a brief glimpse of Rufus's life," she said. "But even so, it couldn't have been more clear that he had a boundless spirit and loyalty that did honor to all of us. Rufus risked his life, and lost it, for the sake of his friends. There is no greater act, no greater love. Let us honor him by never forgetting that."

Charlotte removed her cloak and covered Rufus's body. The tightness in her throat was painful when she laid the fabric over his face. Scoff and Birch came forward; Scoff lifted Rufus from the shoulder, and Birch, the feet. They carried the body to the open door of the boxcar and cast him out, where he rolled into the tangled wilds that edged the rails.

Charlotte watched him flop away from the train, rag-doll-like, until his corpse disappeared into the trees. It surprised her that she hadn't cried since the attacks at the rail yard. No tears came when she first laid eyes upon Rufus's torn and broken body. No tears came now. She didn't feel grief, or fear. Only hollowness accompanied by a deep chill, the sort that comes from standing too long in a cold, hard rain.

. . .

Hours later, as the train rolled westward along the tracks, silence hung heavy in the boxcar. The children had gathered into something of a heap on one side of the car, clustered together for a sense of security while they slept. Birch, Scoff, and Pip were each stretched on the floor nearby, having also succumbed to exhaustion. Moses had found his own roost in the high corner of the car and was hanging upside down, wings folded about his tiny body.

Only Grave and Charlotte remained awake. The pair sat at the far end of the car, away from the others, not sleeping, but letting time pass without conversation.

Lulled by the quiet, Charlotte was caught off guard when Grave said, "I felt it die."

Shaking away the fog that had settled in her mind, Charlotte said, "I'm sorry—what?"

"The catamount." Grave didn't look at her when he spoke, but stared ahead, his face troubled. "When its bones began to break. When it coughed blood. I could feel it fighting to stay alive . . . and then it stopped. Then it wasn't an animal anymore; it was a sack of blood, meat, bone. It was nothing."

His tone made Charlotte's blood curdle.

"That happened to me . . . for a time I was nothing," he continued.

"Grave, I—" Charlotte struggled for some helpful

thought, a few words of comfort. "I don't think you were nothing. An illness took your life and then Hackett found a way to bring you back."

"No," Grave said. "The Maker didn't bring 'me' back. I'm not the boy who was Hackett Bromley's son."

Charlotte didn't protest; she couldn't. If anything about Grave had become clear, it was that his resurrection wasn't a simple returning of a lost child to a broken body. She saw no purpose in clinging to that idea, even if it offered a simpler, less frightening explanation of Grave's existence.

"I don't know what I am." Grave held his hands out in front of him, turning his palms up. "I don't know where I was before this, but I wasn't that sick boy."

"You're human," Charlotte told him. "You may not be that boy, but you're one of us."

"I think I am those things," Grave said, then sighed. "But I think I'm something else as well. And I don't like what I can do. How easy it is."

"What do you mean?" Charlotte asked.

Grave was still looking at his hands. He closed them into fists. "Killing. Making something become nothing."

"That's not what you did." Charlotte put both her hands over one of his fists. "You were defending us. If you hadn't, the catamounts would have killed me and Scoff."

She didn't bother adding "and you," because she didn't believe the catamounts could have killed Grave. Teeth and claws would never be a match for him.

"Don't forget that I killed two of the catamounts," Charlotte told him. "Sometimes we're forced to take a life to protect our own."

"And for that reason, the war?"

There was no malice, no provocation in the question, but all the same it made Charlotte bristle. Having been born into the Resistance, she'd never been interrogated about its rationale. "It's not that simple." She wished she could have instantly offered a more substantive reply.

Grave was silent.

"I told you about the war," Charlotte said, making another effort. "The Empire is greedy, cruel, and petty. It beats and bruises the very body upon which its gold-crowned head rests. Think about Jack and Coe—their father is an admiral, one of the highest-ranking officers in the Empire's army, and yet his sons would fight to overthrow Imperial rule. Even those inside the Empire see its corruption."

"And you think the Empire's corruption makes killing just?" Grave asked.

"You don't?"

He frowned. "I don't know yet, but—"

Still defensive, Charlotte countered before he could go on. "I know there has been much confusion about your past and what's to come, that's it's been a trying time for all of us, but especially you—to be thrown into a conflict in which you had no part and knew nothing of. Yet all you've seen since then . . . what the Empire is, what it does—"

"I know what I've seen," Grave cut in. "And all I've learned about the Empire proves the truth of your claims. But is this war the answer? Your Resistance has been fighting for decades. And the more you fight, the greater the violence, and the more terrible the weapons."

Grave paused, his voice dropping to a murmur. "And now Rufus is dead."

Charlotte had been lining up further justifications for the Resistance's tactics, but her arguments vanished. Grief and trauma. Grave had killed for the first time, and he'd witnessed the death of a companion, an innocent child. His questions weren't truly about the war; they were much more intimate. He was desperate to understand who he was and how he fit into this bloody puzzle of a conflict. They weren't questions Charlotte could answer for him. No one could.

"Grave," Charlotte said softly. "You'll find your place. These burdens upon your mind have already given you an answer you've been seeking."

"What is that?" Grave finally looked at her, his brow crinkled in concentration.

"You're human," Charlotte answered. "And without a doubt, you have a good heart."

Sadness lingered in Grave's eyes, but he smiled. "I hope so."

They fell back into silence, but Charlotte didn't let go of Grave's hand.

5.

CHARLOTTE LEANED AGAINST the boxcar wall, peering through the narrow gap between the door and the car, where a strip of morning light speared the dark interior. Steady pellets of rain beat on the metal roof and the sky was filled with bloated, low clouds of steel gray. While her companions slept, Charlotte's mind chewed on the next stage of their journey.

The Imperial train was bound for Moirai, a trio of settlements clustered at the junction of the Ohio and Mississippi Rivers. Of the three sites, West Moirai alone was a proper town. One of the many free black towns that had been established along the western bank of the Mississippi, West Moirai was the type of place Madam Jedda had intended for her daughter to call home. Independent of the

Empire, self-governing, and located on the greatest trade route of the continent—Charlotte could understand why Jedda would have preferred Meg relocate to West Moirai rather than live in the shadow of Britannia.

North Moirai served as the administrative center of the river junction. Managed by representatives from West Moirai and delegates of the Delaware, Illini, Chicaksaw, and Shawnee tribes, North Moirai regulated trade routes, shipping corridors, and business establishments along both rivers. Just as vital as general maintenance of the tri-town's quotidian activities was North Moirai's role as a buffer between British and French commercial interests. Both empires needed the revenue offered by these two great waterways, but neither could suffer direct dealings with the other. North Moirai kept coin and commodities flowing along the rivers while preventing bloodshed.

But it was at a railyard just outside of East Moirai that the train Charlotte was on would load raw goods and then make the return trip for the factories of the Atlantic coast cities.

One of the first settlements in the neutral trade zone along the Mississippi, East Moirai itself denied entry to any official Imperial vessels. Makeshift home for the transient, East Moirai was the fertile soil in which hopeful entrepreneurs could plant their hopes and then watch them thrive or wither. Ever changing and yet always the same, skirting the boundaries of two hostile empires, the transport and trading center of greater Moirai would serve up opportunity and danger in equal portions.

Disembarking from the train was by no means easy, but still proved much less of an ordeal than stowing aboard it had been. Birch had calculated from days to hours down to within minutes of the train's arrival at the boundary yards. Exiting the train at or too near the yards posed considerable danger, especially in light of the catamount attacks they'd faced in Albany, so when Birch deemed that they were within an hour of the train's destination, it became a matter of watching for an opportunity to leap from the car without risk of serious injury.

At a sharp bend in the tracks the train slowed enough to make jumps feasible, and they hurried to exit the car. Grave jumped first, carrying two of the smallest children with a third hanging on to his neck and shoulders. The elder children left next, then Scoff, Birch, and Pip, each assisting a child too fearful to jump on their own. Charlotte was the last. She landed on the soft bank, rolling a short distance before her body slowed and then stopped. The children bore some bruises and scrapes from rocks and branches, but they'd been spared any sprained ankles or wrists. Without delay, they distributed packs and set off on foot. The train tracks curved south, but their party turned to the west.

After a half day's walk through the forest, they encountered a narrow road of dirt and grass crushed by wagon wheels, and they turned west to follow it. This road wasn't of the Empire, but a forest track used by trackers and traders, merchants or families making their way to

East Moirai's hubs of commerce, making it safe enough for their troupe to use. Charlotte welcomed the reprieve of walking in the open, on a proper path rather than skulking through the woods on game trails. Soon enough the road traced the course of the Ohio River, a waterway teeming with vessels en route to the Mississippi.

The sounds of the trading center reached them before its buildings came into sight. The creaking of wood and the rushing of water that dropped through a mill, the bright ring of hammers striking iron, the shrill whinnies of horses and baying of livestock. Tucked up against a sloping bank of the Ohio, the outer edge of East Moirai bustled with life. Little rhyme or reason dictated the layout of the settlement's fringes. Buildings had been thrown up as needed, aiming to serve those who sought the resources of East Moirai but preferred not to venture too far into the town proper. Some, like the farrier's shop, showed solid construction and orderly design. Others, like the boarding house, were a slapdash assembly of mismatched wood planks and strange angles. There was even a small tinker's workshop, a narrow rectangular building with wooden walls embellished by sheets of hammered metal, from which a bizarre cacophony of sounds emitted.

Charlotte marveled to see the diversity of people mulling about camps that crowded the roadside leading into town. Voyageur canoes rested on the riverbanks and Frenchmen in colorful shirts and fur caps threw dice with American Indian traders whom Charlotte knew could hail from the

Monongahela, Miami, Shawnee, and Illinois tribes, or the farther afield Lakota, Ojibwe, and Iroquois of the north. Trading posts like this one couldn't be established without the permission and oversight of the local ruling American Indians. The British could have their forts for defense and rail systems to transport goods, but the treaty with Pontiac and his army of united tribes after their uprising in 1763 had placed control of the riverways from the Appalachian Mountains to the Mississippi with the Indians.

In addition to the handful of buildings, traveling craftsmen and women had set up stalls wherever space was available between clusters of tents. They called out to passersby, proclaiming the quality of their weaving or carving or leather goods. More enticing still were the small fires over which cauldrons hung or spits turned. Charlotte's stomach rumbled at the scent of rich stews abundant in savory seasoning, and succulent roasts dripping fat that sizzled on hot embers. Having subsisted on hard bread and salted meats of late, Charlotte nearly swooned at the thought of a hot cooked meal. But that temptation had to be put aside for the moment. Their destination was a structure on the northwestern edge of the post, near the riverside shrine to Athena.

Unlike most of the other buildings in the trading post, the Ohio River Sanctuary was constructed of gray stone. The somber structure marked a break between the vagrant character of East Moirai's outskirts and the beginning of the true settlement. The Sanctuary's only ornamentation was a cluster of copper olive branches that adorned its door post. A symbol of the goddess, the branches signaled to travelers that within these walls they would find a safe refuge from the perils of the outside world. Scattered throughout the British wilderness between the coastal cities and the Mississippi River, Sanctuaries were built by priestesses of Athene to offer wisdom and protection of the goddess to those far from Imperial cities.

But this day, what was of interest to Charlotte was another service the Sanctuary provided—that of the crèche. Not all Sanctuaries served as crèches; only a handful of the religious outposts provided shelter to the young and helpless. Crèches did not serve the Resistance alone. Years of war had made orphans of children throughout the interior of the country. The Empire's practice of forcibly conscripting labor from settlers within the wilds often took parents and older children to the foundries of the East while abandoning the young. The lucky among these foundlings arrived on the doorsteps of a crèche. The rest did not.

The religious orders that served Athene and Hephaestus maintained a position of neutrality from the start of the Revolutionary War and still held to that principle, but that hadn't stopped them from providing care for soon-to-be-mothers and small children of the Resistance. The aid offered at the crèches was determined to be in harmony with their stated neutrality. Children, the high priestesses concluded, could not be held accountable for the wars waged by their elders.

The Empire knew that crèches existed, but deemed it unwise spend its resources investigating any Resistance connections to the sites. Even the most jaded of Imperial politicians and military officers were unwilling to risk the wrath of deities. For the Resistance in particular, these special Sanctuaries remained a haven for any child until the time they could relocate to the place they would remain until coming of age—a protected location like the Catacombs. Some children left the crèches as soon as they learned to walk, others were reared with the priestesses for a handful of years, but none stayed past the age of ten.

As Charlotte and her companions approached the olive-branch-crowned door, she tried to summon moments from her own past, but she had no lucid memories of this place, nor of the journey from crèche to the Catacombs. The images she conjured from the past were little more than shadows and always fleeting.

"You should probably keep Moses out of sight," Charlotte told Birch.

The little bat had taken refuge in Birch's shirt pocket, but Charlotte feared that all the unfamiliar noise might startle the bat into flight.

"He's usually a sound sleeper until dark," Birch said. "But I'll keep an eye on him."

Scoff came up beside them and gave the building a cursory assessment. "Looks just like the one I stayed in. Though I remember it being bigger."

When Charlotte cast a sidelong glance at Scoff, he winked.

"Come on." Charlotte opened the door. "Let's get everyone inside."

She held the door open as the children shuttled in. Grave was the last to reach the entrance, but he hesitated beside Charlotte.

"Is something wrong?" she asked him.

"I didn't like the Temple of Athene in the Floating City," he answered.

"I can't say that I did either," Charlotte said. "But this place is different. The sisters here don't know, and won't be concerned with, who you are. Besides, we won't be here long."

Satisfied with Charlotte's reply, Grave continued into the building and Charlotte followed.

They gathered in the antechamber, a small but airy space occupied by a circular reflecting pool, at the center of which stood a bronze statue of Athene.

A door on the opposite side of the fountain opened and one of the priestesses came forward to greet them.

"May I be of assistance?" She was of middle age with gray-streaked auburn hair. She wore a sleeveless dress of simple gray and a long cloak of the deepest blue.

Charlotte stepped to the front of the group. "We seek the protection of the goddess."

The priestess inclined her head. "No seeker of Athene's mercy shall be denied. My name is Sister Annelle; please follow me."

Falling into step beside Sister Annelle, Charlotte motioned for the others to follow. They left the antechamber by way of the door from which Sister Annelle had emerged. The room they entered was much larger and humming with activity. Other priestesses sat at tables with children of various ages. Some were reading, some practicing their letters, while yet others sketched or were simply at play.

So many. Charlotte winced at the sight, wondering what each child's story could be. What events had driven their short lives along this course? It was impossible to tell who among them had been born into the Resistance and who'd been orphaned for altogether different reasons.

The arrival of Charlotte and her companions drew curious gazes from the children, but none left their places. A few did cast pleading glances at their supervising priestess, as if hoping to gain leave to investigate the Sanctuary's new visitors.

Sister Annelle beckoned two of her peers.

"Please meet Sister Delphia and Sister Elsbeth."

The pair of priestesses were as different as January is from May. Elsbeth was older yet than Sister Annelle. Her snow-white hair ringed the crown of her head in a braid, and her olive-toned skin bore the deep creases of age. Sister Delphia looked barely old enough to have completed her initiation into the temple ranks. She wore her hair long and straight, its shade that of polished ebony, while her skin was a tawny hue.

All three sisters looked at Charlotte expectantly.

"Thank you for welcoming us into your Sanctuary," Charlotte said. "My name is Charlotte."

Sister Elsbeth smiled, causing her face to wrinkle even more. It had the effect of making her look impossibly kind. "Charlotte, your company appears to have traveled many miles to reach us and must be weary from the journey. Let us offer you food and drink to restore yourselves, and then we shall speak further of your needs."

The priestesses demonstrated their familiarity and ease with the circumstance presented by a group of ragged, displaced youths. Without waiting for Charlotte's response, Sisters Annelle and Delphia gathered up the youngest children, shepherding them across the room and through an open set of double doors.

"The kitchens." Sister Elsbeth explained to the remaining travelers. "Why don't the rest us of sit for a moment."

The elderly priestess gestured to an unoccupied table. Charlotte and her fellows drew up chairs. Elsbeth took her seat, and addressed them in a frank but not unsympathetic tone.

"You know the small ones are welcome here," Elsbeth said, looking at each of them in turn. "But the rest of you are too close to being of age for the Sanctuary to offer you shelter."

"Not even for a night?" Pip's outburst was hurriedly shushed by both Birch and Scoff, who sat on either side of her.

Elsbeth offered the girl a patient smile. "I'm afraid even a night counters our neutrality, and if that position is compromised, it endangers all who would seek refuge within these walls.

"Of course," the priestess continued, "if any of you have decided against joining the Resistance—or for that matter the Imperial military—and wish to keep peace in your lives, then I may extend our protection to you."

"We understand the boundaries of your mission, Sister," Charlotte said. "We only seek assistance for the youngest of our party."

"Though I'm sorry I can't offer more, I am happy to share from our stores with you." Sister Elsbeth rose. "I'll gather some provisions that will help you on your way. In the meantime, some of my fellow sisters will bring you food and drink to restore you before you depart."

After the priestess left them, Pip dropped her head into her hands, elbows resting on the tabletop. "I can't believe they won't let us stay one night! I'm so tired!"

"Keep your voice down, Pip," Birch said. "What the Sanctuaries provide helps many in need. The Empire would shut all of them down if they were viewed as full supporters of the Resistance. We're all tired, but that's no reason to be resentful."

"Come on, Pip." Scoff nudged her with his elbow. "Aren't you excited to build a camp? Maybe a voyageur will stop by our fire and teach us songs. It'll be fun . . . I think."

Pip laid her head on the table, grumbling under her breath.

To Charlotte's surprise, Birch perked up. "I quite like the idea of learning their songs. My mother used to tell me wonderful stories about the French trappers, their portages, and all their singing."

Scoff reached over Pip to give Birch a light punch on the shoulder. "See, Pip? Birch is going to sing for us too. Care to give us a preview, friend?"

"No, thank you." Birch slid his chair over so his head was out of Scoff's reach.

"But how will we know whether to cover our ears tonight around the fire?" Scoff asked, elbowing Pip again.

This time she giggled.

As the two boys became immersed in their friendly quarrel, and Pip vacillated between sulking and snorting with laughter, Charlotte turned to Grave.

"You need to know," she said to him very quietly. "If you wanted to, you could stay here."

Grave's eyes filled with alarm. "Stay here? Why?"

"What the priestess said," Charlotte replied. "If you aren't fighting for the Empire or the Resistance, the protection of the Sanctuary is yours."

"You don't want me to come with you," Grave said with a frown.

"That's not it at all," Charlotte told him. "But what you said on the train, about whether the cause of the Resistance is worth waging a war, that's not for me to tell you. You're free to fight or not fight, to go with us or to stay here where it's safer. This choice is yours. No one but you should choose your path."

"But where you're going is dangerous," Grave said.

"I've always thought anywhere but the Catacombs was dangerous," Charlotte said. "But it turned out they weren't safe, either. The world is dangerous when you're an enemy of the Empire."

Grave's jaw tightened with resolve. "I don't want to stay behind while you go to fight. I want you to be safe."

Charlotte was about to object, *I don't need you to protect me,* but a flurry of images silenced her. How many ways had Grave protected their band of exiles? How much more likely was their safe arrival in New Orleans with Grave rather than without him?

So she simply said, "Thank you."

6.

THE OHIO DOCKS of Moirai teemed with the scents and sights of those sorts of labor that followed the course of waterways. There was the warm saltiness of sweat and the cool damp scent of cobblestones. Piles of coal were shoveled into barrows that were rushed onto barges. Gnarled fingers of bent, white-haired women stitched together torn nets. Tobacco smoke curled from the pipes of fishermen who strung up the day's catch, while others wielded knives that sloughed away shimmering scales in steady showers. Sailors, merchants, and travelers crowded the docks, elbowing each other aside as they went. It wouldn't be a hard thing to get lost in this press of bodies, Charlotte thought. She wondered if her little troupe should try to tie on to each other like the boats she'd seen strung together like a necklace as they approached the junction of the Ohio and Mississippi.

Despite the frenetic activity of the docks, Charlotte had yet to pull her mind free of the Sanctuary and all it implied about her past . . . and suggested regarding her future. However brief their time at the crèche had been, it nonetheless pushed Charlotte's thoughts toward her family. She hoped that Ash would still be in New Orleans when they arrived, but whom else might they encounter? The Resistance used New Orleans as a secure site where its leaders could live and continue to develop strategies and issue orders that would further their cause, but the missions executed by its members took them far afield from the French city. It was possible that Charlotte's mother and father would be in New Orleans; any of their parents might be, but it was just as likely—probably more so—that they would not. Charlotte didn't want to hope for something that had little chance of coming to pass. And yet it was difficult not to wish for a reunion with her family. At the same time, Charlotte found it difficult to envision what such a reunion would be like. She hadn't seen her parents in years. Would they even recognize her?

The question troubled her more than she liked, and Charlotte was glad for the distraction of Birch's voice demanding her attention.

"Moirai's split into three parts because of the river crossings," Birch told them. "We're most like to find a passenger vessel at the southwest docks across the Great Iron Bridge."

Scoff grunted as he shifted his load from one shoulder to the other. "Are we finding a boat today?"

"I don't want to rush into a poor deal." Charlotte had reached the bottom of the gangplank and stepped aside to make way for the others. "But I'd like to secure passage on a boat that's heading downriver tomorrow. I'll speak with crewmen from the vessels at port and see what sorts of fares are on offer. If they're within reason, we'll camp near the boat tonight and board first thing in the morning—or even tonight, if they're amenable."

"Hopefully I'll have luck adding more coin to our purse," Birch said. His load was a quarter the size of the others, but its value was likely the greatest, and its contents would suffer only slight jostling. Birch and Pip had spent their days in the boxcar putting together trinkets and gadgets that could be traded in the stores and stalls of Moirai. With luck they'd fetch enough to guarantee passage south and still have some to spare.

"Come on, then." Birch was already pushing forward into the teeming crowd.

"Grave, stay right behind him," Charlotte said hurriedly, for Birch was already being swallowed up by the crowd. "Pip, keep close to Grave. Don't lose sight of him. Scoff and I will follow you."

Pip dove into the current of bodies, intent on her target. The girl's vivid green hair was easy to spot as Charlotte kept after her. Charlotte trusted Scoff to keep up and to not diverge from their intended course. Leaving the Sanctuary had been easy, but getting away beyond the docks proved something of a battle. It seemed to Charlotte that every other step found her fending off an elbow, or keeping her balance when someone shoved into her. The crowd offered no easy channels to follow; instead, people moved every which way, knocking into each other and shouting blame for the bruising traverse at random passersby.

A reprieve from the struggle forward came as they drew farther from the docks. While they remained surrounded by bustling activity, the crowd thinned enough that Charlotte bumped against someone only every few minutes instead of every few seconds. Their pace slowed from a frenzied push ahead to a comfortable but swift clip as the world around them shifted subtly, transforming from a hub of harried labor to a slightly more ordered collection of businesses. The buildings of East Moirai were the result of opportunity rather than method. The only unifying quality of the line of shops, saloons, and inns was that all appeared to have been constructed of wood, and very swiftly. They cut a ragged silhouette of sloped, rounded, flat, and sharp-angled roofs against the sky. Some were freshly painted in pale blue, pine green, or brick red. Others wanted badly for attention—whatever hue had adorned those walls long faded into altogether different shades: blue into dull gray, yellow to muddy brown, violet to sickly rose. New and eager or old and tired, all bore signs proclaiming their purpose.

The Lonely Paddle was a forlorn-looking saloon,

whose decrepit appearance belied the waves of patrons that surged in and out of its doors. Maud's Table offered "home-cooked meals and polite company." Polite company seemed to hold less allure than the Lonely Paddle, given the stout woman standing at the restaurant's door with a spoon in her hand, watching potential customers pass with a mixture of contempt and desperation.

Pandora's Box served as a general store, but Birch suggested that such a name implied potential danger, and thus there must be a tinker's workshop inside the store. Knowing that Birch would likely pepper the local tinker with questions irrelevant to the rest of their party, Charlotte suggested that Birch wait until after they'd surveyed all the shops before committing to trade at this one.

They passed a smithy, a haberdashery, a tanner, and an apothecary with a window display so mesmerizing that Charlotte had to drag Scoff away from it. When they'd finished taking stock of the full array of commercial establishments in East Moirai, the sun sat low on the horizon, lending a bronze gleam to the wide river. Birch and Grave took their leave, heading back to Pandora's Box in the hopes of good trading—both in material and information. Scoff, Pip, and Charlotte had the task of finding a boat that would take them to New Orleans. Dusk's arrival lulled East Moirai to a sauntering pace, its denizens filling the air with effervescent chatter and unrestrained laughter—a welcome change from the gruff determination of the working day. Sounds of mirth grew louder and gained the accompaniment of drums, fifes, tin whistles, banjos, fiddles, and an array of voices belting innumerable songs. This odd chorus filled the air with strange melodies both fascinating and ominous.

"What in Hephaestus's name is that?" Scoff tilted his head, listening intently.

"I have no idea," Charlotte said, but she needn't have replied at all, for the answer loomed before them as the road bent to the south.

Hugging the swath of land at the juncture of the Ohio and Mississippi stood a bizarre, haphazard assortment of tents, stalls, and stages. So tightly packed was this hodgepodge that each structure appeared to be shoving up against its neighbors in a battle for space. A banner strung between two tall, ribbon-wrapped maypoles announced that Charlotte, Scoff, and Pip had stumbled upon "The River Carnival." Signposts at the base of each pole boasted of the fair's "impossible wonders" that "could not be missed!" and lent urgency to their message with the notice that "The Mississippi's Most Marvelous Attraction" would be in East Moirai for "one week only!"

At first glance the carnival's appearance turned Charlotte's mood sour. Her only experience with this sort of attraction had been the Tinkers' Faire in the Floating City, which had been nothing other than a disaster. She was about to walk on when she saw the way Pip's mouth had frozen in the shape of a O; the girl's eyes widened and grew bright with yearning.

I've been too cross with her, Charlotte thought. *She's been through so much with no reprieve.*

"Scoff, why don't you and Pip take a turn around the carnival," Charlotte said. "I can manage the docks on my own."

"Really?" Pip's voice came out as a burst of breath trailed by a hopeful squeak. "Can we, Charlotte?"

"As long as you don't accept any invitations to join one of the acts," Charlotte teased. She saw no harm in letting the pair split off for a brief diversion—and could more than manage assessing the range of fares required for transport from Moirai to New Orleans herself.

Pip beamed at Charlotte. Though he hid his eagerness more ably, Scoff's eyes lit with anticipation too at the promise of a carnival's excitement.

Unable to contain herself, Pip grabbed Scoff's arm and dragged him into the pandemonium.

Charlotte laughed, her heart lightening at Pip's unrestrained joy. As she walked on, that cheer spilled over into her regard for the present state of affairs. It hadn't been an easy journey, but they'd reached the Mississippi and soon they would be en route to New Orleans and the heart of the Resistance. Anxious thoughts had been Charlotte's constant companions from the moment she'd seen smoke billowing into the sky above the site of the Catacombs. For the first time in a long while, the fear knotted in her chest began to untie itself, and she knew beyond a doubt that they needed to do more than survive. Moments like this one, surprises that could foment happiness amid a long struggle, nurtured the spirit as food nourished the body.

The docks on the eastern bank of the Mississippi were only a short walk from the River Carnival and offered just as much for the eye to marvel at. The steamboats at port towered above their moorings, behemoths at rest. Great paddle wheels at the stern of each boat now lay still, but evoked the image of the ferocious churning that would power the vessel downriver. Charlotte approached the line of boats with some consternation; they'd been designed to impress, and she surmised that only passengers with deep pockets could afford travel in any of them.

Dismissing the grand steamboats, Charlotte continued along the docks hoping to find less ostentatious boats farther afield from the center of East Moirai. Though the sun had disappeared, crews remained busy aboard their vessels, scuttling from task to task as they readied for the next departure. The boats were getting slightly smaller, but not as small as Charlotte thought would accommodate her limited means. Unless Birch fetched a handsome price for his trinkets, they had little coin to offer. Perhaps a trade in kind could be made, work aboard ship in exchange for transport.

Rapid and heavy footfalls at her back startled Charlotte from her speculations. She pivoted, bracing herself for a possible attack, but it was Scoff who ran toward her.

"Charlotte!" He gasped, winded and red-faced.

She felt a sudden, bone-deep cold. "Where's Pip?"

Scoff's bleak face confirmed her fear. "I don't know. I mean, I'm sure she's in the carnival, but I lost her. She was with me when I fell into conversation with a purveyor of rare herbs and minerals, but she must have wandered off at some point because the next time I looked she was gone."

"I'm sure she's fine," Charlotte said, but she worried for Pip. Alone in a strange place as the night wore on, Pip would make a likely target for cutpurses or worse.

"I did try to find her." His words rattled out. "But there were so many people. I thought . . . maybe I should have kept looking . . . I just . . ."

Charlotte took his arm and set a swift pace back to the carnival. "You were right to come find me. Two of us will find her more easily and more quickly than one."

"I hope so. Hephaestus's hammer—I'll never forgive myself if anything happens to her. Never."

"It will only do harm to think that way," Charlotte said. "Keep your mind on finding her and nothing else."

When they'd passed under the banner, Charlotte had to confront the nightmare it would be to search for a girl amid the chaos of the carnival. People swarmed around them, visitors and performers, barkers and observers. The crowd was both blinding and ever-changing. It was difficult not to be overwhelmed.

Trying to focus on reasonable methods for solving this problem, Charlotte asked Scoff, "Where was this apothecary you met?"

"This way." Scoff pulled Charlotte into the flow of bodies that was sometimes progressing but also revealed a penchant for stopping abruptly without warning or surging forward as if toward an unseen prize.

Their effort to reach the apothecary's stall involved so many stops and starts that when Scoff drew Charlotte to the side of the path through the carnival, she wasn't sure how far they'd gone.

The stall's owner wore a long black robe and a leather sash, from which hung a dozen or more stoppered glass vials. Liquids of various shades sloshed within a few of them, bits of flora could be found in others, and two seemed to have living occupants of the insect variety.

"The gentleman returns." The apothecary steepled his fingers at his chest and bowed to Scoff. "What will it be? You seemed quite intent on the dried eel bladder. Or perhaps your choice has since shifted to gravestone moss? Or powdered amethyst?"

"I'm afraid I'm still looking for the girl who was with me," Scoff told him. "You haven't seen her, by chance?"

Disappointment flashed across the man's face at the absence of a sale. "No green-haired girls have visited the stall since we last spoke. Green-eyed, yes, but not green haired."

Rueful, Scoff looked to Charlotte. "What should we do?"

Charlotte's gaze swept over the throng of people moving past them. "The path through the carnival is always curving. I think it must be a circle."

Turning her attention to the apothecary, she asked, "Does the path form a circle that rings the carnival?"

"More or less." The man's disappointment had become irritation. "If you aren't serious alchemists in need of re-agents, then please stop blocking access to my wares."

Charlotte ignored his scowl, but said to Scoff, "Go back the way we came, but continue. Follow the path until you end up back here again. I'll do the same from the opposite direction. It may take a few rounds, but eventually we'll spot Pip."

"Move along!" The apothecary's eyes had gone beady.

Charlotte clasped Scoff's hand, squeezing his fingers. "Good luck."

Scoff nodded and moved off in the direction of the carnival entrance. Charlotte set out to follow the counter-clockwise route, happy to leave the muttering apothecary behind.

While it did have a few similarities to the Tinkers' Faire of the Floating City, the River Carnival bore obvious markers of its itinerant existence. Once-bright pennants had faded into lackluster hues, sorrowful with memories of glorious days past. Peeling and chipped paint made many signs illegible. Booths draped with heavy cloth showed crooked stitching of hasty repair, if not slashes and gaps that begged for attention but suffered only neglect. Yet the grittier aspects of the River Carnival couldn't smother its allure. Where the Tinkers' Faire seduced New York's elite from their gilded lofts to partake in scandalous entertainments sought by the lower classes, this caravan of attractions strived to amaze its visitors rather than pander to them. The carnival grounds were charged with excitement as children shrieked and dashed between attractions. Sweethearts strolled among the booths, whispering to each other, taking little note of the activity around them while simultaneously twinning their own burgeoning passion with the evocative setting.

Had Charlotte sought distraction, the flash and sparkle of lights joined with the clashing tunes of so many singers and players offered an endless supply. But for seeking out a lost lamb, the River Carnival presented only obstacles. Flames leapt into the air to her right as a woman spat a fiery plume from her mouth. Jugglers appeared at every turn, tossing rings, daggers, torches. A pair of contortionists blocked Charlotte's path, stopping her hunt altogether when they trapped her in a cage built from their own twisting bodies. Only when a gathered crowd began to cheer and toss coins was she able to escape.

Her ears rang with the tinkling bells that hung from the silken garb of women who danced while live snakes twisted up their ankles and wrists. A chorus of pan flutes enveloped her as a dozen "fauns" traipsed past, followed by a giggling chorus of winged fairies. On the heels of the fairies came a herd of bleating goats that could have belonged to the strange parade, or might simply have gotten away from their herder.

As Charlotte drew deeper into the carnival, far from

the glare of its sparking entryway, its attractions took on a more sinister cast. A small train of wagons advertised as "Forbidden Fruit" allowed entry only to men and promised "delights so strange and tantalizing you risk madness." A booth whose occupant's face was hidden by a cowled robe claimed to offer "exotic herbs and rare artifacts needed for dark magicks."

Passing too close, Charlotte gasped when the merchant seized her arm.

"A virgin's tooth and the wings of a queen bee steeped in rosewater will keep your lover faithful, pretty girl," his voice rasped. "Lucky for you, I have all three."

Charlotte wrenched free and bolted away. She heard the man's croaking laughter chase after her. It was so close, Charlotte looked over her shoulder to be certain he wasn't actually running her down. She saw only other spectators and no sign of the dark magician.

Though her steps slowed, Charlotte's pulse insisted on galloping through her veins. She weaved through laughing and gasping spectators, searching for any sign of Pip. It was hard to believe her efforts were anything other than futile. Between the low light, the crowds, and the erratic demands on her senses, Charlotte didn't know how she'd find any green-haired girl in this place, let alone the one she sought.

She'd reached a grand pavilion that she decided must mark the far boundary of the carnival grounds. A sign outside the massive tent, swathed in emerald green, proclaimed that it housed the "Garden of Mirrors" that was the River Carnival's only "permanent" and "ever popular" attraction.

"Care to have a look about, my dear?" The woman querying Charlotte was leaning on a staff of twisted wood. Her silver hair gleamed like moonbeams and her pupils were so large and dark that the entirety of her eyes appeared black.

Fighting off a shiver that she attributed to ragged nerves rather than reason, Charlotte said, "I'm afraid I'm looking for someone."

"Are you, now?" The woman regarded Charlotte with curiosity. She jabbed the end of her staff at the pavilion. "Could be that someone is inside."

Charlotte ground her teeth. She didn't want to be swindled, but there was the chance that Pip had gotten into the pavilion and couldn't find her way out. Even the idea of the Garden of Mirrors made her a bit dizzy.

"She's in her thirteenth year and she has green hair," Charlotte told the woman. "Have you seen her?"

"Green hair, eh?" She closed her eyes, ruminating on the statement. When she opened them, they seemed to be even blacker than before. "I did see a green-haired girl. She went in. I don't know if she came out. I went for a cup of tea about an hour ago. Might be she came out while I was off."

"Can I ask whoever watched the entrance when you were gone?" Charlotte said, her hope flaring.

The woman shook her head. The long earrings that

dangled from her lobes rattled, drawing Charlotte's notice. They were made of shell or bone. Charlotte wanted to shiver again.

"That boy's away for the night," the woman said, in answer to Charlotte's request. "You can wait here as long as you like to see if she comes out, or you can go in to look for her."

Charlotte didn't like either option, but she fished a coin from her pocket. Searching for Pip was preferable to standing around and hoping she'd turn up.

"Many blessings on you, dearie," the woman said as she accepted the coin. "Hope you find your green-haired girl."

With a nod, Charlotte left the woman and ducked into the pavilion. Though she hadn't expected otherwise, Charlotte was nonetheless disheartened by the dim light within. Negotiating twisting rows of endless, ever-changing reflections would not be easy even in well-lit environs. More disconcerting still, the low light was in constant motion. Tall brass candelabras boasted long branches that rose and fell, all the while spinning very slowly like a wheel on its axis.

The candle-bearing trees weren't the only nod to the attraction's billing as a garden. The entrance to what Charlotte felt certain would be a maze of mirrors was marked by a wrought-iron arbor covered with slender vines of silver. Delicate crystal flowers bloomed along the vines, casting tiny rainbows on the ground whenever the moving candlelight struck their petals.

Under different circumstances, Charlotte might have found the effect whimsical and evocative, but at this late hour, bound by the tension of her search, the dance of light seemed sinister, taunting her as she passed beneath the arch. Beyond the arbor, spinning candelabras continued to light the way. At its outset, the garden was composed of tall mirrors etched with roses and lilies, ferns, and songbirds in flight. Adding to the effect were verdant, living vines of ivy climbing along the glass, interweaving with its twin of wrought iron—though the iron vines bore sharp thorns. At Charlotte's feet, spring moss of deep jade lined the path.

Charlotte wondered about the sign's claim that this garden was "ever popular," given that she seemed to be the only fairgoer within the pavilion. So quiet was the garden of glass and iron that Charlotte could hear candle flames sipping at the air, sometimes choking and sputtering as their short lives burned away. Her own steps seemed obscenely loud as she moved past mirror after mirror.

Then, suddenly, there was no going forward. Directly ahead of Charlotte was a mirror, its surface obscured by green and black vines, blocking her way. She turned to her right and her left, each time confronting her own puzzled face as it gazed back at her. She looked back and could still see, barely, the arbor that marked the beginning of the garden. Placing her hands on the mirrors, Charlotte walked to each corner of the dead end, thinking there must be some way out that had been hidden by the mirrors' tricks. But both sides of the path proved solid, impassable.

Biting back her frustration, Charlotte again looked at the mirror that blocked her path. Halfway down the right side of the glass, an iron leaf protruded that was much larger than its peers. Charlotte assessed the mirror once more and noticed that unlike the other mirrors, the thorned, iron vines framed this one entirely. She grasped the protruding leaf and turned her wrist. There was a loud click and the mirror swung back, revealing its true identity—a door.

Clever, Charlotte thought with a grimace. She didn't want to pass the rest of the night discovering all the "clever" features of this garden.

She left the door open and proceeded along the path. Only a short distance ahead the path split. To Charlotte's right, the path curved and the mirrors on either side continued to mimic the flora of a garden. On her left side the path was straight but the mirrors had changed. No longer ornamented by leaves, real or artificial, the glass stood unobscured. But the shape of the mirrors varied. Some were wide, some narrow. Others bulged or followed bizarre angles.

Abandoning the trail of vines, Charlotte went to her left. Pip, she thought, would be excited by the different rather than comforted by the familiar.

The odd mirrors swapped Charlotte's identical reflections for absurd renderings of her form. She witnessed her body stretched, squashed, broken into pieces, blurred. The transformations became so alarming that Charlotte stumbled, falling forward into a mirror as the path took a hard right turn. Staring back at her was a grotesque caricature of her visage. Eyes bulging, mouth widened to the point that it might have gobbled up a pumpkin without bother. Charlotte pushed back from the mirror with a yelp, embarrassed by the fearful hammering of her heart.

"Hello?" a small voice called. "Is someone there?"

"Hello?" Charlotte stood very still. "Who's that?"

A sniffle, and then, "I'm lost."

"Pip?" Charlotte took a few steps. "Pip, is that you?"

"Charlotte?" Pip sounded near, but Charlotte knew that the girl could be only a few feet away and yet impossible to reach except by the correct path through the maze.

Charlotte's heart was racing now with hope instead of fright. "It is me, Pip. Keep talking. I'll try to find you, but I need you to lead me with your voice."

"I didn't mean to get lost." Pip's voice hiccuped, she was still crying. "It's just . . . oh, it's so stupid now that I think back on it . . . but Charlotte . . ."

"Just tell me, dear one," Charlotte soothed. "I'll be with you very soon."

"I thought I saw . . ." Pip sniffled. "I saw Rufus. I mean, I know it couldn't have been Rufus, but it looked so much like him and before I even considered what I was doing I was following him. He went into this place and I thought I'd just peek in, try to catch him, and then run right back to Scoff. I knew where he was; I didn't think I'd be more than a minute."

"That's all right, Pip." Charlotte listened, Pip's mention of Rufus making her stomach twist with grief.

"It was so pretty inside," Pip continued, a bit of wonder creeping into her tone. "And then so strange. And I never found the boy. I know it wasn't Rufus. I know it, but I . . ." Pip's words drowned in a pitiful sob.

Good, Charlotte thought, *she did take the left path.* With luck she'd soon reach the girl.

"When I realized how silly I was being, I turned around. I didn't think I'd gone so far as to forget the way back," Pip said. "But when I tried to get out, I kept running into mirrors that blocked my way. I don't know where I went wrong."

The path was making constant turns now, right, left, left, then right again. Charlotte wanted to hurry, but she feared that if rushed she might miss an obscured pathway. The path split again; three forks this time.

"Pip, call out again."

"I'm here." Pip's voice now seemed to be behind her. "Charlotte, I'm so sorry. You must be so angry with me."

Careful to hide her disappointment at not having found the girl yet, Charlotte said, "I'm not angry, Pip. I need you to keep talking to me. Was there anything else at the carnival that you liked? What did you and Scoff see?"

"Well . . . there was a snake that I think could have eaten me if it wanted. It was gigantic!"

"What else?" Charlotte asked. The path to her right seemed to lead in the direction of Pip's voice.

"I found a tinker's booth," Pip said. "He had a rabbit that could wiggle its nose and do flips. It was funny but not nearly as clever as what Birch builds. A flipping rabbit doesn't have much use, does it."

"No, I wouldn't think it does."

Charlotte followed the path as it turned left. She stopped when there was no longer a path in front of her, but a large square space—a room of mirrors. There were openings in the other three walls of the room. Four paths in the maze ended here. Charlotte wondered if she might be at the very center of the garden.

Above her, the pavilion's fabric was gone, and in its place was a ceiling of mirrors. The myriad reflections overhead had a dizzying effect. Charlotte quickly pulled her gaze away, and even so, she swayed on her feet.

"Charlotte!" In a corner to Charlotte's right side, Pip hopped up and rushed to her.

She wrapped Pip up in a hug. "Thank Athene."

"Do you know the way out?" Pip asked.

"I can help you find the way out." From the pathway on the right side of the room, a man appeared. He tipped his round, narrow-brimmed hat at them. "Always an honor to assist pretty ladies."

Whether it was the man's tone, his slouching steps, or his sudden arrival, something about him made Charlotte's nerves go taut with apprehension.

"We'll be fine on our own, thank you," Charlotte told him. She put her arm around Pip's shoulders and steered her around to return upon the path from which Charlotte had come.

"A lady shouldn't be without some protection," a man said—a different man. "A lot of strange folk at the river crossing. Drifters. Unreliable types."

Charlotte looked over her shoulder. Two more men had joined the first.

"I appreciate the warning." Charlotte weighed her options. If they made a run for it, she could easily take a wrong turn and end up cornered somewhere else in the maze. Fighting them off wasn't out of the question. She had her stiletto hidden in her boot, but she had no idea what arms, if any, the men carried. Pip was sure to have no weapons at all.

She drew Pip another few steps toward the path.

"In some circles it would be considered rude to walk away from an offer of assistance," the first man called to her. "Some might take offense."

Charlotte heard them coming toward her, their steps quickening.

"Pip, stay behind me." Charlotte whirled around, sliding her stiletto out of her boot.

The trio of assailants balked when she faced them, the steel of her thin blade catching the low light.

One of them guffawed and spat a stream of tobacco juice. He gripped a club that he bounced against the side of his leg. "You fancy yourself a match for us?"

"If you keep coming toward us, you'll find out," Charlotte answered.

"Hey, Roger," the first man said to the one who'd goaded her. "If she beats you, you'll be buying my next pint."

"I'll be buying my own pints with *her* coin," Roger replied. "And you'll see none of it."

"The both of yous shut up." The third man drew a wide-bladed dagger. "You're givin' me a terrible thirst."

Without warning, he rushed Charlotte. She ducked and spun beneath the swipe of his blade. Flicking her stiletto out, she sliced through his shirt and into his side.

The man bellowed, wheeling around as Charlotte darted away. "You'll be sorry for that."

"I'm not sorry yet," Charlotte answered. She needed to hold their attention so they'd forget Pip.

"I think she stuck you good, Jim," Roger said, laughing. "You're bleeding same as the piglet you just squealed like."

Roger sauntered toward her, lazily swinging his club. "What do you think, Billy? She quick enough to stick me too?"

"You are faster than Jim, mate," Billy answered. He had yet to draw a weapon.

Then Charlotte saw the glint of brass along his knuckles. He was moving too, casually making an arc toward Charlotte opposite Roger. "But the young lady's a nimble thing, isn't she?"

"Slipperier than an eel, I reckon," Roger said.

Rather than waiting for the pair to close on her, Charlotte dove past Billy. He cursed his surprise and then groaned as Charlotte leapt up to drive her elbow into his kidney. She turned to see Roger coming at her. He'd seen Charlotte take on his companions and adjusted his attack accordingly. Rather than take a swing, he held his club low, waiting for Charlotte to move. She'd be forced to soon; Billy had recovered from her blow and was ready to charge at her if given the chance.

Charlotte darted toward Billy, hoping Roger wouldn't risk hitting his partner along with her. She didn't find out whether she was right. Billy saw her coming and, guessing her strategy, stepped aside but threw out a foot to trip her. She fell, but twisted before she landed so she could quickly roll to her feet. She was still crouched when Roger swung at her with his club, aiming for her head. Charlotte dropped to all fours and the club whooshed past her. She jabbed upward with her stiletto, hard. The blade sank deep beneath Roger's kneecap. He screamed and dropped back. Charlotte grabbed for her blade, but pain flooded her arm as Billy's metal-wrapped fist slammed into her. Ignoring her throbbing arm, Charlotte flattened against the ground and rolled into Billy's shins. He fell over her, grunting when he hit the earth. Charlotte leapfrogged halfway up his body and drove her knee into the small of his back. She knew she had little time; Billy was a big man who'd have no trouble throwing her off once he got his breath back. She tugged off the leather cord she'd used to tie her hair. Slipping one end around Billy's neck, Charlotte continued to put weight into her knee while hauling her arms until the cord was taut around his throat. Billy began to flail, his arms stretching toward her, fingers clawing at her—but flat on his belly, Billy couldn't reach her. He grabbed for the leather cord, but Charlotte had wrapped the ends around her wrists for leverage. His attempts to stop choking were futile. In another minute he'd lose consciousness.

Someone grabbed a fistful of Charlotte's loose hair and yanked her head back. Then Jim's knife was at her throat and his voice in her ear.

"Let him go, you mangy bitch."

The blade pressed into her skin. Charlotte felt a sting and the warm trickle of blood on her neck.

She dropped the ends of the cord and let the leather slide off her wrists. Billy's head dropped down as he coughed and wheezed.

Pulling on her hair and pressing with his blade, Jim made Charlotte stand.

"That was fun at first," Jim said. "But you probably made Roger lame. It'll take more than your coin to make up for that."

Billy had managed to get onto his knees, but he was still gasping.

"Now Billy, here," Jim told Charlotte with another painful jerk of her hair, "he's the thinker. A creative type. I bet he'll know what's best done with you."

Jim drew a sudden, sharp breath and a tiny, high sound squeaked out of his throat.

"And I bet I geld you before you have a chance to cut her throat."

I know that voice, Charlotte thought. *But how?*

Jim squeaked again and dropped his dagger, at the same time letting go of Charlotte's hair. She jumped away from him.

"You all right there, kitten?" Linnet smiled at Charlotte, but there was genuine concern in her eyes.

Charlotte nodded. She glanced at the bandits, hoping her face didn't mirror their alarm. *Linnet is here?* she thought. Charlotte could fathom neither rhyme nor reason in Linnet's sudden appearance.

"Good," Linnet said. "Why don't you get your stiletto, now. I know you're fond of it."

Roger was still on the ground, clutching at his knee. He spat at Charlotte when she approached, throwing out every insult Charlotte knew, and several she didn't.

Ignoring him, Charlotte grabbed the hilt of her blade and jerked it free. Roger howled.

Linnet tut-tutted. "That's going to ache something awful when there's weather coming in."

Billy was on his feet now, glaring at Linnet.

"Shed that brass," Linnet told him. "Or maybe you don't care if your friend here keeps his small bits. I'm sure they're quite small. Aren't you, Charlotte?"

Charlotte couldn't help but laugh.

"You're begging for—" Billy's threat was cut short by Jim's sudden scream.

"Oh, that was just a tiny prick," Linnet chided, then said to Billy, "I'm sorry, I didn't catch what you were saying."

Billy glowered at her.

"We are going to leave now." Linnet shoved Jim so hard he fell right onto Billy. "It would be very, very foolish for either of you to try to follow. I'm not too worried about your friend there."

Roger spat at her, but given that he was on the ground it had little effect.

"Pip!" Charlotte called, and Pip ran to her, grasping her hand. The green-haired, pigtailed girl was trembling, her eyes still wide with fright.

Charlotte led Pip to Linnet's side.

"The path at your back," Linnet told her. "I'll be right behind you."

The three lowlifes began to shout at each other, casting blame wherever they could, as soon as Charlotte, Pip, and Linnet were gone. The path Linnet had directed Charlotte to was a return to the gardenesque design at the beginning of the maze. The appearance of twisting iron vines and mirrors that didn't turn her reflection into something monstrous brought Charlotte more relief than she would have expected.

"What are you doing here?" Charlotte asked Linnet as they hurried along the narrow path.

"I thought that was obvious—saving you. By the way, do I always have to save you?" Linnet sheathed her dagger. "You seem to like trouble, and I can't always be around."

"It wasn't Charlotte's fault," Pip told Linnet. "She came to help me! Who are you, anyway?"

"Pip, this is Linnet," Charlotte appreciated Pip's attempt to defend her, but she couldn't have the girl holding a grudge against Linnet. "She's a friend from the Floating City."

"Oh," Pip said, still a bit surly.

Charlotte offered Pip a reassuring nod, then said to Linnet. "How in Athene's name did you find me?"

"We started to look as soon as your homing bird arrived," Linnet answered. She'd inexplicably stopped in front of the row of mirrors and was inspecting them. "Ott decided the Moirai junction was our best chance of finding you. We've been here a week. The tinker at Pandora's Box sent word as soon as Birch tried to sell his wares there."

"The shopkeeper works for Lord Ott?" Charlotte found that notion rather startling.

"He's more of an occasional contact than an employee," Linnet said. "But then again, Ott has more occasional contacts than any other type of associate."

"Except you?" Charlotte asked with a smile.

"Yes," Linnet replied. "I'm quite special."

"We should keep moving." Charlotte couldn't wait to be free of the mirrored maze and was growing impatient with the delay in their departure. "Do you know the way out?"

Linnet lifted onto the balls of her feet and grasped one of the thorn-covered metal vines winding along the mirrors. She gave it a twist and the mirror pulled back, sliding to the side with a hiss. On the other side was the green draping of the pavilion walls.

"Oh, kitten," Linnet said. "I always know the way out."

7.

LINNET NOT ONLY knew the way out of the Garden of Mirrors, she also managed to lead Charlotte and Pip back to the center of the commercial hub in half the time it had taken Charlotte to reach the River Carnival.

And when Charlotte suggested that they pick up Scoff before leaving the carnival, Linnet informed Charlotte that he'd already been "collected" by one of her "associates." On their walk, Pip watched Linnet with a kind of awe that Charlotte couldn't help but smile at, and any time Linnet looked directly at Pip, Pip would duck her head with an uncharacteristic shyness. The young girl proved just as susceptible to Linnet's charms as everyone else; any signs of her initial distrust had vanished.

To Charlotte's surprise, Linnet took them to one of the

many inns scattered among the shops. She told Charlotte that, compared to its peers, Abrams's Boarding House offered accommodation neither ostentatious nor dodgy. Simple but clean, the three-story bunkhouse had a sitting room, dining room, and kitchen on its main floor, with the two upper floors dedicated to boarders.

There was a sign hanging from its front door, *No rooms available*, that Charlotte regarded with suspicion, considering that she'd seen no such signs on any other East Moirai inn. When they stepped inside, the air was filled with irresistible scents. The scrumptious tang of slow-roasted game and thick gravy along with the warm, soft allure of freshly baked bread made Charlotte's mouth water, and the sound her stomach made was more of a roar than a growl.

Heavenly odors wafted from the kitchen into Abrams's dining hall, promising scrumptious food to come, but when Charlotte saw the veritable feast laid out on the table she could hardly believe that yet more dishes remained to be served. One platter held a haunch of roast venison. Another, a suckling pig. Not one, but two roast chickens sat plump and honey-gold at the center of the table. Steam rose from carrots that glistened with the promise of butter, and baskets held fat, round loaves of dark bread. And despite the sign's claim of no rooms to be had, the only boarders seated at the long benches were Charlotte's friends. Lord Ott stood at the head of the table as if holding court.

"There you are!" Ott spread his arms wide. "Welcome,

welcome! Good to see you, my dear girl; please sit down. Now that you've arrived, we can partake of these fine offerings provided by Mr. Abrams's cooks."

The rotund merchant wore a crisp white shirt and a silk vest of deep violet, as well as black trousers that accommodated his significant girth. Unable to help herself, Charlotte dashed forward and threw her arms around Ott.

"Well, now." Ott patted Charlotte's head and then winked at her. "It's good to see you too, Lady Marshall."

Embarrassed by her outburst, Charlotte drew back, blushing.

For his own part, Lord Ott looked pleased at Charlotte's display of affection, though he gave her a gentle push toward a chair. "No time to waste on sentiment, though. Business to be done."

Charlotte nodded and sank into the chair. Pip sat beside her, with Scoff in the next seat. He looked relieved to see them safe, but also bewildered by the current circumstance. After giving Pip a hug, he began piling food onto his plate. Grave and Birch sat opposite them. Grave appeared unperturbed by this sudden turn of events and equally uninterested in the food, but Birch wore an expression of wary puzzlement. He served himself just enough of each dish so as not to be blatantly rude.

Instead of joining them at the table, Linnet sauntered up to her employer.

"I trust you didn't have trouble," Ott said to her.

"Bumbling amateurs are an irritation." Linnet snatched

the kerchief from his vest pocket, drew her blade, and began to polish it. "But hardly trouble."

With a brief glance of annoyance at having lost his kerchief, Ott grumbled something unintelligible.

Birch cleared his throat, obviously ill at ease. "This man says you know him, Charlotte?"

"A cautious lot, your companions," said Ott with an approving nod. "An admirable trait, caution. Keeps you alive longer than blind trust. Considerably longer."

Ott's comment didn't make Birch any more comfortable. He fixed a pleading gaze on Charlotte.

"Lord Ott is a friend to the Resistance," Charlotte said. She tore off a chunk of still-warm bread and fended off the temptation to wolf it down. "And this is Linnet, Jack's sister."

"Half-sister," Linnet added drolly. "He'd be cross if you forgot to make that distinction."

"Really?" Scoff eyed Linnet with a new appreciation, though he addressed her around mouthfuls of food. "Jack has a sister? He never said so. That's rather odd."

"Again, half-sister," Linnet replied. She put her blade away and stuffed the kerchief back into Ott's front pocket. "Hence the lack of his ever mentioning my existence."

Ott drew out the tall chair at the head of the table. Its wood creaked when he sat. "Linnet can regale you with her sordid family history after we've taken care of business."

"We have business with you?" Birch frowned at Ott. The tinker had yet to sample the food on his plate.

"I have business with almost everyone." Ott tone was mirthful, but Charlotte took note of the familiar sly cast of his expression. "And at this moment, your endeavors constitute a particularly valuable, but high-risk, investment. I may believe the Resistance has the moral upper hand compared to the Empire, but at times I feel I may as well be juggling hornets' nests. I'm still a businessman and have to be prudent when it comes to managing my involvement in this conflict. Why else would I come personally to set things back in order?"

"It's true." Linnet plopped onto the bench beside Grave and rested her elbows on the table, propping her chin in her hands. "He'd rather sit back and watch things happen than get his hands dirty."

Lord Ott ignored her, focusing instead on wrenching a drumstick from one of the chickens. "I'll be giving you passage to New Orleans, and I'll take care of your accommodation when we reach the city. It's not the sort of place you can stumble into without the right connections. In many ways, New Orleans is more dangerous than the Floating City."

"But the Resistance leadership is there." Pip's reticence had melted away. She waved her own drumstick at him in defiance. "Why wouldn't we be safe there?"

"There's more to New Orleans than the Resistance. Much more," Ott said gently. "It's a strange and complex city that requires careful navigation. The threats therein aren't specific to you, little emerald; they pose a risk to everyone."

Pip blushed at Ott's new pet name for her. "But you'll tell us what we need to do? Where to go?" She suddenly remembered that the chicken leg was food rather than a weapon and began to chomp on it.

"I'm not just going to tell you," Ott said, helping himself to a pile of carrots. "I'm going to show you."

"So does that mean I'm off?" Linnet quipped. She stabbed one of the carrots on Ott's plate with her fork. "It sounds like you'll be doing all the work."

Ott sighed, adding dryly, "I should say, I will show you with the invaluable assistance of those in my employ."

"That's better." Linnet batted her eyelashes at him and took a bite of the carrot.

"You're never like this with Margery," Ott said. "You do realize you work for her, too."

Linnet smiled sweetly. "She's nicer than you. You're quite irascible."

Ott spared her a flat, unsympathetic look, batting her fork away when she angled for another carrot.

"What about the others?" Charlotte's appetite flagged as the question prodded at her nerves. "Do you have any news about Ash?"

She wanted to say, "And Jack," but stopped herself at the last moment. Now that Lord Ott had taken charge of their journey, the chances of reuniting with Ash and Jack were greatly improved. Charlotte had been trying to keep Jack from her thoughts, but now she needed to consider what she would do when she had to face him again. The back of her neck heated when she caught Linnet watching her, one eyebrow arched, with a smile that made her feel like the other girl knew exactly what she was thinking.

"We know he's arrived without incident in New Orleans," Ott told her. "That means he and Jack will have begun their attempt to unite the Resistance and the dissenters within the Empire. Not a simple task. The potential for treachery will be the foremost thought among the Resistance's leadership."

Birch leaned forward, his food as yet untouched. "I must confess, as much as I trust Jack, I find it hard to believe that any among the upper echelons of Imperial society would be happy to see it toppled, much less help bring it down."

"Your doubts aren't unreasonable," Ott told him, sopping up gravy with a hunk of bread. "And I'd think the same if I didn't see the cracks in the Empire's foundation multiplying every day."

"But why is that?" Birch asked.

"The problem with empires is their inability to accommodate change," Ott said. "Britannia often behaves like a sullen child, nursing old rivalries and treasuring antiquated ideas. As the Empire ages, so do its rulers, but the longer in years they become, the more unwilling they are to relinquish control. In their fear of their losing grip on power they refuse to share it, thus denying would-be heirs a place among them."

"*Um noff shoe a fuloh,*" Scoff said, then finished chewing and repeated, "I'm not sure I follow."

But Charlotte thought she did. "Coe, Jack, other young officers like them. They can't advance in the ranks of authority, can they?"

"To be honest, the situation in the military isn't nearly as dire as it is elsewhere." Ott sliced himself a good section of the roast venison. "The greatest tension lies among those seeking lordships and the lands that go with them."

Linnet flipped a pea off the flat of her knife and caught it in her mouth. "It's tough, you know, when everyone wishes they could live on the same little island."

"What a clever observation." Ott smiled at Linnet, until she flipped a pea that hit him in the middle of the forehead.

Pip began to giggle, but Scoff asked, "What about all the land between here and the eastern seaboard? That all belongs to Britannia."

"Indeed it does," Ott said. "But doling out that land would mean handing over its resources to whatever lord builds his estate there. The wildlands are valuable to the empire because they feed its machines. The decision to prevent private settlement away from the coast was made with absolute purpose. Wood, stone, farms—the wildlands offer an endless harvest, and all the goods and all the profits go directly into Imperial coffers."

"And they won't give that up," Birch said, finally taking a bite of pork.

Ott leaned back in his chair, folding his hands atop his great belly. "There is always talk of expansion to the west, past the Mississippi. But should the day come when Britain tries to claim the west, it will surely mean war with France and likely Spain as well, which means that the Empire's leaders spend most of their time squabbling with one another and nothing changes."

Birch was chewing his meat slowly, thinking on Ott's words.

"But what about you?"

Everyone looked at Grave in surprise. He'd been so silent that Charlotte assumed he had no interest in the conversation.

Grave kept his attention on Lord Ott. "Why do you want the Empire to fall? You're already a lord."

"Yes." Ott's eyes narrowed very slightly. "I do hold a title and have lands to my name in the north of England."

Charlotte was taken aback by Grave's question, but she realized she'd never thought to seek the reason for Ott's position herself. Her trust in Lord and Lady Ott had been an extension of her faith in Jack—and Charlotte no longer had that same faith.

Grave's face was open, bearing not a hint of hostility, as he waited for Ott's answer.

Lord Ott scratched his beard, smiling to himself. "It would be a fine thing if I could claim some noble purpose or staunch belief as the source of my . . . disloyalty, but the truth of my tale is that the life of a lord proved too dull for my taste. I still hold my lands and collect revenue from them, but my interests lie here. I prefer to be a mover of pieces, a player of the game."

"I don't understand," Grave said. "You speak of a game. Of taking joy from it. But all I've seen in this war is violence, death, pain. How is that a game?"

Ott's smile vanished. "Have you succeeded in retrieving your memories, boy?"

"I'm—"

"Some of them," Charlotte broke in. Given Ott's sources, Charlotte wouldn't have been surprised if he knew the truth about Grave's past. All the same, if Lord Ott didn't know that Grave had once been a sickly boy who, if Hackett Bromley was to be believed, returned to life through a mix of mechanical invention and dark magic, then Charlotte wanted to keep that information hidden.

"We've come to believe he once was very ill," Charlotte continued. "And while pieces of his past have resurfaced, it may be that his memory will never be fully restored."

"I see." Lord Ott gave away nothing in his expression, but he said to Grave, "*Game* is a metaphor. I merely wished to convey that I am not content to watch the world transform while I remain still. I choose instead to be a traveler of the times."

Ott pushed his chair back and stood. "I'll bid you all a good night, then. Linnet is spending the night here and will bring you to the *Calypso* in the morning."

When he'd gone, Linnet pulled his plate over and picked at the roast pork he'd left behind.

"That may be the first time I've seen Lord Ott ruffled

by someone," she said. "Then again, most people know better than to ruffle him."

"It was an innocent question," Charlotte said. Uncomfortable as the exchange had been, Charlotte didn't fault Grave for inquisitiveness.

"I agree," Linnet replied. "Though I might call that question 'tactless' rather than 'innocent.'"

She glanced down the table. "If you'll pardon my saying so, Grave."

Grave shrugged. "I just wanted to know."

"And that's fair enough," Linnet said. "Don't worry, Ott'll get over it. He's not used to being challenged."

"You challenge him all the time," Charlotte said.

An impish smile overtook Linnet's mouth. "Really? I hadn't noticed."

8.

THE *CALYPSO* BORE no resemblance whatsoever to the trading vessels lining the Ohio docks. Charlotte and her companions had arrived on the shore of the glittering Mississippi early that morning. Now porters carried their belongings to quarters provided by Lord Ott, and while the others reveled in the fine appointments of their rooms, Charlotte returned to the shore with Linnet to take another look at the vessel. The *Calypso* rested at the dock, pristine, elegant, and white as a swan, except for the great blue paddlewheel at its stern. The giant steamboat's four decks were ringed by promenades decorated with intricately carved arches inlaid with mother-of-pearl. When sunbeams hit the boat, the *Calypso* threw back a gleam so intense that Charlotte had to look away.

"It helps if you shade your eyes," Linnet said, holding her hand horizontal against her forehead. "Still pretty bright, though."

Imitating Linnet's pose, Charlotte still had to squint, but was able to continue her examination of the boat.

"She's kind of a beast," Linnet said. "Lord Ott hates it when I say that, but I always tell him that there are plenty of attractive beasts in the world. Elephants, whales, moose. Well, maybe not moose."

In terms of size, Charlotte had to agree that the *Calypso* was indeed a beast. If the boat had a great maw it could have swallowed four smaller vessels abreast with no trouble. Passengers kept the decks teeming with activity. Couples strolled arm in arm along the promenades while children raced past, consumed with their games of tag. Whether an unspoken rule or an expectation of travelers, it appeared common practice to garb oneself in pastel hues that complemented the shining surfaces of the *Calypso*.

Charlotte gazed at the well-frocked passengers and uttered a soft curse. "Who do I have to be for this trip? And what will I have to wear?"

It had been a relief to return to her familiar, if limited, wardrobe when she left the Floating City, and she wasn't eager to trade in her clothes for society's costume.

Linnet gave a little cough of laughter. "River life isn't city life, kitten. You'll discover that all manner of folk seek passage aboard Lord Ott's steamboat. From this angle it might appear only the refined and dainty are traveling south, but that's a fiction. A good many of the passengers are still sleeping off last night's fun. They won't show their faces before noon; some don't bother to leave their quarters in daylight hours at all."

When Charlotte answered Linnet's narration with a puzzled look, Linnet said, "Better to see for yourself."

"So we'll be mingling with the other passengers?" Charlotte asked. "And no one will be suspicious of who we are?"

"Plenty will be curious," Linnet answered. "But I'd be very surprised if anyone made that admission. But you needn't concoct an elaborate identity like that of 'Lady Marshall' on the *Calypso*. Not that you'll be honest about who you are. Don't *ever* be honest about who you are— and I mean that as a life rule, not just in this instance."

"Does that mean I've never witnessed who you truly are?" Charlotte asked, her mouth twisting as though she'd bitten into something sour.

"I didn't mean when you're among friends," Linnet said, resting her hip against a dock piling. "But it's the wisest course in mixed company."

Charlotte spared her companion a sharp smile. "Is that your answer to my question?"

"Hmm." Linnet drummed her fingers along her cheekbone. "I suppose it is. Would you like me to concoct another answer?"

"You're a terrible and dangerous friend, I think." Charlotte's smile became part grimace.

"Of course I am." Linnet pushed off the piling and

walked to the end of the gangplank. "But that's why I'm your most irresistible and wonderful friend."

Charlotte didn't bother to comment. She followed Linnet up the walkway and onto the vessel.

They stepped onto the broad main deck, where a troupe of musicians welcomed them with a cheerful melody played on fiddle, drum, flute, and accordion. A celebratory, playful air suffused the steamboat. Everywhere around her, Charlotte heard laughter, singing, a lightness of spirit in snippets of conversations. Giddiness fluttered through her, a welcome change from the tension that had been her companion mile after mile. A white-gloved butler bearing a silver tray laden with fresh fruit paused beside the girls, inviting them to partake of the bounty. He was trailed by another servant who provided them glasses of champagne. As peach juice mingling with the crisp effervescence of champagne tickled her tongue, Charlotte felt she could have floated right off the deck from pure delight.

"Oh dear." Linnet's sour mutter curbed Charlotte's sensory transport.

"What?" Charlotte asked, and, unable to resist, took another bite of peach and sip of champagne.

Linnet cast a sidelong glance at her. "I was hoping we'd have a little more time, but there's no use avoiding it."

Charlotte's brow crinkled, but Linnet's eyes were focused on a point behind Charlotte.

"A lovely morning," a man's voice said, quite near Charlotte's shoulder. "One to be savored."

"If you start spouting poetry, don't think I won't hit you." Linnet's smile didn't quite reach her eyes.

Charlotte turned to find a tall, lean figure standing so close that it startled her into faltering back.

"Hello, Charlotte. It's a pleasure to see you again." Commodore Coe Winter was much as she remembered. His bright blue eyes, speckled with brown, were intent upon Charlotte. He wore his dark brown hair loose so that it brushed his shoulders, instead of tied back in the popular style of Imperial society. Coe had also traded his clean-shaven face for a close-trimmed beard.

Charlotte suddenly wondered if she had peach juice running down her chin. Her stomach had tied itself into a knot, but one not altogether unpleasant. Coe wasn't wearing his uniform, having abandoned his military garb in favor of a linen shirt paired with a dark vest and trousers. A pair of gun belts were slung low on his hips. The changes in his hair and clothes made Coe appear more rugged, like he could have grown up in the Catacombs, but also less severe.

"Coe!" Her voice came out much too high. "I didn't . . . how . . . this is a surprise. With your beard I almost didn't recognize you." She bit her tongue for allowing such foolish words to roll off it.

Linnet snickered, and Charlotte took another step back, so she could stomp on Linnet's toe. Linnet hissed an oath, but Charlotte kept smiling at Commodore Winter.

Coe took Charlotte's hand in his and bent to kiss her

fingers. His lips lingered on her skin just long enough to send a shivering warmth up her arm.

"How is it that you're away from the city?" Charlotte kept her voice low to avoid other passengers overhearing. "Won't you be missed?"

"I'm enjoying a leave that's been long coming." Coe smiled.

Charlotte had forgotten how disarming the Winter boys' smiles could be. Her body's reaction unsettled her. On the one hand these waves of sensation were sweeter than the loveliest of daydreams, but Charlotte couldn't separate Coe's physical effect on her from the similar feelings Jack provoked. She pulled her hand away from Coe's, hoping he wouldn't think her rude. She tried to make up for it with a fond smile.

"And you thought a holiday on the Mississippi was the best place to spend this leave?"

Coe laughed and raked his hair back from his face. Charlotte's throat tightened. *Had he been this handsome in New York? Or has the journey here left me ravenous for affection?*

"I will be quite happy when the world has become a place in which I'm able to take holidays in good conscience," Coe said.

Linnet stepped alongside Charlotte. "Jack sent word that the leadership of the Resistance was amenable to talks. Coe's high rank in the military made him the best emissary for dissenters within the Empire. He's coming to New Orleans to discuss the possibility of an alliance."

"And when I learned that Lord Ott was also traveling to New Orleans, I decided to join him," Coe added.

"It would have been faster if you'd flown," Linnet snipped.

Coe grinned at her. "How could I miss the chance to spend day after day with my beloved sister?"

"What a sentimental creature you are, dear brother." Linnet smiled back at him. "If you'll excuse us, I'd like to show Charlotte the rest of the *Calypso* before it's overrun with passengers."

"Never in a thousand years would I attempt to thwart your noble task." Coe moved aside and bowed deeply. When he lifted his head he winked at Charlotte.

Linnet stuck her tongue out at Coe, and Charlotte covered her mouth to stifle a laugh. Light in spirit from their encounter, she threaded her arm through Linnet's as they walked along the deck.

"When he's not in that uniform he becomes a complete rascal," Linnet said.

"It did seem quite the change in character," Charlotte said. It seemed silly that she was still smiling to herself, but she couldn't stop.

Linnet cast a sidelong glance at Charlotte. "He's much more like Jack this way, isn't he?"

Charlotte's smile stiffened.

"I've always thought they seem more like brothers when they're apart," Linnet continued. "When they're together they spend too much time snapping at each other. It's easy to forget they have much in common. Don't you think?"

"I don't think I've known them long enough to make a judgment." All the bubbling joy in Charlotte had drained away.

"Spear of Athene." With that mutter of frustration, Linnet disengaged her arm from Charlotte's. "You know them. Granted, you know Jack better than Coe, but you know them."

Charlotte jerked back, resentful and defensive. "Why are you badgering me about this?"

"Because I care about you," Linnet snapped. "And, boorish as they may be, I care about my brothers, too."

"I haven't done anything wrong," Charlotte said.

Linnet shook her head and let out an exasperated breath. "This isn't a matter of right and wrong."

"Then what is it?" Charlotte's hands were tight fists at her sides.

"Remember what Lord Ott said, about playing the game?"

When Charlotte nodded, Linnet went on. "War isn't the only game. People are always playing games of all kinds. There are no rules, but there are very real costs. And the one you've stepped into can be devastating."

"I'm not playing a game." Charlotte glared at Linnet. "Do you think me that fickle?"

Linnet's gaze remained steady. "You might not want to believe you're playing a game, but you are. We all play this game. From everything I've seen of this world, there is no way to avoid it."

A kindness crept into Linnet's eyes, the same blue eyes that Coe had. Tears began to well in the corners of Charlotte's eyes and she hated it. She wasn't sad, she was furious.

I will not cry. I will not.

"I don't think you're fickle, kitten," Linnet said softly. "But I hope you know what you're trying to win."

Though they each enjoyed a cabin of their own, Charlotte and her friends still ended up gathered in Charlotte's cabin in the late afternoon and into the evening. The relief of Lord Ott's assistance and the excessive comforts of his steamboat had buoyed their spirits, leaving them eager to share stories and laugh with one another. Birch confessed to an excess of joy at being able to retain the profits from selling his trinkets. When he began to describe the designs of new gadgets he hoped to build, Grave and Pip were enraptured, while Charlotte and Scoff soon fell to their own conversation. Scoff, too, wished for the chance to return to creating his experimental concoctions in New Orleans.

"I know it's where I lost Pip, and I still feel horrible about that," Scoff told Charlotte. "But speaking with that apothecary at the River Carnival gave me all sorts of ideas.

I'm going to have some fantastic formulas as soon as I'm able to gather the necessary equipment and ingredients."

Scoff was near feverish with excitement as he rattled off the potential benefits of his elixirs. Charlotte resisted the temptation to ask him what the anticipated side effects of said elixirs might be. She also decided against inquiring what dried eel bladder was used for.

As Scoff and Birch reminisced while expressing such optimism for the future, Charlotte began to wonder about her own hopes. Scoff longed to return to a laboratory, and Birch to a workshop. Pip would be eager to continue as Birch's apprentice and, given Grave's inclination toward mechanics, he'd likely be content in a workshop as well. But Charlotte wasn't sure what she hoped to return to, or rather, to make anew when they reached New Orleans. She was neither an inventor nor an apothecary. At the Catacombs, she'd been a scout and a fighter. Since Ash left, the role of leader had been foisted upon her, and while no one had complained to her or contested her authority, Charlotte wasn't at all sure of how she fared at the helm of this group.

Thinking of Ashley caused a twinge in Charlotte's chest, and she knew what she wished she could return to. Her brother. As often as she had resented being the little sister to Ash's older brother, the comfort of his guidance had been ever present through her childhood. That innocence wasn't something she could regain, but she could be reunited with Ash again. The burst of hope Charlotte felt at that thought was so powerful it made her chest ache. She was so engrossed in her own thoughts that it wasn't until Birch called out "Who is it?" that she realized someone must have knocked on her cabin door.

Embarrassed that she'd drifted away from the conversation, Charlotte was about to apologize to Scoff, but before she could, he waved his hand and said, "Oh well, I guess I'll tell you more about the Fang and Claw tonic some other time."

A voice from the other side of the door called, "Linnet."

Charlotte stood up and went to answer the door, though she dreaded opening it. Her parting words to Linnet earlier that day had been, "I'll explore the rest of the ship on my own. Thank you," before she'd stormed away. She hadn't explored the boat at all, but returned to her room full of anger and guilt. Charlotte stayed there until long after the *Calypso* had left Moirai and Pip came looking for her. Even so many hours later, Charlotte remained embarrassed by her outburst, but also still upset by the conversation that had brought it on. Whatever discomfort she'd endure now, hiding from Linnet was both childish and ludicrous.

She opened the door. "Good evening, Linnet."

"Good evening, Charlotte," Linnet replied. Lowering her voice, she asked, "Are you still cross with me?"

Charlotte felt a rush of affection for her friend, so unafraid to confront their quarrel. She shook her head.

"Good." Linnet's expression was one of genuine relief.

She grabbed Charlotte's hand, giving it a tight squeeze. Then she peeked her head into the cabin.

"Do you mind if I steal this lovely maiden for a bit?" Linnet glanced at Charlotte and added, loud enough for all to hear, "You are still a maiden, aren't you, Charlotte?"

Pip gasped, Scoff guffawed, and Birch and Grave simply looked uncomfortable, until Charlotte jabbed Linnet in the ribs. Linnet feigned a wince and they both fell to laughing.

After Charlotte bade the others good night, Linnet took Charlotte to her own cabin.

"I have a surprise for you," she told her. "I hope you like it."

Charlotte didn't know if she could endure another surprise, but when Linnet turned the wheel that made her cabin's lamps glow bright, Charlotte gasped at what she saw. Gowns covered Linnet's bed. Crafted of smooth silks and rich taffetas, these were not the high-waisted, flimsy gowns of the Floating City. The dresses laced at the back like a corset and their skirts bloomed into fullness below the narrow waistline.

"Are you giving me a dress?" Charlotte asked, delighted but a bit perplexed.

"If you find one you *must* have, then you can keep it," Linnet said. "But I was more inclined to *lend* you a dress appropriate to tonight's festivities."

"What festivities?" Charlotte grew wary again.

"Lord Ott is hosting a party," Linnet told her. "And invitations are very hard to come by. Unless you're me."

Charlotte laughed.

Linnet clapped her hands. "Oh good! We'll have such fun. Now pick a dress."

"No wonder Lord Ott complains about your taste in fashion," Charlotte said, as she held up each dress in turn. "These must cost a fortune."

"I'm worth it," Linnet replied. "Ooh, of course you can wear whatever you like best, but I think that olive green would be so lovely on you."

Charlotte agreed that the gown in question was extraordinary, and the silk felt like liquid moonlight. "Will you help me put it on?"

Linnet wasted no time in helping Charlotte into the dress. The skirt's draping fell into unique lines, forming a pattern that mimicked the movement of pliant fabric if one should spin in rapid circles. The bodice wrapped around her torso, snug but not too tight, even after Linnet had finished tugging on the lacings.

Stepping back to observe her handiwork, Linnet said, "This gown is much more suited to you than me. I'm afraid you *will* have to keep it."

For herself, Linnet selected a gown the rich hue of hammered steel. A layer of sheer gray chiffon encircled the skirt, adding both intrigue and elegance.

The girls took turns arranging their hair into suitable styles held in place by pearl-laden silver combs.

"I have to say," Linnet told Charlotte just before they

left her cabin, "I've never partaken in this women's tradition of preparing for a public outing before, but it's rather fun, isn't it?"

Charlotte kissed Linnet on the cheek. "It was tonight."

Lord Ott's exclusive gathering, contrary to Charlotte's expectations, was not taking place on the upper decks of the ship, but rather in its bowels. The heavy, metal door Linnet stopped in front of at the end of their descent looked like the entrance to the engine room or storage for coal. But stepping through the door, Charlotte found herself in another world entirely. Not of the passenger decks nor of the mechanisms that propelled the vessel, this dimly lit space looked like the den of a warlock as rendered in an old folktale. Smoke curled through the room, carrying with it the scent of tobacco and other, more exotic aromas.

Charlotte hoped to Athene that Linnet wouldn't leave her side, because the room was as intimidating a labyrinth as the Garden of Mirrors had been. Lamps encased in red glass lit the room, filling it with a ruddy glow that barely pierced the shadows. Linnet drew Charlotte to a velvet settee.

"I think we'll have a fine vantage point from here," Linnet said.

"What do you mean?" Charlotte asked, not bothering to suggest it unlikely that Linnet could see anything beyond the length of her arm.

"Parties, balls, dinners—all sorts of gatherings, in truth—if viewed as occasions for making merry, are wasted," Linnet said. "They best serve as sites for observing and learning."

Charlotte sat up a bit straighter, her interest piqued. "Are you planning to teach me to be a spy?"

"If you're going to ask questions like that, I might as well not make the effort." Linnet waved her hand and a man appeared—from where, Charlotte had no clue.

"What may I bring you?" the man asked. He wore the formal suits of all serving staff aboard the Calypso, but tonight his features were partly hidden by a black mask that covered the top half of his face.

"Peach nectar," Linnet told him. She smiled at Charlotte. "You looked like you enjoyed it this morning, but for our purposes now we'll forego the champagne."

Speaking to the servant again, Linnet added, "We'll have a plate of strawberries as well."

The room was gradually filling with guests. Men in fine suits, women in exquisite dresses. Charlotte decided that it didn't matter what gown she wore, because the crimson light rendered everything murky and unidentifiable.

"Keep watching the crowd," Linnet said. "In a few minutes I'm going to ask you what you see."

"Won't I see the same things you see?" Charlotte peered into the dim features of the room.

Linnet sighed. "I think we need to establish a rule about asking questions."

"What's the rule?" Charlotte asked.

"No questions."

Charlotte didn't want to start another argument, but she was irked by Linnet's demeanor. "I hardly—"

"Don't hiss at me, kitten." Charlotte would have taken offense, if not for the mirth in the other girl's voice. "Under other circumstances questions are prudent, but for now they'll only distract you from the task at hand. Espionage is mostly quiet waiting, patient gathering. You are a collector, not an inquisitor."

"Very well."

Until that moment the air had been occupied with the low buzz of hushed voices and the rapid footfalls of servants who glided to and fro, but Charlotte detected a new sound. At first it was only a gentle rumble. But the rumble took the shape of a note that grew louder, as the strings of a violoncello poured out a melody soft as velvet and sweet as wild honey. Charlotte couldn't see the player, who must have been tucked into a shadowed corner. The musician's invisibility enhanced the mystique already possessed by this strange, dark room. Ribbons of smoke followed the trail laid by the cello, curling in time with the rhythm.

The masked servant returned with a silver tray laden with sliced strawberries and two crystal flutes brimming with peach nectar. Charlotte lifted her glass and sipped; the liquid sparkled on her tongue and danced down her throat. Every aspect of the room seemed to flow with the music, bodies turned, sat, leaned closer to one another. Conversations continued, but in a quiet drone, ever beneath the cello's rich voice.

Charlotte bit into a strawberry slice. The bite of the fresh berry mingled with sweet peach, turning into a heady bouquet.

Then Linnet whispered, "Tell me what you see."

Charlotte swallowed more juice, letting her eyes sweep the room. "I see very little, but I don't think that's important."

"If that's not important, than what is?" Linnet asked. Even her voice matched the pace of the cello's song.

"What I feel," Charlotte said. "This place wants to tell me how to feel. It's trying to lull me into the dream it's spinning and make the real world fade away."

There was a long pause before Linnet said, "Very good, kitten. Very good."

"What does it mean?" Charlotte set down her glass and looked at Linnet.

"No questions." Linnet smiled at her. "I think you know what it means. Just speak from your instincts."

Charlotte breathed in the smoke and spice of the air. "I should be wary, lest I forget myself."

Linnet picked up Charlotte's glass and returned it to her, then lifted her own glass and clinked it against the rim of Charlotte's. The ring of crystal pierced the room's spell in a way that made Charlotte feel as if she'd been shaken out of a beautiful sleep . . . when she'd believed she'd always been awake.

Linnet's face came into focus, her eyes alert and intent on Charlotte. "You have great potential, Charlotte. I'm impressed. And I don't impress easily."

"But I . . ." Charlotte's head was still muddled. "I was taken in."

She pinched the bridge of her nose, waiting for her mind to clear.

"You were, but just a bit." Linnet patted Charlotte's hand. "Most people have no resistance."

When Charlotte lifted her face the room appeared brighter, the guests more easily seen, and the cello's melody—while still pleasing—was no different than that produced by any skilled player.

"What was that?" Charlotte asked Linnet. "What happened?"

Linnet took a lingering sip of nectar and ate a slice of strawberry before she answered. "The cellist is a mesmer."

Charlotte frowned at her. She knew of mesmers, though only from tales and not experience. She'd thought of them as traveling hucksters, trading sleights of hand and tricks of the eye for food and goods as they moved from place to place. But what she'd just witnessed was nothing of that sort.

"Is it magic?"

"Magic?" Linnet lifted an eyebrow at Charlotte. "I couldn't say, because magic isn't something I know about or believe in. But there is something real about what mesmers can do. Where it comes from, how it works, I don't know. It's an innate talent, though, and it manifests in various ways. Zephyr—that cellist—bends the wills of listeners and alters their perceptions through his music, but I've seen it done through speech, dance, song . . . it's an incredible talent."

With the mesmer's veil lifted, Charlotte could see its full effect on the other guests. Their gestures and movements were languid—almost drunken, but without the sloppiness. The sight filled her with chagrin, drawing a soft growl of frustration from her throat.

"Still troubled?" Linnet offered Charlotte a strawberry.

Charlotte waved the fruit away and Linnet popped the slice into her mouth.

"I would never have known," Charlotte said. She couldn't stand the idea of being the puppet in another man's play.

"Actually, you did," Linnet said. "You always knew that something about this situation wasn't quite right. If the mesmer had full control of you, you wouldn't have been able to answer my questions. The attempt to alter your mind would have bothered you until you broke free."

Linnet's explanation had yet to reassure Charlotte. "I thought the ringing of our glasses pulled me out of the illusion."

"It hurried along the process," Linnet said. "But I only did that because I knew you could do it yourself. I didn't feel like waiting."

When Charlotte's skeptical countenance remained unchanged, Linnet huffed, "Stop nursing your doubts, kitten. It's a waste of your time and an insult to your talent."

Linnet waved at the roomful of somnambulists. "You were never one of them and you never could be. Mesmers can't take hold of anyone with a strong will."

"Are we two the only strong-willed ones at this party?" Charlotte didn't believe that could be the case.

"Your talent shines through again." Linnet smiled as she ate the last strawberry slice. "No. We are not. So what do you make of that?"

Charlotte cast her gaze about the party as she answered. "If all appear to be affected by the mesmer, then some must be pretenders."

"Yes." Linnet took a sip from her glass only to find it empty. "We need more nectar."

"And strawberries." Charlotte flashed a teasing smile at her friend.

"And strawberries." Linnet waved the servant over again. When he'd refilled their glasses and taken their empty tray, Linnet said to Charlotte, "Revelers are not all alike. Some of the guests here have come to lose themselves. The mesmer's presence is a boon to them and they will happily swim through this dream until the party ends. Others have come to benefit from the first lot, who can be easily manipulated while mesmerized."

"Criminals?" Charlotte was taken aback, though she quickly realized she shouldn't have been. Lord Ott had his hands deep in things above and beneath the law. His party guests would also hail from both sides of legality.

After a throaty laugh, Linnet answered, "That's a base way to put things. But, yes, quite a few could be classified as criminals, though most aren't of the sorry type you encountered at the River Carnival. Those at this party would call themselves artisans rather than criminals. Their services come at a high price."

"They're spies." Charlotte wondered if she would be able to differentiate the lucid guests from the mesmerized if she could study their behavior more closely.

"Spies, of course." Linnet waited for the servant to set down a tray newly filled with strawberry slices. "Also assassins, concubines, pirates, and swindlers."

"You can't be serious about the pirates," Charlotte told Linnet.

"Pirates are very serious," Linnet replied. "And there are definitely a few aboard the *Calypso*. There will be many more in New Orleans. Should you meet one, I wouldn't advise making light of his profession."

Charlotte didn't know if Linnet was attempting to tease her or offer a true warning. Probably a bit of both.

"The original point I was trying to make," Linnet said, "is that your strong will kept you from succumbing, but even more importantly, now that you know how mesmerization takes effect, you'll recognize any time it's happening—and it happens more often than most ever realize. Only mesmers lacking talent ply their trade on the road;

the best mesmers operate in the guise of ordinary performers, but they're paid for the rarer skill they command."

Given that Charlotte's life had been devoid of performance artists until very recently, she was glad to know there was little chance she'd encountered these hidden mesmers in the past.

"Since we've taken care of that, you're ready." Linnet stood up.

Startled, Charlotte stood as well. "Ready for what?"

"To take a turn about the room," Linnet told her. "Mingle. Practice your social graces. You can even flirt if you like. You probably need practice."

Charlotte ignored the jibe. "Is there a reason you want to mingle?"

"There is ever but one reason I engage in these mundane affairs," Linnet said. "I'm a collector."

She put her arm about Charlotte's waist and turned her toward one side of the room. "And tonight you are, too. I'll meet you here in an hour."

"We're not staying together?" As much as Charlotte appreciated Linnet's confidence, she wasn't convinced that parting ways would yield a good outcome.

"You'll be fine, kitten," Linnet replied. "Make me proud."

And then she was gone.

9.

THE TREPIDATION CHARLOTTE felt upon Linnet's departure fled at the thrill of this unexpected adventure.

I have the advantage, Charlotte reminded herself. *The others are caught in a dream state. I'm here to observe. To collect. There is no danger.*

She first encountered a trio of ladies whose features were slack with pleasure, but bore faint lines that suggested haughtiness as their most commonly worn expression. They were the wives of shipping barons and their home was the port of Charleston. Lady Gordon and Lady Firth were sisters and Lady Rothmore was their dearest friend. Their husbands wished to explore the potential profit of investing with a few of the more illustrious river merchants. The ladies shared their exuberance about their courageous foray—with their husbands, of course—into the wild territory so far from the coast. The stories they'd heard about New Orleans were indeed somewhat intimidating—those awful French and their scandals!—but the journey thus far had been surprisingly pleasant.

When Charlotte pressed a bit more about the lords' business venture, Lady Firth admitted that the rivers had become alluring when several cargo-laden ships had run afoul of pirates. Lady Gordon confided that even without losses to the brigands of the river, the costs of the raw materials needed to build new ships had been raised by the Empire to the point where her husband had been forced to take on a large debt to afford them. When Lady Gordon mentioned "debt," Lady Rothmore's lip began to tremble, and soon enough she was tearfully recounting her discovery of Lord Rothmore's fondness for gambling and his reckless squandering of her inheritance. Charlotte took her leave of them when Lady Rothmore was sobbing into Lady Firth's bosom.

No sooner had Charlotte walked away from the now-forlorn ladies than a pair of gentlemen waved her over. Their youth struck a discord with their suits, which bespoke wealth exceeding that of many others in the room. They introduced themselves as Mr. Lannock and Mr. Hume, further evincing that their fortunes had been made, not inherited. The charming, self-possessed gentlemen proved to be on the happier end of Lord Rothmore's sorrow, for Lannock and Hume, by their own testament, were the best card players on the Mississippi. Neither man had set down roots, but spent their days and their nights aboard the great steamboats. They'd played the tables on every vessel that ran a game worthy of their skill, but the *Calypso* was their favorite.

"She's the only vessel that has good drink, soft beds, and beautiful women." Mr. Hume winked at Charlotte.

Mr. Lannock nodded. "It's true; the others all lack at least one."

"And sometimes all," Mr. Hume said mournfully.

There was a light touch on Charlotte's wrist. When she turned, a masked servant took her near-empty glass and offered her a crystal tumbler of dark liquid.

"Fresh blackberry juice from the host, with his compliments," the man said. He left without further explanation.

Charlotte's current companions regarded her with new admiration and obvious interest.

"You've been listening to our tired stories when we should have asked for yours," said Mr. Lannock. "You have friends in high places."

"To the best kind of friends." Mr. Hume lifted his glass. "Those with power."

"To the best kind of friends," Mr. Lannock intoned.

They looked at Charlotte expectantly. She hesitated a beat, then lifted her drink to join their toast. When she brought the glass to her lips she recognized the biting scent of anise under the sweetness of blackberries. Though

Charlotte much preferred the peach nectar, she appreciated Lord Ott's beneficence. She wouldn't have been surprised if he was watching from another part of the room, making sure she could hold her own while circulating through the party. She took another swallow and smiled at Mr. Lannock and Mr. Hume. It occurred to Charlotte that this pair of gamblers might be the very sort to take advantage of a mesmer's sway over others, but nothing in their conversation had indicated that they'd resisted the cello's spell. She'd have to remember to ask Linnet how to recognize signs that a person had been unaffected by mesmerization. She also realized she needed to know how to mask her own lucid state in this sort of situation.

"I should find our host and thank him," Charlotte told them.

They bowed, and Charlotte went in search of new fonts of information to add to her collection.

The elderly Monsieur Bellard was escorting young Mademoiselle Joliet from the headwaters of the Missisippi to New Orleans. Charlotte became enamored of the story Monsieur Bellard spun. She sipped her blackberry tonic while he regaled her with his life's story. Having made his fortune in the fur trade, Monsieur Bellard stood to lose everything when England defeated France in the Seven Years' War. Bellard weighed his options and chose prudence over patriotism. He won the right to remain on English lands and continue his commerce by giving the Empire a sizable percentage of his profit. He had amassed enough wealth that he continued to enlarge his fortune from this arrangement. He'd married late, his long-stoic heart softened by a métis woman, Ma'iigan Joliet, the daughter of an Anishinaabe woman and a voyageur who had long supplied Bellard's storehouses.

Mademoiselle Joliet was Monsieur Bellard's only child. Her given name was Namid, which meant "star dancing" in the language of her mother's people. Ma'iigan had fallen ill shortly after Mademoiselle Joliet's second birthday. Grief laid waste to Monsieur Bellard, and to his shame, Namid's care fell to her maternal grandparents for several years. Though he still regretted such a long absence from his daughter's life, Monsieur Bellard had resumed the duties of a father by the time Namid saw her sixth year. To honor both his wife and her parents, Bellard gave his daughter their surname rather than his own.

Now that Mademoiselle Joliet had reached a marriageable age, her father had decided that a suitable husband would more likely be found in New Orleans than elsewhere. Their homeland in the north suffered a dearth of men who could offer Mademoiselle Joliet the quality of life Monsieur Bellard wanted for his daughter. And he would, in his own words, "first send her like Persephone to Hades to be wed than see her marry some ass of an English lord."

As Bellard's tale went on, Charlotte was transported by its tragedy and romance. She could envision strapping voyageurs as they hauled piles of furs from their canoes.

She saw the rippling water of deep rivers and the froth of their rapids.

"My dear, are you well?" Mademoiselle Joliet's voice was lovely and sonorous, like the ringing of a distant bell.

"Yes," Charlotte said. "I'm quite well."

It was strange that her own voice echoed around her as though she'd spoken within the depths of a cavern. And she couldn't quite escape the vivid images of Bellard's story. The rippling of water still played before her eyes, making the room's walls appear to undulate all around her.

A small voice within Charlotte whispered, *Find Linnet. All is not right.*

"If you'll excuse me," Charlotte said to Monsieur Bellard and his daughter, "I must return to my friend."

"Of course." Bellard inclined his head, and Mademoiselle Joliet bobbed in a curtsy.

Charlotte thought the way they stared at her when she left them was a bit rude. She simply hadn't seen the chair she walked into. It was a silly mistake, but hardly something to gawk at.

Though unsure of how much time had passed since she and Linnet parted ways, Charlotte decided it best that she return to their settee and wait for the other girl. Continuing to mingle with other partygoers before her head cleared of these lovely but intrusive visions could prove embarrassing.

Where had they been sitting?

The walls were still rippling, and the crimson light of

the lamps twined with the smoke in the air to form shapes that Charlotte was convinced she should recognize.

Are they pictures? No, letters. Letters forming words. A message in the smoke.

How wondrous.

Charlotte squinted at the curling smoke, trying to keep track of the letters as they formed, then disappeared. If only she had something to write with.

She wasn't aware that she was still walking through the room until she stumbled into someone.

"I beg your pardon, madam—Charlotte?"

Charlotte blinked up at the speaker, rather cross that his body had destroyed a smoky letter before she could determine what it was. And he'd almost made her drop her glass.

"Charlotte." Hands were on her shoulders. A face peered into hers. She thought she might recognize that face. "Has something happened? Your eyes . . ."

"Ahhh. I know you." She raised her free hand and put them on his whiskered cheeks. "Coe. You have a beard now."

"Yes." Coe sounded worried. Didn't he know that nothing should worry him? Nothing should worry anyone. "How long have you been like this?"

"Mmmmm?" Charlotte rubbed her palm against Coe's whiskers. She giggled. His beard was soft but scratchy at the same time. She wanted to rub her cheek against his to see how that would feel. She lifted on her tiptoes to do just that, but without warning, she began to tip over.

"Ooooh!"

Coe grabbed her around the waist, stopping her fall. Charlotte put her arms around his neck and laughed. What fun this was!

"We should dance!" Charlotte swayed in Coe's grasp. She didn't know if the other guests were dancing, but she didn't care; there were shadows frolicking in every corner of the room. She would dance with them if no one else cared to.

"Try to keep quiet, Charlotte." Coe spoke in a hushed tone, as if something terribly serious had taken place. "I'm going to take care of you."

Charlotte didn't argue, because the idea of being cared for by Coe sounded very nice. They could dance later, when he was done being serious. Her feet brushed the ground on occasion as Coe helped her through the room, bearing most of her weight. For a time she was aware only of the swishing of her skirts and the taut sinews in Coe's arm. Then she was falling. No, someone was lowering her. Velvet brushed her skin, Charlotte shuddered at the fabric's caress, and a moan slipped from her throat. Cushions yielded to her body's shape, molding around her in an embrace. She continued to sink in an ocean of velvet, until Coe's voice reached out, drawing her to the surface.

"What ails you?" Coe asked. "You sound as if you've been hurt."

"No." Charlotte's eyes wouldn't focus on Coe's face, but she knew he was close. She'd felt his breath touch her cheek when he spoke. "I feel wonderful. Just wonderful."

"I should get someone to help you back to your cabin." He began to retreat and Charlotte grabbed his shirt, jerking so hard that Coe stumbled and fell on top of her.

"My goodness," Charlotte laughed. "I'm very strong. Aren't I strong, Coe?"

"Surprisingly so." His voice came out rough. Charlotte liked that, though she wasn't sure why. "It's not right for me to stay with you like this, Charlotte."

"Why not?"

"For many, many reasons," Coe said. "But foremost that we're not alone. I tried my best to find a place as out of sight as I could manage, but that's not really what matters."

Charlotte had no idea what he was prattling on about. She let go of his shirt and put her hands on his shoulders. "You're strong, too. Stronger than me, I think."

Coe didn't respond. He seemed to be trying to catch his breath.

Charlotte found it marvelous to learn the shape of Coe's muscles. He had so many, all so fascinatingly contoured. She was particularly interested in the sudden change from the broad muscles of his chest to the narrowing ridges of his abdomen. She thought it would be a stunning contrast. Deciding she must see it for herself, Charlotte set to unbuttoning Coe's shirt. She'd only loosed two buttons when Coe seized her hands.

"By Hephaestus, girl," he growled. "What are you doing?"

"Trying to look at you." Charlotte told him, surprised

that he sounded so angry. "Don't be cross with me. I only want to because I'm certain you're very beautiful. Possibly perfect. But I need to see to be sure."

Coe groaned, dropping his head so it leaned on Charlotte's shoulder. "Athene have mercy. Charlotte, you don't know what you're saying."

Charlotte knew very well what she was saying and had a mind to explain to Coe that he was the one making things difficult, but his forehead was touching her collarbone, and his loose hair brushed against the top of her bodice. Her ideas about looking at Coe were shoved aside by much more powerful notions.

Taking Coe's head in her hands, she lifted his face and brought her lips to his. Charlotte felt him tense, but she was more intrigued by the way his mouth felt against hers. His lips were soft, but his whiskers rough. Her fingers wound through his hair and she opened her mouth, breathing in the taste of him. She kissed his upper lip and his chin. He was salt and juniper. She wanted to devour him.

Coe stayed very still.

"I'll burn in Hephaestus's forge if this goes any further," Coe said, and pulled away from her.

"But—" Charlotte couldn't form any more words. Her skin was burning and her body so light. Except for the damnable heavy skirts of her dress. Oh, to be free of them. She'd be much happier if she could rid herself of the gown entirely. When had the room become hotter than a furnace? She tugged at the neck of her dress, pulling it down over her left shoulder, but there it stuck, her shoulder free, but the rest of her still enclosed.

Coe would help her escape from this excess of fabric if she told him how she felt, that her flesh had become the petals of a sun-warmed rose and she needed to bask in the cool night air. She couldn't breathe.

"Help me take it off," she begged. "Please."

The world outside her fiery veins slowly came into an unsteady focus and a voice other than Coe's filled her ears.

"I should geld you right now!"

"That's a bit harsh," Coe said.

He was so far away—at least it felt that way, though somehow Charlotte knew he was still seated beside her. She could barely make out his features. Her head throbbed.

"You might not think so if you were surprised by the scene I just discovered." The voice belonged to a woman. An enraged woman. "Button your shirt."

Coe's voice carried more than a little anger as well. "And you might not condemn me if you'd had to take care of her in the state I found her."

"And your idea of taking care of her involved a state of undress?"

Charlotte had a fuzzy sense that she might know the angry woman, but she was also quite sure she must not like this interloper. How could she?

"You don't know what happened," Coe said. "I brought her here and I was trying to find out what happened. Then things . . . became more complicated than I expected."

"Well, I beg your pardon, then, brother," the woman was obviously being sarcastic. Charlotte thought that was terribly haughty of her. "A complex situation completely absolves you of what appears to be an unforgivable act. How could you take advantage of her in this state?"

"I would never hurt her," Coe's voice was hushed, but carried a deadly note. "You've gone too far."

"No," the woman said, her words like ice. "You are the one who has gone too far."

Brother. Charlotte struggled to join their words with her scattered thoughts. *I know Coe has a family. This woman . . . his sister.*

With considerable effort, Charlotte pushed herself into a sitting position. "Linnet," she said, pulling the name from the fog in her mind. "Stop badgering him."

"Thank Athene." Linnet knelt beside Charlotte, clasping Charlotte's hands in hers. "What happened? How do you feel?"

Nothing Linnet said made sense to her. She frowned at the other girl. "I don't know what you mean."

Linnet looked at Coe. "Did you even try to find out why she's like this?"

"Of course I did," Coe said.

"Why are you being so horrible to him?" Charlotte asked Linnet. "He hasn't done anything wrong."

"I'll let that go for now." Linnet put one hand on Charlotte's cheek. "Charlotte, try to concentrate. Did anyone give you something? Food? A drink?"

Charlotte knew that Linnet was her friend, but she wished the other girl would go away. A drink did sound very nice, though. Her throat had gone dry and scratchy, as though she'd been swallowing sand. She needed another drink, something sweet and smooth to cool the fire on her tongue.

"Yes." Charlotte glanced around. "I'm very thirsty and I was drinking something lovely."

"Did you see what she was drinking?" Linnet asked Coe.

When he didn't answer, Linnet snarled. "Of course you didn't."

"There it is!" Charlotte saw her glass lying on its side on the floor. "Oh no. It's empty. Can you get me another?"

Linnet picked up the glass. "I'll get you something else."

Charlotte shook her head. "No. What I had was lovely. I'd like more."

Since Linnet's attention had shifted to Charlotte's empty glass, Charlotte rolled over so she was sitting in Coe's lap.

"Charlotte—" Coe's demeanor had changed after his sister's arrival and Charlotte did not like it at all.

She put her arms around his neck. "I'm sure she'll be gone soon."

"I don't think she will," Coe said, but Charlotte smiled when his arms encircled her waist.

Charlotte stroked his cheek. The scratch of his whiskers on her skin still fascinated her. "She can't stay here forever. But I'll wait. I can wait until the stars burn out."

Linnet began to make sounds as though she were choking.

"She did not say that." Linnet was speaking to Coe, but she stared at Charlotte as though Charlotte were some sort of monster.

"Do you think it's fair to geld me now?" Coe asked his sister. "I've been trying to keep her safe, but she's been very . . . persistent."

Linnet spared him a flat stare. "I don't think you want me to answer you honestly. Never mind. I don't care what you want. You're in command of your mind and body. She is not. That is all I need to know."

Charlotte sighed. Their quarreling was awful and none of it would have happened if Linnet hadn't intruded on her and Coe. "Please go away, Linnet. You're my friend and I'm very fond of you. But I was so happy until you came. You're ruining everything. Don't you want me to be happy?"

Linnet ignored Charlotte, but sniffed the empty glass. "Absinthe. But it can't be that alone. Even several glasses of absinthe wouldn't have this effect."

"You think someone poisoned her drink?" Coe asked. His arms tightened around Charlotte. She mewled with pleasure and kissed his neck.

"Stop that," Linnet snapped at her.

"Why are you so mean?" Charlotte whimpered, snuggling into Coe. "He smells wonderful. I need to taste him."

Coe gave a polite cough and pushed Charlotte's mouth away from his neck.

"That's not very nice," Charlotte told him. "Neither of you are very nice." She glared at Linnet. "I wish you would leave. I asked nicely. Now you're just being rude."

"You'll realize how thoughtful I've been in the morning," Linnet replied. "There's already plenty for you to be rueful about. Now it's just a matter of preventing further injury."

"Am I hurt?" Charlotte asked. She held her arms out and stared at them. "I don't see any blood. Is there blood on my dress? Maybe it's under my dress. Should I take it off?"

"Spear of Athene," Linnet muttered. "That is not absinthe. I have no idea what it is."

"I don't want to wear this gown." Charlotte reached around her back and attempted to undo the knot of her corset lacing. "I'm terribly warm. Why is the room so warm?"

Coe grabbed her wrists and pulled them into her lap. "You're keeping the gown on, Charlotte."

"I hate you!" Charlotte burst into tears.

Linnet gazed at Charlotte. "I know you won't care right now, but I'm going to kill whoever did this to you."

Charlotte sobbed, swung her arm out, and fell over.

"I think she just tried to punch you," Coe said, cradling the now-wailing Charlotte in his lap.

"And I think you know how lacking in judgment she is in this state," Linnet replied.

Charlotte sat bolt upright and thrust one pointed finger in Linnet's face. "You! You . . ."

The fire heating Charlotte's limbs no longer brought pleasure. It seared every inch of her flesh. She screamed in agony. Linnet seized Charlotte, holding her tight as Charlotte cried out and jerked violently in Linnet's arms.

The flames coalesced into a thick, molten tar that covered Charlotte's skin and poured down her throat, drowning her.

10.

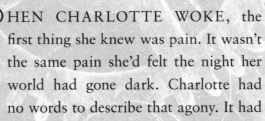

WHEN CHARLOTTE WOKE, the first thing she knew was pain. It wasn't the same pain she'd felt the night her world had gone dark. Charlotte had no words to describe that agony. It had been beyond comprehension and Charlotte believed she'd sell her soul before willingly enduring that sort of torment again. Even so, the pain she woke to was no easy thing. She groaned and opened her eyes.

The first thing Charlotte saw were wide eyes staring down at her. Tears welled in those eyes and dripped onto Charlotte's cheeks.

"Charlotte!" Pip threw herself against her. "I prayed to Athene every day. I was so afraid for you."

Charlotte put her arms around Pip, giving her a hug.

Charlotte's nerves were raw, but she took comfort in Pip's affection. The few memories she could muster before this moment were troubling at best, and incredibly difficult to comprehend.

"Thank you, Pip."

After crushing Charlotte in a hug for several minutes, Pip jumped up, ran to the door, threw it open, and shouted, "She's awake!"

Charlotte had just enough time to prop herself up before her friends streamed into her cabin.

Birch reached her first. "We've been so worried."

Scoff was right behind him. "They made me concoct an antidote. By Hephaestus, Charlotte, I've never been so scared. Don't ever do that again. I don't like saving lives. It's far too much pressure. I am so relieved it worked, though."

"Leave some air for the girl to breathe." Lord Ott's booming voice made Scoff and Birch scuttle away from Charlotte's bed. Ott tossed an apologetic glance at the pair. "Didn't mean to frighten you, but I'd be much obliged for a moment alone with our patient."

Charlotte nodded, and Birch and Scoff hurried out of the cabin.

Lord Ott drew up a chair. His face was etched with concern when he looked at Charlotte.

"You were almost stolen from us," he told her. "And that would-be thief is aboard my ship. I take great offense at that."

"I was poisoned?" Charlotte asked. "How long have I been unconscious?" She was remembering more with each minute she was awake. She wasn't sure she wanted to remember all that had happened.

"Yes." Lord Ott took her hand. "And you've been out for a day and a bit."

The mischief that Charlotte had come to recognize in his expression was gone, and she saw fear in his eyes. "From Linnet and Coe's accounts of what transpired and their descriptions of your behavior and physical symptoms, we were able to narrow down possible substances you were dosed with."

He grimaced, shaking his head. "Whoever meddled with your drink was more foolish than a Dionysian—an obvious amateur. You had a near-fatal reaction. If not for the cleverness of your boy, Scoff—what kind of a name is that . . . never mind—we wouldn't have been able to save you."

Charlotte didn't know how to reply. Her skin was terribly cold, as if it might never warm again, and her heart was cramped. She felt so much like a little girl about to cry and the only person she wanted to see was Ashley.

"You'll be all right, my girl." Ott's voice was gruff, but thick with sentiment. A tear leaked from Charlotte's eye and he gripped her fingers tight. "You're stronger than steel. I saw that from the first moment I met you. Don't let this fester. Fear can do that to you. It's just like the poison some coward handed you in a glass. But only if you let it."

Charlotte nodded, clinging to the certitude of his words. "But if my death wasn't the purpose behind the poisoning, then what was?"

"Scoff recognized your reactions as potential side effects of a concoction he'd been working on for some time: an elixir of truth, he called it," Ott told her. "But the body is extremely sensitive to the combination of herbs used in such a potion. The effects vary wildly in relation to a person's weight, age, or any number of variables. Whoever targeted you either had no regard for your safety, or was too hurried to bother with making sure they'd used the proper dosage. In any case, though the fiend may only have wanted information, it nearly cost your life."

"Do you have any idea how this happened?" Ott asked gently. "I don't want to ask questions you aren't ready to answer. If trying to recall that night is too much, then wait. You shouldn't tax your body or mind until you're well again."

Though every movement made her body ache, Charlotte refused to be manipulated by her unknown assailant for a moment longer. She fought for her memories.

"I'm sorry." She cringed as she spoke. "I'm still trying to understand the way that night . . . how I was taken so far from what I know of myself . . . But I don't know what I would know that could be of such great value. I'm a refugee."

"There is no circumstance in which you should apologize." Lord Ott's eyes were filled with fury. "You were attacked while under my protection. The fault lies with me. I beg your forgiveness for failing you."

Charlotte wanted to cry again, but she refused to break down. She needed to remember her strength. "There is no blame that lies with you, only with the one who poisoned me."

"You have a kind heart." Ott smiled at her.

"I don't know that kindness has any part in it," Charlotte replied. "But I trust that you bear me no ill will. Someone tried to harm me, but you took no part in whatever plot was at work. Of that I have no doubt."

Ott regarded Charlotte for a long moment. "I will retract my suggestion of kindness and instead offer shrewdness. Linnet speaks of your sharp mind with admiration. She's right to do so."

"Thank you for saying that." Charlotte tried to sit up straighter and winced, regretting that Ott should witness her discomfort.

But he quickly said, "There's no shame in honest suffering, my dear. You're enduring more than many could."

Charlotte offered him a wan smile. "I want to remember as much as I can about that night, unpleasant as it may be."

"Unfortunately the most significant moments of our lives are often unpleasant," Lord Ott said. "I wish I could say otherwise."

Charlotte nodded. "It didn't start out as an ill-fated evening. I was with Linnet."

"She told me that she engaged you in a game of

collection," Lord Ott said, chuckling. "She has an enterprising spirit."

"And I was happy for it," Charlotte said. "The night took a turn for the worse when you sent me a drink."

"I'm sorry?" Lord Ott's expression clouded.

"I was conversing with two gentlemen," Charlotte told him. "Gamblers by the names of Lannock and Hume."

Lord Ott inclined his head. "I know those men. Scoundrels, but the harmless kind. Harmless to the body, that is, not to the coin purse."

"That's how I regarded them," Charlotte said. "But while I was speaking with them a servant came to me and gave me a drink."

"What kind of drink?" Ott asked.

"I don't know," Charlotte told him. "I had a glass of peach nectar and he took that. He gave me a tumbler of something else. It tasted like licorice and blackberries."

"Linnet thought it was absinthe," Ott said. He rose from his chair, pacing along her bedside. "And while many attribute visions to the green fairy, those with real experience know such stories to be exaggerations. Absinthe may have been the greater part of what you were given, but that was not the substance that put your life at risk."

"But you did send me a drink?" Charlotte didn't know what troubled her more, that Ott could have requested the glass be sent to her only to have it tampered with, or that she accepted the drink without question.

Lord Ott smiled at her, but his eyes were regretful. "I did not. In truth I was not in attendance that night. I served as the host in name only. While it is unfortunate that your trust in me was a means to put you at risk, it does offer a clue about the fiend that perpetrated this crime."

"Whoever poisoned me knew that I trusted you," Charlotte said.

"Yes." Ott clasped his hands at his back, frowning. "Though that fact in itself is troubling."

"Because the person who sent the drink to me knew enough about both of us to be confident I'd accept it," Charlotte said. The pain she'd experienced when she'd woken had begun to fade, but the conclusions this conversation had drawn presented a much greater threat than whatever physical burdens Charlotte anticipated in the wake of her ordeal.

Lord Ott turned a steady gaze toward Charlotte.

"What happens now?" Charlotte was glad her voice didn't tremble, because she thought it might.

"Vigilance," Ott said.

While Charlotte didn't believe vigilance in and of itself was without value, she still asked, "Is that all?"

Lord Ott chuckled. "That was my sage advice, dear girl."

"And other than your sage advice?" Charlotte regarded him with a new curiosity.

She hadn't known until that moment that Lord Ott's smile could be full of daggers.

"A great deal more than an old man's wisdom remains at my disposal, Charlotte," Ott said. "But if I revealed anything further, by necessity I'd be the next man putting poison in your glass."

When Lord Ott took up her hand and pressed his lips to it, Charlotte was still staring at him in disbelief.

Charlotte was contemplating Lord Ott's words when someone else called her name.

"May I come in?" Coe was standing at her cabin door.

The heat of embarrassment flooded Charlotte's cheeks, while another heat altogether fought for attention in a very different part of her body.

Ignoring the strength of both physical reactions, Charlotte forced her voice to remain calm. "Please do, Coe."

Charlotte took note that Coe closed her cabin door after he entered, whereas her other visitors had left it ajar. She wasn't sure if she was pleased or disconcerted by the difference.

Coe was obviously hesitant to approach her. His eyes traveled swiftly over her body and Charlotte became horribly aware that she had no idea what state of appearance she was in. She fought the overpowering desire to dive beneath her bed linens and carry on whatever conversation Coe wished to have from the safety of her cotton defenses. Given that such action would make her incredibly cowardly as well as vain, Charlotte endured Coe's inspection and tried not to think of all the awful transformations she might have undergone while fighting off the toxins she'd ingested. She didn't even know if her hair was the same color, much less if it resembled anything other than a thatched roof of straw.

Her mind was still running through the best and worst possibilities when Coe came to stand beside her bed.

"I don't mean to be forward," he said quietly. "But I'd like to sit beside you."

All thoughts about how she might look fled Charlotte's mind and she nodded, shifting her body to make room for Coe.

He sat, but he didn't look at her. His head was slightly bowed when he said, "Charlotte, you must think me the worst sort of man."

Charlotte had pulled as many memories from that night as she thought possible, but none of them cast Coe as the villain.

"How can you say that?" Charlotte laid her hand on his arm. "I should beg your pardon for my inexcusable behavior."

"You weren't yourself," Coe said.

"Still . . ." Charlotte's eyes were downcast. She knew that someone had stolen her senses when handing her that drink, but she couldn't shake off the shame of losing control. What a fool she'd played that night.

"Stop that," Coe said. He laid his hand atop hers. "I can see that you're punishing yourself. Nothing that happened was your fault."

Charlotte looked up at Coe. His expression was full of kindness and entirely absent of judgment.

"Thank you," she murmured.

Coe smiled and brought Charlotte's fingers to his lips. "I will always do whatever I can to keep you from harm. You have my word."

His pledge took her aback. She wasn't certain what she'd done to earn such devotion from the elder Winter brother. They'd just barely begun to know each other.

"Ahem." Linnet stood in the doorway. "If I might interrupt."

"I was just leaving." Coe dropped Charlotte's hand and stood up. "Good day, Linnet."

"Good day." Linnet gave a sarcastic little curtsy as Coe brushed past her to exit the cabin.

Charlotte gazed after him, still puzzled by his declaration and his abrupt departure. Did he think Linnet had overheard him? Was he embarrassed? Coe had left so suddenly, he hadn't bothered to bid Charlotte farewell.

"Charlotte." Linnet's voice was like the crack of a whip, drawing her attention.

"It's good to see you," Charlotte said. "I know you did so much to help me after I'd been poisoned. I wish I could remember more so I could fully appreciate all you've done."

Linnet smirked at her. "If you did remember, you might not thank me."

"Why is that?" Charlotte's question carried an edge that made Linnet's friendly demeanor go rigid. She quickly tried to compensate. "That came out other than as I intended."

"And what did you intend to say?" Linnet asked coolly.

"My memories of that night are still muddled," Charlotte said, which was not altogether untrue. "I'm finding it difficult to admit I wasn't in control of my own actions."

Linnet sat on the edge of Charlotte's bed. "Being robbed of your own will is a terrible thing. I hate that it happened to you."

The depth of Linnet's expression made Charlotte uneasy.

"So do I," Charlotte said. "But I'm grateful it wasn't worse. I'm fine now, thanks to you."

"And Coe," Linnet added.

That admission surprised Charlotte. Linnet never seemed that happy to encounter her brother. "Yes. I'm grateful to him as well."

Linnet sighed, offering Charlotte a smile she could only describe as tolerant—like the kindness a loving parent thought was obligated to a misbehaving child.

Charlotte bristled at Linnet's condescending manner. "You don't trust me with him. Is that it?"

"I trust *you*. Coe, on the other hand . . . ," Linnet replied. "It's not that I think he would intentionally hurt you."

"What is it, then?" Charlotte asked, hoping her animosity wasn't obvious, though she couldn't understand Linnet's hostility toward Coe.

Flopping back onto Charlotte's bed, Linnet sighed again, but this time the sound was one of frustration, not impatience.

"To be honest, Charlotte, sometimes I wonder if it's anything at all."

Charlotte lay down beside Linnet. "I don't understand."

Linnet glanced at her. "When I'm at my worst I'm afraid it's jealousy."

"Jealousy?" Charlotte turned on her side so she could look at her friend. "Of what?"

"Both of my brothers want you," Linnet replied. She stared at the ceiling. "I know they'll fight over you, for you."

Charlotte didn't know what to say, but Linnet laughed to herself bitterly. "I'm their sister and neither of them cared enough to compete for my affection." She laughed again. "Don't take that the wrong way. I don't mean anything like what they're fighting for when it comes to you."

"I don't really know that they're fighting over me," Charlotte said. "Jack isn't even here."

She pretended not to feel the sharp pinch in her chest when she spoke of Jack, further muddling her sensibilities toward Coe.

Linnet smiled, but no joy infused her words. "You can tell yourself whatever you need to, kitten. But I'll bet my next payment from Ott that we'll be tearing the Winter brothers apart because of you before the year is out."

"I don't want that," Charlotte said softly.

"I know you don't." Linnet took her hand. "And that's why I keep getting in your way."

Whatever pettiness had dug its claws into Charlotte's

heart couldn't withstand the strength of affection she held for Linnet.

"I hope you always will," Charlotte said to her. "Though I've never thought of it as getting in my way, so much as keeping me on the right path."

Linnet laughed. "Athene spare you that you should trust me so much."

Charlotte rested her head on Linnet's shoulder. Linnet folded her arms around Charlotte.

And fear could not touch them.

11.

ITH THE NIGHT of the party drifting further and further into the past, doubts began to pepper Charlotte's recollection of what had transpired. Not only did her memories feel unreliable, but she also questioned how lingering the poison's effect might have been. She told herself that the nagging uncertainty about her soundness of body and mind was an offshoot of her need to be as helpful as possible to the investigation Lord Ott had underway. Should she offer false leads or imagined clues, Charlotte might delay or misdirect all attempts to apprehend her assailant.

But all the rational explanations with which Charlotte

girded herself couldn't fully obscure what she believed to be a shameful truth. All of her misgivings and hesitation about closely examining that night had to do with Coe. Linnet's pointed words about the Winter brothers made it impossible for her to let herself be swept up in fanciful daydreams about a romance with Coe. There was no simple love story to be enjoyed.

I told Jack I love him.

Charlotte might still feel pangs over Jack's deceit. She might be justified in questioning whether the attachment they had to one another was simply another fabrication, an artifice that aided Jack's mission in the Catacombs. But Charlotte could not take back her words. And she could not pretend she hadn't meant them.

Under the influence of whatever toxins had been in her drink, Charlotte had sought Coe's touch, his embrace. The response his body stirred deep within her might have been enhanced by the altering substance in her blood, but the sensations themselves were not a fiction. Charlotte had come to accept that her desire for Coe was real and weighty enough to give serious consideration, but she couldn't disentangle her feelings for him from those she still had for Jack.

Was her attraction to Coe only derivative of the original passion she felt for Jack?

Or was her attachment to Jack simply a glimmer of what she might eventually have with Coe?

Any which way Charlotte considered her predicament, she could find no resolution.

So she made the choice to act in the only way she thought reasonable until she solved the puzzle of her heart: she would avoid being alone with Coe. Or with Jack—if and when she crossed paths with him again. Unpleasant as that choice would be, Charlotte much preferred it to a dance of ever-changing partners where she didn't know in whose arms she wished to end up.

Enacting her new strategy proved easy enough. After Charlotte's run-in with a poisoner, her friends became increasingly vigilant. Lord Ott insisted that she stay abed another full day and never be without a companion. Charlotte enlisted Linnet's aid so that whenever Coe arrived to serve as Charlotte's companion, Linnet turned up as well. Though Linnet was polite enough not to mention it, Charlotte had no doubts that her friend more than approved of Charlotte's arrangement. Coe, however, being denied time alone with Charlotte, chafed at Linnet's presence and soon gave himself over to leveling stony glares at his sister. Linnet had no trouble ignoring his silent complaints.

Lord Ott himself turned up to reintroduce Charlotte to the world outside her cabin and to present an entirely new vista for her admiration. Charlotte stood arm in arm with Ott at the *Calypso*'s bow, waiting for their destination to appear.

Linnet strolled up to them. "Kitten's finally out of her cage, I see."

"My cabin was hardly a cage," Charlotte said, patting Lord Ott's arm. "I do appreciate the beautiful room. Few patients enjoy such comforts while their bodies mend."

"So this is what it's like to have a charming young lady around," Ott said to Charlotte, but his grin was for Linnet.

"If you like that sort of thing." Linnet shrugged.

Letting Linnet's comment slide, Lord Ott said to Charlotte, "It pains me to say it after your gracious words, but I'm afraid I can't afford you the same quality of accommodation in New Orleans you enjoyed on the *Calypso*. For appearance's sake I'll be staying at the *Belle Fleur*, which is in the Salon district."

Charlotte had no idea what that meant.

As if expecting an objection, Ott raised his hands in defense. "It's not an issue of coin, I assure you. But the eyes of New Orleans are always upon the occupants of its finest inns. You need to escape notice."

"He means that you're staying on the dodgy side of the city," Linnet said.

"Hardly," Ott snorted. "*Le Poisson Noir* is modest. Not dodgy."

"Delude yourself if you will, old man." Linnet grinned at him. "I've seen some questionable deals made in the Black Fish—I've made some of them myself."

"Perhaps *you're* bringing in the criminal element," Ott prodded.

"Of course I am," Linnet quipped. "That's what you pay me to do."

Looking a bit injured, Ott said, "It's not as though I've put them in the Quay."

"That's like saying, 'At least I didn't give them mud pie' when you've fed them moldy bread," Linnet replied.

"Careful, darling." Ott's thick mustache began to twitch. "I could just as easily banish you from the *Belle Fleur.*"

With fluttering laughter, Linnet replied, "You know I'd just talk my way into one of their finest suites."

Exasperated, Lord Ott adopted a mournful tone. "Must you torment your benefactor so?"

"You'd lose all respect for me if I didn't, you old bandit." Linnet rose to her tiptoes and kissed him on the nose. Then she turned to Charlotte. "All jibes aside, don't go into the Quay without me or someone from the Resistance."

"What's so terrible about the Quay?" Charlotte asked. She didn't like the implication that she wouldn't be able to defend herself against any brigand who dared attack her.

"Oh, I wouldn't describe it as terrible," Linnet replied. "As far as appearances go, the Quay looks friendly enough. But once you're inside you'll find it very difficult to leave with your coin, or your life."

Charlotte suspected Linnet exaggerated the dangers of the Quay, at least in part. "What if I accidentally wander into the Quay?"

"You can't wander into the Quay," Linnet told her. "You have to descend into it."

"I'm sorry?" Charlotte frowned at her.

Lord Ott lifted his chin toward the steamboat's prow.

"You'll find out what she means soon enough. There lies the Iron Wall."

In the Catacombs, Charlotte hadn't been inclined to imagine what New Orleans was like. Though the French city had long played an exceptional role in the survival of the Resistance, Charlotte's life had been too filled with work and responsibilities to squander time wondering about far-off places she might never see. Even now she thought she could recall only one or two occasions where the grandeur and might of the city's river gates had come up in conversation, but those memories were hazy at best, and most definitely unreliable.

Therefore, when the immense structure that was the New Orleans Iron Wall came into sight as the *Calypso* rounded a bend in the Mississippi, Charlotte gasped.

A great iron wall spanned the river, its black hulk stretching into the sky and completely hiding the city it protected. The only break in the wall was an immense portcullis. At this hour the portcullis was raised, sharp points at the bottom of the metal lattice giving the impression of a gaping maw.

"Lest their Imperial rivals forget the French still wield power on this continent," Lord Ott said, smiling at Charlotte's awestruck expression.

Embarrassed, Charlotte quickly shut her mouth and nodded. Nonetheless, she couldn't take her eyes off the gates, which grew impossibly larger as the steamboat approached.

Linnet scrunched up her face in disapproval of the gates. "Don't worry. The city is much nicer on the inside."

"Since the American rebellion was quashed, the French have poured resources into the defense of this city," Ott told Charlotte. "It's been built to withstand a long siege and to repel any would-be conquerors. New Orleans can be accessed only by waterways. There are no airship docks here, not that the lack will prevent an airborne assault."

"Yes, yes," Linnet gave a dismissive wave of her hand. "The show of brute force is well and good, but the rules once you're in the city proper are quite brilliant."

"Rules?" Charlotte had hoped to avoid the social strictures that prevailed in New York.

"It was an interesting choice the French made, to be sure." Ott scratched his beard as he mused. "Utterly changes the dynamics of city life."

"You love it," Linnet said with a snicker. "It's the most interesting place to play the game."

"Mmmmm . . ." A smile played at the corners of Lord Ott's mouth, his thoughts drifting to another time and place.

"What are you talking about?" Charlotte had lost patience with this strange turn in the conversation.

Ott snapped out of his wistful reverie, but his eyes were full of mischief when he answered her. "New Orleans has another name. The City of Masks."

Charlotte swallowed a groan. Her most recent association with masks was the man who'd handed her a poisoned drink. She wasn't eager to have another encounter of that sort.

Reading Charlotte's pained expression, Linnet said, "Don't fret. I know you'll find it fascinating. A bit silly, but still fascinating."

"Since I'm going to be fascinated, you should tell me exactly what I'm to be fascinated by," Charlotte said with a grimace.

Linnet glanced at Lord Ott. "Your charming girl has gotten a bit peevish."

"No one's perfect." Lord Ott winked at Charlotte.

"Except me," Linnet sniffed. "I'm quite perfect."

"Careful, Linnet," Ott said. "You know what happens to braggarts whose boasts reach the ears of the gods."

"It's not bragging if it's true."

Ott made a sound that was both sigh and laugh.

"Masks." Charlotte withdrew her arm from Lord Ott's so she could poke Linnet. "Tell me about the masks."

"Poking someone isn't just peevish, it's rude." Linnet rubbed the spot on her arm that Charlotte had jabbed with her index finger.

When Charlotte offered her a bland smile, Linnet relented. "New Orleans belongs to France, but it's hardly a French city. It's an asset, one of the most valuable assets on this continent, and everyone wants to exploit that to their own advantage."

"You mean through trade?" Charlotte asked.

"There are many kinds of trade," Lord Ott replied. "Commerce, of course, plays a vital role in the city, as it stands between the interior and the southern coast, but many of the merchants who come to New Orleans are in search of something other than coin or wares."

The twinkle of anticipation in Ott's eyes prompted Charlotte to say, "Information. They come to trade in intelligence. Like you."

Ott's face fell. "I suppose—"

"He doesn't like to think anyone else is like him," Linnet broke in. "Just humor him."

"Since you're so fond of offering comment—" Lord Ott drew out a pocket watch and checked the time. "I'll leave Charlotte's introduction to the city with you. We'll be docking soon and I should speak with the pilot."

When Lord Ott had gone, Charlotte asked Linnet, "I didn't really offend him, did I?"

"Of course not." Linnet took a pistol from its holster and a kerchief from her pocket. "He loves attention, is all. Should've been an actor."

She began to polish the gun's mother-of-pearl grip. "All fun aside, it is important that you understand the way New Orleans operates."

"I'm listening," Charlotte said.

"The French don't openly support the American rebellion," Linnet said. "But it's no secret that the Resistance's base of operations is New Orleans. The only reason the Empire hasn't laid siege to the city is that they aren't yet ready to declare all-out war on France. But it won't be that way forever."

"And that has something to do with masks?" Charlotte leaned out over the deck railing, watching as the Iron Wall grew impossibly taller. In a few moments the *Calypso* would pass into its long shadow.

Linnet holstered her gun and drew another, to set about polishing its ebony grip. "It has more to do with irking the British than with brilliant political strategizing."

Charlotte nodded, listening but keeping her eyes on the wall. They were close enough that she had to tip her head up to see the battlements running along the top of it.

"The British knew their victory was due in large part to France's refusal to enter the fray," Linnet continued. "Not wanting to antagonize their oldest enemy, the Empire decided against pursuing rebels who were granted sanctuary by the French. But that didn't mean they lost interest in what happened to the revolution's ringleaders. When France fell into the storm of its own revolution, the American rebels there went into even deeper hiding and lost contact with their peers across the Atlantic. The Resistance formed and began its steady, if rather ineffectual, attacks on the Empire. After Napoleon took New Orleans from the Spanish, the connection between France and the Resistance was reestablished, which raised a fair amount of alarm in Britannia. They couldn't send troops to capture Resistance leaders without sparking a war in America, and they were already embroiled in one in Europe. New Orleans, then, became the heart of British covert operations, and within a year it was overwhelmed by the chaos of intrigue, assassinations, and subterfuge."

Managing to tear her attention from the fortifications, Charlotte said, "I thought it still was."

"It is," Linnet said. "But not in the bedlam manner it once was. The masks reined in chaos by making New Orleans a center of bizarre spectacle, drawing visitors who had no interest in Imperial conflict, just entertainment."

"You're not making sense," Charlotte said.

"That's because it's such an unlikely solution." Linnet smiled at her. "And it was completely happenstance. Only the French could have decided to make it a fixture of the city."

Charlotte turned her back to the wall, its mass finally too intimidating to stare down.

"*Le droit des masques* took effect in 1803," Linnet said. "When control of New Orleans transferred from Spain back to France. The crown-appointed French governor, an eccentric fellow by the name of Guy de Rohan-Rohan, despite the gift of noble blood bore a birthmark that by rumor gave him the appearance of an octopus latched onto his face."

Charlotte scoffed in disbelief, but Linnet only grinned at her.

"Unwilling to show his face, Rohan-Rohan never appeared in public without an elaborate mask. When he assumed rule of New Orleans, his first decree was to establish a law that requires every man, woman, and child in the city to hide their face while in public. The masks, of course, brought widespread attention to New Orleans, and visitors began to descend on the city in unprecedented numbers; when the tourists brought their wealth, merchants followed in droves. New Orleans was transformed into an oasis of rare entertainment and unmatched spectacle. All of these changes tempered the level of political machinations that had overshadowed all other enterprises of the city."

"That's just . . . strange." Charlotte still didn't like the wall, but Linnet's description had piqued her interest.

"It's very strange," Linnet said. "And that's why you should go explain it all to your friends before they get off the ship."

Charlotte nodded, but when Linnet continued to stare at her pointedly, she said, "Now?"

"Yes, kitten. Now."

12.

LINNET HAD BEEN right to send Charlotte back to her friends with plenty of time to spare before the *Calypso* docked. It took three repetitions of Linnet's story for the others to comprehend it fully.

Scoff tugged on his suspenders. "You know, I'm pretty sure Jack told me about this once, but I thought he was lying."

"I can't fault you for that," Charlotte said. "It sounds like something Jack would make up."

"It certainly does," Birch said. "What a bizarre law."

"I like it." Scoff bobbed his head in an exaggerated show of approval.

"What do the masks look like?" Pip was sitting on Charlotte's bed. "Do we get to choose what mask we wear?"

Charlotte answered, "I don't know. I'm sure we'll find out soon enough."

"I've always had the notion to create an elixir that alters facial features," Scoff said. "I wonder if I could brew it up here and sell it."

"Since it's a law that requires your face to be hidden, I don't think it matters if you've altered the way your own face looks. It's still a face." Even as she said it, Charlotte felt confused.

"I suppose," Scoff grumbled.

"I don't think they'd object to modifications of one's mask, though." Birch scratched at his chin. "Do you?"

"I really couldn't say," Charlotte answered.

"Oh! Oh!" Pip jumped up and down, tugging at Birch's sleeve. "I want to modify my mask, too. Will you help me?"

"Let's make sure modifications are permitted before you start to draw schematics," Charlotte told her.

Pip stuck her lower lip out. "Even if they're just tiny modifications?"

"Who's modifying what, now?" Linnet asked. She and Coe carried a large trunk into the room.

Pip dashed to it and opened the lid before they could set the trunk down.

"Masks!" Pip's eyes were wide. "They're sooooo pretty."

Pip's body obscured Charlotte's view, but she could see an array of bright colors peeking from within.

"And they're animals." Pip held a mask aloft. It had

been crafted of leather in a deep, mottled green and shaped to have the blunt snout of a serpent. "I'd rather not be a snake." She tossed the mask aside.

"Ummmm." Linnet frowned when the mask hit the floor. "Maybe take a bit more care with the masks. They're quite expensive."

"Oh, a butterfly!" Pip brandished another mask. "I want this one."

She put the mask up to her face. Wings of turquoise rimmed in black spanned Pip's cheeks, the butterfly's wing-tips reaching just beyond her temples and jaw. She tied the ribbon around her head.

"That's not an animal," Scoff said. "It's an ornament."

Pip ignored him, asking Birch, "Can we make the wings beat?"

Linnet glanced at Charlotte, eyebrows raised.

"The modifications," Charlotte said.

"Ah." Linnet smiled at butterfly Pip. "Small mechanical mods are permitted. So long as the movement doesn't reveal the face."

Pip squeaked her delight.

"The rest of you should find your favored animal quickly," Coe told them. "We'll be docking within the hour."

"And don't become too attached to one mask," Linnet added, with an eye to Pip. "You should put on a different mask whenever you leave a private space to go into the public. It discourages would-be spies from identifying you without making at least a little effort. More importantly, it's considered fashionable to wear a variety of masks rather than adopting a signature visage."

Pip nodded at her, then said to Birch, "We'll have to modify a lot of them."

The corners of Birch's mouth twitched in the hint of a smile, but he answered in all solemnity, "Yes. I suppose we will. I'd hate anyone to think we're less than fashionable."

The *Calypso*'s passengers emerged from their cabins transformed into all manner of fauna. Charlotte passed a spider, several owls, a handful of cats, a horse, a few bulls, and even an elephant as her company disembarked from the steamboat. The docks teemed with masked people swarming into the city proper.

Coe, masked as a wolf, walked at Charlotte's right hand, and Grave's snowy egret was at her left. Charlotte had taken on the guise of a fox for this first venture into New Orleans. Pedestrian traffic from the riverside docks accessed the city platforms by stepping onto ascending ramps that twisted in tight spirals. New Orleans may have been an elevated city, but it bore no comparison to New York. Stout iron ribs held the city aloft, high above the river and bayous.

"The city is divided into quadrants," Coe told Charlotte as the corkscrew took them upward. "The Garden is exactly what its name suggests, a verdant space in a city otherwise dominated by metal. The Salon plays host to the wealthiest and most powerful in New Orleans, both residents and visitors."

"That's where Ott is staying?" Charlotte asked.

Coe nodded. "The *Belle Fleur* is located in the Salon quadrant."

"Where will we stay?" Grave asked. His gaze was fixed on the docks as they grew more distant.

"*Le Poisson Noir* is in the Domicile quadrant," Coe answered. "The Domicile and the Market are the largest and liveliest of the quadrants. Like the Garden, the Market's name disguises nothing about its purpose."

"What about the Quay?" Charlotte wondered if the area she'd been warned against was wedged somewhere within the quadrants.

"Who told you about the Quay?" The sharpness in Coe's voice made Charlotte bristle.

"Why shouldn't I know about it?" Charlotte rested her palms on her gun belt.

Grave's eyes were drawn from the riverbank by the newly tense exchange. "What's the Quay?"

Coe leveled a disapproving stare on Charlotte.

"I've been told it's a dangerous place," Charlotte said to Grave. "One to be avoided."

"At least you got sensible advice," Coe muttered.

"And if you want me to adhere to that advice, I should know where the Quay is." Charlotte resented Coe's attitude, as if she were a foolish girl in need of protection.

Had he forgotten the brigands she'd fought off in the Iron Forest? Without his aid?

Coe glanced at Grave, then lowered his voice so only Charlotte would hear. "I don't mean to upset you, Charlotte. But the Quay can't be taken lightly."

"And why would I be careless about it?" Charlotte snapped. "Do you think I'm that naïve?"

"Of course not." Coe rested his hand on her arm, and she felt her pulse quicken. "But your anger makes me worry you've forgotten that only recently someone attacked you. We still don't know who or why, but we do know they were on the *Calypso*, and that means they are now in New Orleans just like us. I don't want you to put yourself at greater risk than you already are."

Charlotte's throat grew thick with embarrassment. "Oh."

Coe offered her a thin smile, then said to both Charlotte and Grave, "The Quay isn't a single place; it's scattered throughout the same area as the city, only beneath it—with the exception of the docks, which are heavily regulated by the French and therefore avoided by those for whom the Quay's offerings hold allure. Merchants, saloons, and brothels in the Quay are in clusters near the three lakes inside the city walls: Pontchartrain, Borgne, and Catatouatche."

"If it's so dangerous, why do the French let it exist?" Grave asked.

"The Quay is the underbelly of New Orleans," Coe

said. "Ugly as it may be, to slice it open would be fatal to the city."

Grave shook his head. "It can't be a good city, then, to be reliant on such a place."

"All cities are reliant on such places, Grave," Coe told him. "At least every city I've known."

Grave's sigh was so deep that Charlotte took his hand.

"The more I'm in the world the less I like it," Grave said softly.

"It's not all ugly," Charlotte said, wishing she could offer greater assurance. But they'd come to New Orleans because of a war. Charlotte knew far uglier things could lie ahead than what Grave had already seen.

"The lady's a prophet." Coe smiled as he stepped off the ramp and waved his hand at the scene laid out before them. "Look at all this beauty."

The spare design of the docks and iron foundations of the city belied the wonder that waited above. Pristine buildings in pastel hues greeted them, their structures curving alongside walking paths of mosaic tiles. Fountains of copper and marble bubbled cheerfully beside bushes studded with exotic blooms, the likes of which Charlotte had never seen.

"This must be the Salon," Charlotte said as they followed the path.

Upon closer inspection she could see that the images in the mosaic were great tales of myth. Their steps traced Actaeon's doom as his own dogs hunted him down, a man transformed into a stag for the transgression of spying on the virgin goddess Artemis as she bathed.

"No," Coe said. "This is the Domicile."

"But—" Charlotte swept over her surroundings, searching for some flaw. She found none. "By Athene, what is the Salon like?"

Coe laughed and when he offered Charlotte his arm, she took it.

Le Poisson Noir sat in the middle of the quadrant. A fat little building painted sea green, the inn had a wrought-iron balcony that was decorated with swimming black fish that reminded Charlotte of Pisces. Linnet and Coe shepherded the others into the foyer, and after a few quick words from Linnet, they were given keys to a large suite on the upper floor. Ott's servants brought what few belongings Charlotte and her companions had to the inn, though given the change in circumstances Charlotte didn't know what value, if any, their salvaged items from the Catacombs continued to have. Lord Ott's resources appeared limitless, and as far as Charlotte could tell he withheld nothing in his efforts to help them.

Except for a room at La Belle Fleur, Charlotte thought with a smile.

Linnet and Coe went to arrange contact with the Resistance, leaving Charlotte and the others to settle into their rooms. The suite was enormous. Charlotte entered a spacious sitting room appointed with satin-upholstered settees supported by delicate, curving wooden legs polished to a bright sheen. Glass doors opened to the wide balcony, where iron fish swam across the railings. She heard Pip gasp in delight from one of the adjoining rooms.

"This bed is enormous," Pip called out to no one in particular. "It has ten pillows! Who needs ten pillows?"

Charlotte laughed to herself, but chose to visit the balcony before exploring the rest of the suite.

As she leaned on the railing, Charlotte could see the expanse of the city. The iron wall rose above all else, but its presence was less ominous within the city than she had perceived it to be from the outside. *Le Poisson Noir* faced north, and from her perch on the balcony, Charlotte could spy in the distance what she assumed was the Garden quadrant, given its emerald hue and lack of buildings. She'd seen little of this city, but already she found more to like here than she had in the Floating City. New Orleans embraced its strange nature and welcomed its visitors to take part in its game, where New York condescended, ordering all who entered to conform to its rigid structures.

Charlotte had to admit her own bias. She'd reached the end of a long, arduous journey and New Orleans had long been a refuge for those like her, those fleeing the grasp of the Empire's iron fist. Only with time would she know if New Orleans offered a true respite, a place that could become home. The glimpses of the city gave her a nagging desire to explore the other quadrants.

Had Linnet and Coe said anything about when they'd return? Had they been explicit about not leaving the inn? Obviously the Quay was to be avoided, but the rest of the city wasn't brimming with threats.

Charlotte decided she would tell Birch she planned to go out into the city for a bit. If he balked, she could take Grave along. No one could argue that Grave wouldn't offer protection, and Charlotte wouldn't mind his company.

When she'd returned to the sitting room and closed the balcony doors, Charlotte removed her mask. The confines of the suite would be one of few places where a mask wasn't required. Wearing the mask had been unusual, but neither uncomfortable nor cumbersome. Charlotte didn't think she'd be too irked by the *droit des masques*.

Birch sat on one of the couches with Pip's butterfly mask in his left hand. With his right, he dug through a sack that jangled as he shuffled through metal parts and scraps.

"Moving wings?" Charlotte asked, sitting beside him.

Birch smiled. She could see that tension had eased from his face now that they were in New Orleans.

"It's a way to pass the time," Birch said. "I'm not sure how long we have here or what comes next, but I prefer to have something to work on rather than being idle."

Charlotte leaned over and kissed his cheek. "Only one of the reasons we could never manage without you."

Birch guffawed, pink dusting his features.

His reaction gave Charlotte pause. She'd been wrestling with her divided heart, but what of her friends? Had Birch fallen to Eros's arrow? Had Scoff? Pip was too young to be ensnared by romance, but the others weren't. Charlotte knew of her brother's attachment to Meg, and the heartache he'd felt when she left them to join the Sisters. Aside from Ash, Charlotte had no inkling of where her friends stood in relation to love.

And what of Grave?

The question chilled her for reasons she didn't grasp.

"Are you unwell, Charlotte?" Birch had stopped searching the sack and was peering into her face. "You've gone rather pale."

Charlotte didn't know how to answer. Her thoughts had led her down a path that ended in a place unfamiliar and deeply unsettling. She sensed that having arrived here, there would be no going back.

"I—"

Whatever jumble of words was about to pass her lips, it was stopped by a knock at the door.

Pip bolted into the sitting room. "I'll get it!"

"Find out who it is, Pip." Charlotte stood up. "Don't just open the door."

"I *know*." Pip gave a little huff, then her voice became sugar when she asked, "Who is it, please?"

"It's Ash, Pip."

Charlotte wanted to run to the door and fling it open, but she was frozen where she stood. Her limbs locked with anticipation.

Ashley is here. He's here!

Pip had no run-in with paralysis. She opened the door, bouncing up and down with glee.

"Ash! Ash! Ash! Oh, you're an eagle. Who's she?"

Ash hadn't come alone. A tall woman stood beside him in the doorway, her face hidden by that of a badger.

Ashley put his arm around Pip, gently moving her aside. The woman came into the room and closed the door.

When Ash took his mask off, whatever held Charlotte in place let go.

"Ash!"

She ran across the room and jumped into her brother's arms.

"Lottie. It's so good to see you."

Charlotte couldn't stop an embarrassment of tears from fleeing her eyes. "I've missed you so."

"Charlotte." The woman had spoken, and the sound of her name in that voice rang with a familiarity that echoed in Charlotte's bones.

Charlotte turned to see that the badger no longer covered the stranger's face. But she wasn't a stranger.

"Lottie." Ashley gripped her hand. Her fingers wrapped tight around his.

When Charlotte spoke, only a whisper emerged.

"Mother."

13.

CAROLINE MARSHALL STOOD taller than her daughter by a head and a half, but Charlotte recognized features they did share: a straight, thin nose, brown hair, long fingers, and a sharp chin. Charlotte remembered her mother's face as softer than the stern, angled visage gazing back at her now. She attributed the difference to naïveté of childhood. All the world had seemed a gentler place before Charlotte grew into a young woman; why should her mother be any different?

She wore a crisply pressed white shirt and draped trousers of deep gray silk with a cuff that hit just below her knee. Silver hilts flashed from their sheaths at the mid-calf of her boots, and smooth bone gleamed on the grips of the guns holstered at the bottom edge of her wide leather belt.

When her mother extended a hand, Charlotte was taken aback by how shy she suddenly felt. She wanted to duck her chin and keep her eyes on the ground, perhaps even hide behind her brother, but she forced herself to stand straight, let go of Ashley's hand, and approach with a confident bearing no matter how madly her heart drummed against her ribs.

Charlotte took her mother's hand, and Caroline leaned down to place a cool kiss on Charlotte's cheek.

"How you've grown."

Unable to find words, Charlotte simply nodded.

Caroline smiled the barest of smiles. "And you've led those who escaped the Catacombs to New Orleans. That's a remarkable feat, Charlotte."

"Thank you," Charlotte said. "We left the youngest children at the crèche in East Moirai."

"You kept a level head when following protocol," Caroline replied. "One must be pragmatic in trying circumstances. If sentiment had lulled you into an attempt to bring them along, I doubt you'd be here today."

That was something of a compliment, and Charlotte stood up a bit taller.

"Ashley showed wisdom in handing leadership to you," Caroline said, casting her smile of approval in his direction. "I hope you'll continue to demonstrate the same qualities here. Fighting for the Resistance, giving your full commitment to the cause, requires sacrifice. Difficult decisions."

"I understand," Charlotte said, though her mother's

proclamation made Charlotte's heart stutter with uncertainty, as did the hard cast of her mother's face. Something about her expression was unyielding to the point of severity.

"I've asked your brother to take charge of introducing your companions to the world, and rules, of the Resistance and our operations here," Caroline said. "But I'd like you to accompany me to the Daedalus Tower."

The burst of surprise and delight made Charlotte almost giddy. Her mother wanted to take Charlotte, and only Charlotte, to . . .

"The Daedalus Tower?" Charlotte didn't want to appear ignorant of anything, so pleased was she with her mother's approval, but she knew better than to pretend knowledge.

Caroline touched Charlotte's cheek, and for the first time her smile emanated warmth. "Where we spend all our days and many of our nights. The home of the Resistance."

Despite wanting to give a little shriek of excitement, Charlotte managed to retain her composure. She felt a tentative tug on her sleeve. Pip had snuck up beside her. The green-haired girl had wide eyes, and an uncharacteristically timid demeanor.

"Who have we here?" Caroline asked.

Pip's cheeks went rosy. With her own reticence so fresh in her mind, Charlotte put her arm around Pip's shoulders to encourage her.

"This is Pip," Charlotte said. "Pip, this is my mother, Caroline."

"Hello, Mrs. Marshall," Pip's voice squeaked out.

"Pip." Caroline tilted her head, assessing Pip's face and hair. "Cressida and Lark's daughter?"

Shedding her trepidation like a husk, Pip skipped forward at the sound of her parents' names. "Yes! Yes! You know them? Are they here?"

The corners of Caroline's mouth tightened ever so slightly. "Of course. But I'm afraid they aren't in New Orleans at present. A mission required them in the field."

"Oh." Pip's face fell.

Charlotte drew Pip back to her side. "It's all right, Pip. Why don't you see how Birch is coming with your mask's wings?"

"I think it's going to work!" Birch called to Pip.

Though her eyes still shone with disappointment, Pip joined the tinker on the sofa. Caroline watched the pair, then laughed.

"Are your experiments as incendiary as your aunt's, Birch?" Caroline asked.

Birch startled at her question, but Pip caught the mask he dropped before it hit the ground. "Aunt Io?"

"The very same," Caroline replied.

He cast a guilt-ridden glance at Pip before he asked, "And . . . is she here?"

Caroline nodded, then laughed again. "She oversees the Daedalus Tower workshop. Your aunt is brilliant at design, but can be a bit careless when it comes to execution. When we put her in charge, we continued to benefit from her exceptional mind, but significantly reduced the number of accidents in the workshop."

Birch wore a lopsided smile. "That sounds like Auntie Io."

"Ash can bring you to her office," Caroline told him. "She'll be thrilled to see you."

She looked at Pip, who was fidgeting with the mask in her hands, her eyes downcast.

"And I know she'll want to meet your young protégée," Caroline added.

Pip's head bobbed up, a little color and a tiny smile returning to her face. She glanced at Birch. "Do you think so, too?"

"Without a doubt." Birch patted her green hair.

Caroline's gaze moved from the pair on the couch to the solitary figure who sat in the chair beside them.

"Another introduction is needed, I think."

Charlotte's mother was looking at Grave. Surely, Ash had told their mother about him. He must have. Charlotte turned her head, looking to Ashley for guidance. Her brother gave a brief nod.

"Mother . . ." Charlotte walked to stand behind Grave's chair. "This is Grave. Our friend."

Caroline stayed where she stood, her eyes searching Grave's face. "It's a pleasure to meet you . . . Grave."

"Hello," Grave said.

"We should be on our way," Caroline said to Charlotte, but her focus remained on Grave. "Don't forget to choose a different mask than the one you wore earlier today. Ott should have left a variety for you. Pick one for me as well."

Charlotte went to the bedroom that housed the trunks Lord Ott had sent to them. Scoff was sprawled on the bed, snoring. Charlotte quietly retrieved two masks, one composed of rose petals and the other in the likeness of a bear. When she returned to the sitting room, she offered the flower mask to her mother.

"Lovely," Caroline murmured.

While her mother put on the mask, Charlotte went to hug Ash once more.

"I wish we could talk," she whispered to him. "I have so many questions. And so much to tell you."

"We'll talk soon," Ash replied. "But you should go with Mother."

"Ash." Charlotte held on to him a moment longer. "Where is Father?"

She hadn't wanted to ask her mother in front of the others. It was a question to which there were more grievous possible answers than happy ones.

"She'll tell you," Ash said.

Charlotte wished his reply had been more reassuring.

The walk from *Le Poisson Noir* to the Daedalus Tower didn't afford Charlotte the opportunity to share an intimate conversation with her mother. Caroline moved at a swift clip along the Domicile walkway, without so much as looking toward Charlotte. Charlotte resigned herself to waiting until they'd arrived at their destination before trying to ask about her father, or anything else.

They crossed the covered metal bridge that linked the Domicile with the Market. While the Domicile didn't lack for activity, the Market was a riot by comparison. Tents and booths crowded with vendors and shoppers lined the sides of the walkway, while behind the transient sellers of crops and small crafts, buildings housed all manner of goods. The shops boasted sparkling windows, polished to give browsers an unimpeded view of the wares within.

Charlotte had been impressed by the variety of shops she'd seen in East Moirai, but those shops offered a mere pittance compared to the grand displays of New Orleans' Market. A grand purveyor of furnishings displayed pieces with slender, curving legs crafted from exotic woods of all shades. Ladies in delicate masks and pastel bustled skirts stepped primly through the doors of a dressmaker. Automatons waved and twirled behind the store windows, their metal bodies bedecked in velvet, silk, and lace. There were stores that Charlotte couldn't believe existed: a shop that sold only toys, another stocked treasures of spun sugar and sculpted chocolate whose scents made her mouth water, and yet another offered musical instruments—Charlotte lagged behind her mother to watch the fiddler who stood on the store's broad porch, luring customers with his intricate melodies.

Hurrying to catch up with her mother, Charlotte resisted the dazzling sights of the storefronts with a pang of regret. She wondered if there would be time to explore the city, to wander at her leisure. She followed Caroline around a corner and discovered that, unlike the single walkway through the main thoroughfare of the Domicile, the center of the Market quadrant had a second row of buildings and an accompanying walkway. The most vibrant and fanciful stores occupied the first row, while the stores residing behind had purposes more familiar and practical. Butcher, baker, tanner, cooper. Tinker, alchemist, gunsmith, clockmaker.

Caroline turned off the walkway when they reached a long building bearing the sign *The Sintians' Warehouse.* This store had no bright windows. The small openings in its walls were caked with dust. Charlotte followed her mother into the store. Inside, the air smelled of oil and metal. Tall shelves and squat crates filled the store, loaded with parts of all kinds. The only order Charlotte could discern was that the goods appeared to have been sorted by type of metal. There were shelves laden with bronze gadgets and tubes. Others were overburdened by copper, brass, silver, and gold. It was a maze of broken-down machines and half-assembled weapons.

Birch would call it heaven, Charlotte thought.

They passed the rows of shelves, heading for the back of the store, where a man stood behind a simple counter. He looked up at Caroline and nodded. She walked past him without a word, going through a door behind the counter.

The door led to a room stacked with empty crates. Charlotte watched her mother go to one of the crates on the floor and reach inside it. When she lifted her hand, the bottom of the crate came with it. A trapdoor.

"Go ahead," she told Charlotte.

When Charlotte looked into the opening, she saw a wooden ladder descending to a cellar. She climbed down quickly as she could. Caroline followed, closing the trapdoor behind them. The cellar was empty except for one wall covered with hooks from which an array of masks hung. When Caroline reached the bottom of the ladder, she untied her rose mask and placed it on one of the hooks. Charlotte did likewise.

Caroline crouched down and turned the lowest hook on the right side. A panel on the opposite wall slid open, revealing a long metal corridor, round in shape like a large drainage pipe. Charlotte surmised that it probably was, or had once been, a real drainage pipe.

Leading the way, Caroline stepped into the corridor. When Charlotte joined her, Caroline said, "There's a wood handle hanging from a chain on your left. When you pull it, the panel will close behind us."

Charlotte took that description as a direction as well, and tugged on the chain. The wall panel slid back into place. A string of glass globes ran along the top of the corridor. Inside the spheres, clumps of moss gave off a blue-green light that reminded Charlotte of the glowing fungi that grew in the Catacombs. Their footsteps echoed along the metal tube, but Charlotte's mother didn't pause to speak to her. Charlotte wondered when the appropriate time might be to ask her mother questions. Caroline's bearing and purposeful stride didn't invite conversation, but Charlotte was beginning to grow frustrated by her mother's silence.

She was working up the courage to speak, when they reached the other end of the tube. Caroline turned a wheel to open a round brass door. Natural light poured in from the other side of the door, as well as a rush of fresh air tinged with brine. Charlotte stepped out of the pipe and found herself in another corridor, but this one was wide. To either side of her, four staircases built of metal grating climbed up each of the corridor walls, and above her, walkways connected the opposite landings as far as she could see, up and down its length.

"Welcome to the Daedalus Tower," Caroline said. Charlotte heard pride in her mother's voice.

Charlotte turned in a slow circle, trying to make sense of this place. "Where are we?"

"In the wall," her mother replied.

"The Iron Wall?" Charlotte asked in disbelief.

With a smile, Caroline said, "Yes. It takes some adjustment to orient yourself to this space, since the interior of the wall has no defining features. Take note of where you came in."

She pointed at the brass door. The image of a hammer had been stamped onto its face.

"There are other entrances?" Charlotte wasn't only thinking about getting in, but about getting out. What came as a surprising comfort were the similarities of the narrow passageways and cavernous spaces in the Daedalus Tower to those of the Catacombs. With bolstered confidence, Charlotte waited eagerly for further details from her mother.

"Of course," Caroline replied, starting down the corridor. "Some are known to all members of the Resistance; others are hidden from all but a few."

They passed other doors on both sides of the wall. These were numbered.

"Do people live here?" Charlotte asked.

"We do have living quarters available. Most are on this level, in the interior wall," Caroline said. "But they serve as temporary homes for Resistance members who frequently move to and from field operations. Those of us who serve indefinitely in the city have residences in the Domicile."

Charlotte seized the opportunity to query her mother. "Do you and Father have a home there?"

"I keep a modest apartment," Caroline answered stiffly.

"And Father?" Charlotte had to ask, no matter how awful the answer.

Caroline stopped and faced her daughter. "Your father is gone, Charlotte."

"But . . . how?" Her mother's answer had been not only abrupt, but so stark, so empty. "What happened?"

Charlotte's breath became shaky. Though she had few

memories of her father, those she'd retained were full of warmth and comfort, glimpses of walks among tall pines, and laughter while riding high atop his shoulders and pretending she could fly into the treetops. She knew these images were what little she remembered of her father's visits to his children while they lived at the crèche, but she couldn't keep a firm hold on the past. Each memory slipped through her fingers as soon as she touched it. Those elusive, ghostly moments would be all she ever knew of her father.

Caroline gazed at Charlotte for a long moment, then gathered her daughter into a careful embrace. "Sorrow is an indulgence. I know it seems cruel, but a long mourning period is something we cannot afford."

Not wanting to disappoint her mother, Charlotte shed a few tears, but kept the rest at bay—though doing so was no easy task.

Was she right? Her mother had seen years of war, had somehow lost her husband, and this was the conclusion she'd arrived at. There must be truth in what she'd said, even if it flouted convention.

Charlotte's mind continued to accept the finality of her mother's declaration, but it couldn't stop Charlotte from feeling sick. Like she'd eaten something rotten and her body was desperate to purge the toxins.

Caroline's fingers loosened and her next words were gentle. She gathered Charlotte into a brief embrace. "Forgive me, Charlotte. It appears in the time we've been apart the war has hardened me and I've forgotten what it is to be a mother. I should have found a better way to tell you. But give me your trust, and believe that it's a mistake to linger in the past, on things that can't be changed. Put your heart into what you can change. And Charlotte, you can make an incredible difference."

Charlotte still felt unsteady, but she let her mother lead her up two staircases and through a door in the exterior wall. A large square table was in the center of the room. A map was unfurled on its surface with markers of iron, brass, and copper situated at different points.

"Iron for the Resistance, brass for the Empire, and copper for the French." Caroline walked up to the table. "This is where the officers gather and determine every move that must be made."

Charlotte buried the quivering bits of her heart as far from her present mind as possible. Her mother stood over the map, her eyes sweeping across the figures and narrowing as she assessed their positions. Her bearing was one of absolute authority.

"Mother, are you one of the officers?" Charlotte asked.

"I'm Commander of Special Operations," Caroline said. "And, yes, that means I have a place at this table."

This news sparked pride in Charlotte's chest, which helped to chase off some of the sorrow that lingered after raising the subject of her father.

"Then may I . . ." Charlotte hesitated, awash with excitement yet a bit overwhelmed. "May I ask for an assignment? I want to do my part here."

Caroline smiled at her, and Charlotte lifted her chin, ready to receive what orders her mother was ready to give.

"Since you've only just arrived, I should take some time to consider a formal appointment for you in the Tower," Caroline said. "But I do have a task in mind for you. An important one."

"Yes?" Charlotte clasped her hands at the small of her back to keep herself from fidgeting with excitement.

"You know your companions better than anyone," Caroline told her. "Having undertaken the journey you just did, you've seen how each of them responds to challenging situations. Within the Resistance, we believe it imperative that each person play the role best suited to their talent and their character. I'd like you to provide me with a detailed assessment of each member of your party and make recommendations as to how they might best serve our cause."

Charlotte's eyes widened slightly, which prompted her mother to smile again.

"I'm glad to see you understand what an important task this is," she said. "And, Charlotte, don't hesitate to include any conclusions you come to regarding the limitations of your peers. You shouldn't think of your critiques as passing judgment on your friends, but as the means for ensuring they end up in the right place within the Resistance."

"I can do that." Charlotte had already begun to catalog the variety of skills her companions might bring to the cause.

"I know you can," her mother replied.

Caroline walked around to the other side of the table, trailing her fingertips over one of the maps.

"There's another matter I'd like to discuss with you," she said, looking at Charlotte. "I need to know more about the stranger you found in the wilds. The boy."

"Grave," Charlotte said. "His name is Grave."

"Yes." Caroline nodded. "Ashley said Grave's origins are something of a mystery. His father was an inventor?"

"Hackett Bromley." Charlotte's skin prickled. She wished she knew exactly what Ash had told their mother. *Does she know everything?* It bothered Charlotte that she was reluctant to share the story of Grave's past. Her mother was an officer of the Resistance who had just entrusted her with an assignment she was honored to undertake. She knew her mother wouldn't ask about Grave if it wasn't important, but she found it difficult to resist the impulse to shelter Grave from scrutiny.

"Bromley, yes," Caroline murmured. "But before the boy became . . . Grave, he was Bromley's son. A sickly boy?"

"Very sickly," Charlotte said. "He died."

Caroline drew up a chair alongside the table and gestured for Charlotte to sit.

"But Grave lives." Caroline tapped her chin with her index finger. "That's quite the puzzle. To be honest, Charlotte, I don't know if it's a puzzle that we can solve. Do you understand how this inventor, Bromley, revived your Grave?"

Did Ashley withhold Bromley's revelation about the Book of the Dead? Does Mother know that Meg joined the Sisters in the Temple of Athene in the hope of learning more about Grave's creation?

"I'm inclined to believe it doesn't matter," Caroline went on. "How he came to be might be much less relevant than what he is now."

"He's a person," Charlotte blurted.

Caroline leveled a cool gaze on her daughter. "I never said he wasn't."

"I just meant . . ." Charlotte was tongue-tied. Of course her mother would disapprove of such an outburst. It had been both unnecessary and disrespectful. "I don't like it when people treat him like a thing."

"Of course you wouldn't," Caroline replied. "You've made it clear that Grave is a friend to you. And that's good. But Ashley told me Grave is different. I'm not denying that he's a person, but I am acknowledging that he boasts qualities unknown to most people. And part of what serving the Resistance includes is gathering any intelligence that may be relevant to our struggle—even things that appear strange or unlikely to bear weight on the outcome of this war. We know that Hackett Bromley was taken into Imperial custody shortly after your encounter with him. If the Empire deems Bromley a person of interest, then we must assume his work, and Grave's existence, are important to the Resistance as well."

Charlotte nodded, despite the stubborn persistence of her hesitation to speak about Grave.

"Strength." Caroline paced in front of her. "Imperviousness."

"Yes."

"Grave remained with you when Ashley left," Caroline said. "Is there anything else you've observed in the time that's elapsed since you parted ways with your brother? Anything more that sets him apart?"

He doesn't sleep. He never tires. He thinks about his actions. He is loyal. He has a conscience.

"No."

"Still . . . ," Caroline said quietly and to herself, lost in thought.

The sound of boots striking the metal grate of the staircase snapped Charlotte's mother from her musing.

"The other officers will be arriving soon," Caroline said. "But I've arranged for someone to show you the rest of the Tower. Someone who's very eager to see you."

"I don't know if I'm fond of the word 'eager' as a defining quality of my character." The quip came from the door.

Charlotte went rigid. She closed her eyes, willing herself to be calm.

Why does it have to be here? Why now, with my mother?

Swallowing hard, Charlotte opened her eyes and smiled up at her mother. Then she stood and turned to face Jack.

14.

HE HADN'T CHANGED. The face smiling at her had the familiar impish cast Charlotte knew so well. She'd missed it. She'd missed *him*.

Charlotte gripped the back of the chair, hoping to rid herself of the nervous energy surging through her.

A part of her wanted to run to Jack and throw her arms around him. It was a relief to see him, to know he was safe and well.

But Charlotte's other inclination was to run from Jack as swiftly as she could. She wasn't ready for this encounter. She didn't know how to be near Jack, given the things that had happened on the river with Coe. She didn't know if she was ready to forgive him for deceiving her. For pledging his affections to another.

"It's good to see you, Charlotte." Jack's voice had a catch when he said her name.

"Thank you." Charlotte let go of the chair. "I'm glad you and Ashley arrived here safely."

More footsteps rang against the metal in the corridor. Jack stepped out of the doorway and into the room just in time to let a man with thick silver hair and a mustache pass through.

"Captain." Caroline inclined her head. He responded with a curt bow.

Charlotte was waiting for her mother to introduce the captain when Caroline spoke again, to someone following behind him. "Commodore."

"Commander," a familiar voice answered.

No.

No. No. No.

This isn't happening. I'm caught in a dream. A terrible, terrible dream.

"I didn't expect to find you here, Charlotte," Coe said. "You're making an impressive leap up the ranks."

"Hello, Coe." But it wasn't a dream. He was walking toward her.

Coe gave a polite bow, then clasped her hand in both of his. "How do you like the Daedalus Tower?"

Charlotte glanced at her mother and saw Caroline's

eyebrows rise with interest. Charlotte quickly stepped back.

"I have yet to see all of it," Charlotte said. "But my mother has arranged a tour."

"Glad to hear it." Coe smiled. "Though I'm sorry for such a brief meeting. May I call on you this evening?"

"I—"

Jack coughed loudly.

"And here's another surprise," Coe said, sounding much less enthusiastic about Jack's presence.

"Athene's blessings on you, brother," Jack said in a wry tone. "Don't worry, I'm not here to take up your time. Are you ready?"

Coe looked at Charlotte. "What's this?" His voice had an edge.

Charlotte was startled when her mother answered.

"I've asked Jack to take Charlotte through the Tower," Caroline told Coe. "It can be overwhelming at first."

"It can."

Caroline fixed Coe with an expectant look, and Coe joined her at the table.

Jack had already ducked out of the room, and Charlotte found him waiting for her on the landing. Two more officers, a man and a woman, came up the stairs. They greeted Jack before going to join their peers. The door closed and Charlotte stood alone with Jack.

For what felt like ages, they simply looked at each other. Then Jack moved toward her.

"Don't." Charlotte backed away. "Please don't touch me."

Jack stopped, looking terribly awkward with his arms half raised. "If that's what you want."

I have no idea what I want.

"You're supposed to be introducing me to the Daedalus Tower," Charlotte said.

Jack frowned. "Can't we at least talk?"

"Do you really want to talk here?" Charlotte glanced at the closed door, then wiggled her fingers at a passerby on the stairway below.

"I—" Jack leaned against the railing. "No. I suppose not."

"Then show me this place, so I won't get lost," Charlotte said. "I'm sure you can find someplace along the way that's more suited to a private conversation."

Jack brightened, and Charlotte's heart crumpled. She was only delaying the inevitable, but for the moment it would have to serve.

"Follow me, dear lady." Jack spun on his heel. "I could not bear it should you become lost in these halls."

"Ugh." Charlotte folded her arms across her chest and fell into step beside Jack.

He lowered his voice. "To be honest, they all go on about how confusing and intimidating the Tower is to newcomers. It is nothing compared to the Catacombs."

Charlotte laughed, but immediately wished she hadn't. She wasn't ready to invoke their shared past or indulge in nostalgia about the home they'd lost. She glanced at Jack and saw a shadow passing over his expression as well. He glanced back at her.

"I'm so glad you're safe," he said, all teasing gone from his voice. "And that you made it here. I wanted to go out to search for you, but the officers wouldn't hear of it."

"They were right," Charlotte said. "It could have exposed all of us. A Dragonfly combing the countryside wouldn't have gone unnoticed."

"I didn't care," Jack replied. "I had to know you were all right."

"I am all right." Charlotte needed to cut off this line of conversation. "You haven't told me anything about where we are or where we're going. I will definitely get lost if you don't start doing your job."

Jack gave her a withering look, but he dove into an explanation of the Tower's layout. Serving as both a refuge for the Resistance and a defensible position in the event of direct assault, the Daedalus Tower had been designed to provide everything needed for day-to-day operations and to weather a long siege. Links to the city and the Quay channeled supplies into the Tower. Air shafts and repurposed piping brought light and air into an otherwise austere space. Despite the presence of people moving from one floor to the next and in and out of doors, the inside of the Iron Wall was so gaping that it gave the impression of emptiness.

As they descended the stairs, Jack explained that, other

than the War Room—where the officers were meeting—the third floor served mostly bureaucratic functions: relaying intelligence, archiving records, managing accounts. The second floor exterior wall was lined with hatches. Jack opened one. The light from above shone on massive artillery.

"All of the hatches lead to gun wells?" Charlotte gasped. The Tower truly was equipped to repel an assault.

Jack nodded. "The guns and the operating capsules are anchored to the wall. The outer doors are kept oiled but opened only when absolutely necessary for maintenance. The Resistance believes the Empire does not know about the gun wells, and they want to keep it that way."

They descended to the bottom staircase, and Charlotte learned that in addition to the living quarters, the first floor was home to a basic foundry for metalwork and munitions productions and the tinkers' workshop.

"Scoff will be disappointed there's not an apothecary," Charlotte said. Perhaps that was a recommendation she could give her mother. While some of Scoff's experiments were bizarre, he had real talent. With practice and refinement, he could make important contributions in the form of his tonics and elixirs.

"The Resistance prefers to work with apothecaries by contract," Jack replied. "Apparently it wasn't always that way, but somewhere along the line the decision was made that having an apothecary in the Daedalus Tower posed more risk than reward."

As they neared the workshop, Charlotte slowed. A barrage of sounds emitted from within—whirs, clicks, buzzes, whizzes, jingles, jangles, pops, and hisses—along with the acrid scent of smoke and charred leather, layered in strength from dangerously recent to faint and stale. Curiosity made Charlotte pause and peek inside.

In the Catacombs, Birch often had the workshop to himself, with Pip appearing on whatever days she styled herself his apprentice. The workshop Charlotte now entered was far from a space for solitary creation. Tinkers crowded the room, hunching over tiny contraptions that they concentrated on through magnifying goggles, soldering components that would eventually form a gun, poring over schematics for surveillance equipment, consulting with one another about recent innovations.

She wondered if Birch would welcome the change or feel burdened by the presence of so many others in his workspace.

"Charlotte!"

Pip came bounding down the corridor.

"Jack!" she cried again.

Pip jumped up and Jack caught her, swinging her around in a circle. She laughed and hugged him, and Charlotte was a little envious.

"How are you, Pip?" Jack batted at her pigtails. "Keeping Birch out of trouble?"

Pip grinned, nodding. "We came to see his aunt. She has blue hair. Scoff's gonna try to make a tonic for me so I can get it too."

Charlotte smiled at Pip. Envisioning a role for the enthusiastic girl was easy enough—she'd been Birch's de facto apprentice in the Catacombs for almost a year. Making that an official relationship would be the most logical step in the development of her skills. But would it better serve Pip to separate her from Birch? She obviously adored the tinker and they had a strong bond, but sometimes comfort and familiarity undermined growth and innovation. These were considerations Charlotte would have to weigh before making her recommendation.

Birch, Grave, Scoff, and a spindly woman whom Charlotte assumed was Aunt Io came up the corridor at a less energetic pace. Aunt Io's hair was not only blue, it also shimmered and sparkled, giving the appearance of a river of sapphires cascading down her back. Blue hair was only one of several distinguishing features. Birch's aunt had two pairs of goggles pushed up onto her forehead, and another dangling around her neck. She wore a leather apron similar to the kind Birch donned when he was working. Thick-soled boots reached past her knees, and gloves with blackened fingers stretched well past her elbows.

"Aunt Io." Birch grinned. "I'd like you to meet Charlotte and Jack."

Charlotte thought she'd never seen Birch so happy. If Pip were to suggest that he skip up and down the corridor, Charlotte wouldn't have been surprised to see him do it.

"Everyone here knows Jack," Io said, with a flap of her

hand. "But this is the girl who hacked her way through the forest to get here? It's a pleasure."

"I'm glad to meet you." Charlotte didn't want to be rude, but she couldn't quite take her eyes off the length of Io's tresses.

Io followed Charlotte's gaze and chuckled.

"Observant, this one is," Io said to the others. "Go ahead, ask your question."

Charlotte hesitated. "I don't want to give offense."

"You won't," Io replied. "Go on."

"Given your vocation," Charlotte said, "doesn't your hair present a hazard?"

"Well, yes, it did." Io pulled off a glove and gathered her locks so they fell over her shoulder. "But I like having long hair. And I don't like wearing it up. Wearing it up always gives me a headache."

Charlotte decided against asking how wearing her hair up gave her a headache when wearing multiple pairs of goggles did not.

"I complained about it to a friend of mine who happened to be an alchemist and apothecary." Io smiled wistfully. "And he suggested I make it fireproof."

Scoff made a strangling sound. Pip stared at Io's blue hair in awe.

"He came up with the mixture," Io continued. "I drank it. And then we tried to set my hair on fire."

Jack began to cough violently, but Charlotte suspected it was to hide a fit of laughter.

Io tossed her hair back over her shoulder with a flourish. "His experiment was a success! My hair is completely fireproof. And the side effects weren't bad at all."

Scoff had managed to recover, but where Pip was mesmerized by the color of Io's hair, Scoff looked at it with the pained expression of an artist who'd just come upon a skill he believed he could never master. "What side effects?"

"Well, the color, obviously." Io put her glove back on. "And it doesn't grow anymore. It doesn't fall out, but it doesn't grow. Oh, yes, and for about a month if I ate anything with lemon in it, my face developed purple stripes."

"Is there any way you could introduce me to your friend?" Scoff was grabbing tufts of his hair and tugging on them, his eyes wild. "I have a lot of questions. And some theories I'd like to discuss with him."

"You're a budding alchemist, then?" Io asked.

Scoff nodded. He was still giving mad tugs on his hair. Charlotte was fairly certain he had no idea he was doing it.

"I wish I could introduce you," Io sighed. "But I'm afraid dear Albion blew himself up years ago."

Scoff turned a shade of green not unlike Pip's hair.

"He actually blew himself up?" Birch asked. "I always thought those stories were exaggerations."

"Mostly," Io told them. "And he might not have blown himself up. We only found the feathers."

"Feathers?" Scoff squeaked out the word.

"He was working on an elixir that he hoped would allow him to transform into a bird at will," Io said in all seriousness.

"And I sincerely hope that's what happened. I still scatter seeds in the Garden every Saturday, in case he's there. Now if you'll excuse me, I need to assign my nephew a workstation. I am ecstatic over what he did not only to aid a poor little beast, but in doing so, also to gain a marvelous companion."

Charlotte gave Io a puzzled look, but when Birch's aunt clucked her tongue, Moses crawled out from beneath her waterfall of hair.

"I've never been so enchanted by a creature." Io scratched beneath Moses's chin with the tip of her pinky. "My nephew is brilliant and pure of heart."

Birch ducked his head, his cheeks reddening. "I just wanted to help him."

"Of course you did." Io beamed at her nephew. "And you will continue to do great things now that you're here."

She put her arm around Birch and steered him into the workshop. Pip trotted after them; Scoff stumbled.

Grave, who in his usual manner had been observing the conversation in silence, smiled at Charlotte. "She's very strange. I quite like her."

Still somewhat bewildered by Io's tale, Charlotte made an affirmative noise.

"Hello, Jack," Grave said.

"Grave." Jack shoved his hands into his pockets, doubtless mindful of how much Grave knew about his troubled relationship with Charlotte.

Charlotte broke the awkward pause by saying, "Do you want to come with us, Grave?"

She knew Jack was glaring at her, but she ignored him.

Grave shook his head. "I'd like to stay here. I enjoy watching Birch work. And Aunt Io has asked me to complete some tasks for her."

"What kind of tasks?" Charlotte asked with a small frown.

"I don't know," Grave answered. "But she said it would be helpful to the Resistance if she could observe me and take notes."

He smiled at her again. And then, to her surprise, he reached out and clasped her hand. "Take care, Charlotte."

"Thank you?" Charlotte stared after Grave as he left.

"What was that about?" Jack asked. He sounded as perplexed as Charlotte felt, but not angry.

"I have no idea." Unease stirred in Charlotte's chest. Io's quirkiness had been disarming, but Charlotte didn't like the idea of anyone running experiments that involved Grave.

Oblivious to Charlotte's troubled thoughts, Jack glanced at the workshop and shrugged. "There's one last thing to show you."

Deciding there was nothing she could do at the moment short of storming into the workshop and demanding to know what Io's plans for Grave were, which seemed both impractical and ridiculous, Charlotte followed Jack beyond the workshop to another row of hatches in the wall.

"More guns?" she asked.

"No," Jack said. "These are escape hatches. If the

Tower should be taken, this is the way out. Each hatch contains a capsule that, when activated, will be propelled down a chute and into one of the surrounding lakes. The capsules will float, so they won't be stuck at the bottom."

"Good to know." Charlotte hoped she never had cause to think about the escape hatches again.

She was still thinking about the chute and the lakes when she noticed that Jack hadn't said anything else. He was just looking at her. Then she noticed that the escape hatches were tucked away, removed from the working spaces of the Tower.

"Is Ash here?" Charlotte asked, in an attempt to dodge whatever conversation Jack hoped to have. "I should find him."

"Charlotte." Jack took one step, and he was standing right in front of her.

She could feel her pulse jumping at her throat. "I really should find him. There are things—"

Her words died, because Jack had reached out and was curling strands of her hair between his fingers.

"It's not blue," Charlotte said with a nervous laugh.

"I know." He touched her temple and slid his hand around to the nape of her neck.

Charlotte couldn't move. She couldn't look away from Jack's face. She knew he was about to kiss her and she wanted him to. She could let everything else go for just a few moments. Just enough time to know Jack's kiss again.

But he didn't kiss her. Jack folded Charlotte in his arms, holding her against him. His palm still cradled the back of her head. She rested her cheek on his chest, listening to his heart. Listening to him breathe.

"I'm so sorry about your father," Jack murmured.

Charlotte's throat burned and her head throbbed. She pushed Jack away because she was about to cry. Not only cry, but give herself over to sobs that would wrack her body until she couldn't breathe. She didn't want to let that happen. She didn't think she could bear the shame.

She hissed at him, "Don't you dare try to follow me."

She fled.

Charlotte didn't run. She didn't want to draw anyone's attention. All she had to do was find her way back to the door stamped with a hammer. She walked close to the stairwells, feeling too exposed in the broad corridor. She thought she must be close, and she slowed, trying to get her bearings. It wasn't easy; everything in the Tower did look the same. But it was a straight line from where she had left Jack to the door she was seeking. It had to be nearby.

Voices on the landing above Charlotte brought her to a complete stop. They were voices she recognized. Her mother's. Coe's.

The upside of their proximity was that it meant Charlotte had almost reached her goal. But she was desperate to keep either of them from seeing her. She glanced around. If she ran forward, they would spot her. If she ran back the way she'd come, she risked meeting Jack. She took in her surroundings once more, and decided on scrambling beneath the stairwell to wedge herself between stacks of boxes that had been stored there. She tucked her knees to her chest, making herself as small as she could.

Their footsteps were louder, their voices becoming more distinct.

"Gladwell is getting restless," Caroline said. "He's wearing on my patience."

"I'll try to find something to keep him busy," Coe replied.

"I'll be indebted to you." Caroline laughed.

Their footsteps stilled, and though Charlotte couldn't see them through the boxes, she realized with horror that they had to be standing at the bottom of the staircase.

"Now that you've spoken to Ashley and Charlotte, what do you think of my proposal for your next operation?" Coe asked.

A shudder traveled down Charlotte's arms.

"It's intriguing and not without merit," Caroline said. "But I have very little to go on. Both of my children seem reluctant to talk about him."

"Ashley's nature is to be reticent," Coe remarked. "And Charlotte is protective of the boy because she's tender-hearted. Though I wouldn't recommend ever telling her that."

"Her father was tenderhearted," Caroline said. "It didn't help him in the end."

A sob tried to crawl from Charlotte's throat. She clamped her hand over her mouth and struggled to hold back her welling sorrow.

"Despite my children's reluctance to divulge more about Grave, we can build upon what intelligence we've gleaned from the Empire," Caroline continued. "Our sources report that they plan to break Bromley in order to recover the process by which he resurrected his son. Once they've managed to bend his will, they'll have the means to repeat his work. We need that information first."

"I know Charlotte." Coe sounded smug. "With a little time, I'll convince her that Grave belongs with the Resistance. And she'll persuade him to assent to our designs. He does whatever she asks."

"How strange," Caroline said. "Very well, Commodore. I'll give you your time, but Grave cannot leave New Orleans. If all that you believe about him is true, we can't risk losing him to the Empire. And given that the man who invented him is in Imperial custody, they'll soon be searching for the boy—if they haven't already begun."

"As long as Charlotte stays in New Orleans, Grave stays," Coe told her. "And I'll give Charlotte all the reasons she needs to be here."

"Watch your tone, Commodore," Caroline snapped. "She's still my daughter."

"I believe your words to me were 'whatever you deem necessary'," Coe replied. "If you want soldiers who boast the strength and resilience of Grave, you'll let me proceed without hindrance."

A frustrated huff followed by rapid boot strikes that began to fade signaled to Charlotte that her mother had gone. She heard Coe sigh, whether from weariness or frustration she couldn't divine, and then his footsteps, too, faded.

Charlotte stayed beneath those stairs for a long while, too shocked to move. She sat with her arms wrapped around herself, but it was no longer to aid her hiding. Her body was numb, her mind in denial.

What she'd overheard couldn't be true. She must have misconstrued their words. Or missed some essential part of the conversation that made it obvious Caroline wasn't so calculating, and that Coe hadn't revealed his intention to manipulate Charlotte.

Ashley. When I tell Ash what I heard, he'll explain everything.

But the thought of finding Ashley didn't compel Charlotte from her hiding place.

Grave.

They wanted Grave. But not because of who he was, but what he was. Soldiers alike to him? How did her mother plan to achieve that end? What would they do to Grave to ensure success?

Horrible images and scenarios crowded Charlotte's mind until she couldn't bear them. Losing herself in those thoughts would only mire her in dark emotions. She had to act, to do something to work against the plans her mother and Coe hoped to set in motion.

It was Grave that Charlotte needed to find. She couldn't leave him alone in the Daedalus Tower. Not until she knew more about what she'd overheard.

She climbed out from between the stacks of boxes and slowly moved to the edge of the stairwell. She stood up casually, hoping no one had been watching her. As she hurried toward the workshop, she did her best to ward off imminent panic. She had no idea what to do beyond getting to Grave. Her mind was grasping for explanations that would make everything all right again. How could she have doubts about the motivations of the Resistance? Her entire life had been molded by the endless rebellion for which her parents fought. So many had died. So many still would.

It's not that they're wrong. A dry, pragmatic thought managed to wriggle its way through the otherwise hysterical chorus. *Coe agrees with my mother about Grave. He* could *be the perfect weapon if he was trained to fight and his loyalty to the Resistance was secured. Coe made that assessment because he's a soldier. The Resistance is made up of soldiers; if they discovered something that could turn the tide of the war, what else would they do but make use of that asset? But what would it mean to create others like Grave?*

That rationalization offered Charlotte no comfort. While she could understand its logic, her stomach knotted at the ease with which so many people seemed to recategorize Grave from a person to a thing. Establishing a distinction of such gravitas should be difficult, and yet somehow Charlotte found herself again and again put in the position of defending Grave's humanity and denying the dominance of whatever machinery had brought him back from death.

It wasn't just machinery. Charlotte shivered, remembering her brief visit to the Hive. Yes, Hackett Bromley had employed his expertise as an inventor to create the mechanisms that accounted for Grave's strength, speed, and agility, but Grave had always been more than machine.

He's the echo of a person.

Charlotte remembered Meg's hiss of fear and rage when Bromley had revealed the Book of the Dead and admitted his reliance upon its secrets to complete his work. So powerful had been Meg's reaction that it prompted her to abandon her friends and join the Sisters of Athene's Temple to learn more about the arcane mysteries that could breathe life into dead flesh. Having witnessed the things Grave could do and heard the tale of his origins, Meg had taken on the personal responsibility of seeking out the greater meaning of Grave's existence.

But what are my responsibilities?

Speaking out on behalf of Grave was something Charlotte took to without hesitation; her instincts compelled her defense of the strange boy. But she sensed that a time loomed not far off when words would not be enough.

What then would she do? What choices did she even have?

No, Charlotte chided herself. *What choices does Grave have?*

Charlotte picked her way through the room, avoiding fountains of sparks and discarded hunks of metal. The tinkers were cloaked by leather aprons and goggles of all sorts, making it difficult to discern any person's identity. Pip's bright pigtails saved Charlotte from tapping on shoulders until she found Birch and Grave. The trio had been set to assemble constrictor slings. Grave and Pip were measuring out lengths of slender metal cable while Birch fine-tuned the trigger mechanism.

Birch pushed his goggles up onto his forehead when Charlotte joined them. "Meeting done?"

"More or less," Charlotte said. "Can you spare Grave for a bit?"

"I don't think that will cause a problem," Birch said with a shrug. "They're just trying to keep us busy, from what I can tell. No one will be assigning me vital tasks until they've seen more of my work."

"Do you need me too, Charlotte?" Pip asked. She glanced at the length of cable in her hands with disappointment, none too taken with her current work.

Charlotte gave her an apologetic smile. "I don't want to steal both of Birch's apprentices."

"Chin up, Pip." Birch nudged the girl with his elbow.

"If you like, I can show you how the trigger functions and let you have a go on the next one."

Pip brightened instantly, hopping up on a stool beside Birch at the workbench.

Charlotte waited while Grave returned his protective goggles, gloves, and apron to their appointed hooks and drawers just inside the workshop's entrance. They exited the room and Charlotte gestured for Grave to follow her. She chose a route that would take them back to the boat-houses while also avoiding the commons. She walked at a quick clip, but hoped her swift retreat wouldn't draw unwanted attention. Grave matched her pace and imitated her silence. As they walked, Charlotte played out scenarios in her mind, considering the outcomes that could result from her next act. She couldn't stand by while Grave was put to use as a weapon for the Resistance without regard for his willingness to do so. But how could she stop it? Could Grave be hidden? Could he run? Could he simply refuse and face whatever consequences resulted from that disobedience?

It troubled Charlotte deeply that the last option struck her as the most dangerous. The Resistance was something she'd always trusted to be in the right, but she couldn't imagine her mother or the other leaders leaving Grave to his own devices while they continued to fight. If Grave didn't fight for them, he became a liability. At best, he would become their prisoner. At worst . . .

They reached the ladder exit and climbed up to the

trapdoor that opened into the storeroom that was the secret entrance to the Daedalus Tower. After they'd collected
and donned their masks, they ascended the stairs to the
shop and made their way to the front door. Outside the
store, the Market paths were abuzz with festivity. People
filled the paths bearing cups brimming with drinks, each
so potent that Charlotte's eyes watered when a vendor
shoved a cup toward her and its vapors filled her nostrils.
Street performers dazzled children with feats of balance
and contortion. Men and women shouted and bellowed as
their fortunes grew or shrank at various games of chance.
Musicians were everywhere. Some paraded through the
streets in vivid costumes, frolicking as their bugles blasted
and drums thundered. Others occupied those places where
paths met and crossed, the players' bright tunes drawing
throngs of attentive listeners.

Charlotte took Grave's hand and led him into the crowd.
She'd gone only a short distance when she came up against
a wall of bodies. She couldn't see over the heads and shoulders of onlookers, but she pushed her way through without
garnering the ire of any spectators. Whatever performance
had captured their attention must have been riveting, for
nary a person paid notice to Charlotte and Grave as they
squirmed through the crowd.

In her attempt to go through the ring of onlookers,
Charlotte somehow ended up at the front of the group.
The object of the crowd's attention was a duo of musicians
and a dancer. The musicians were men; one played a fife,

the other a drum. The dancer was a woman clad in scarlet that flamed against her dark skin. Charlotte slowed, not wanting to look away from the dancer. The woman's movements were impossibly fluid. She bent and twisted, rose and fell, flowing with the drums' persistent rhythm and the frenzied pace of the fife's melody.

Charlotte felt each strike of the drum in her pulse, its vibrations somehow thrilling and calming her simultaneously. Though she stood still as stone, Charlotte became aware of every sinew in her body. She knew its power, its potential. She was the dancer. She was every drumbeat and each soaring note of the flute. They all were.

This isn't right.

The small voice whispered to Charlotte, its message pushing past the captivating art of the dancer and her musicians.

She's not a dancer. Entertainment is not her aim.

Though she felt a bit silly doing so, Charlotte answered her conscience. *Of course she's a dancer. Isn't she dancing?*

Is that all? The voice answered. *Look around you. Look at what's happening.*

Pulling herself out of the torpor induced by the performance, Charlotte observed the rest of the crowd. Glassy-eyed, bodies swaying with the drumbeats but never moving from the place where they stood, the audience wasn't enjoying the music or the dancer's skill. They were caught in an invisible snare.

A mesmer. The dancer is a mesmer.

The moment Charlotte realized what was happening,

all lingering drowsiness and befuddlement departed as if blown away by a sudden gale. Charlotte viewed the scene with clarity, and alarm. While they watched, the crowd had grown. Anyone who stopped to listen and watch became rooted at that place, which left Charlotte and Grave surrounded by a thick wall of bodies.

Charlotte didn't know the end goal of this mesmer—it could be something as petty as pickpocketing—but she had no desire to find out. She grabbed Grave's arm.

He looked at her, his eyes not as unfocused as those around him, but still altered. "I feel strange."

"I know." Charlotte tugged on his shirtsleeve. "Come with me. You'll be fine once we're away."

Grave frowned, and when his attention returned to the dancer his face filled with contentment. "I like it here."

"That's the problem."

She was about to wrap her arms around his waist and haul him backward, when she caught a movement in her peripheral vision. Charlotte turned, trying to pinpoint the flicker of speed that had been such a contrast to the sluggish shifting of the bodies around them.

There it was again, but only for an instant. And Charlotte was certain the second flash of movement had been too far removed from the first to have originated from the same place.

"Grave." Charlotte gripped his arm. "We have to get out of here."

"I like it here," Grave said again.

"Please, Grave." The movements in the crowd were becoming more frequent. As much as Charlotte chased them with her eyes, her gaze couldn't catch whoever or whatever it was.

Suddenly, a tall shape loomed behind Grave. Charlotte reached for her dagger, but a hand clamped down on her shoulder and spun her around. She looked into a skull, or rather a skull painted on a face. Her hand closed around the dagger's hilt, but not before the skull-faced man hurled Charlotte into the crowd and away from Grave. Charlotte slammed into spectators' bodies as she fell. They stumbled away from her but otherwise paid no attention to the struggle unfolding. The dancing mesmer still held their minds captive. Charlotte landed on her side, pain shooting up her elbow when it took the brunt of her landing.

Charlotte rolled to her hands and knees, anticipating another attack. Instead, the crowd closed around her, blocking the path between her and her assailant. Staying on all fours to avoid detection, Charlotte crawled back in the direction from which she'd been tossed aside.

I need to get Grave. She scrambled through the forest of legs and feet, keeping watch for imminent danger while she sought out her friend.

When she noticed a scuffle of feet nearby, Charlotte crawled faster. As she neared the site of the activity, a figure collapsed to the ground. Behind shins and knees, Charlotte recognized Grave's face. His eyes were closed and he lay very still. She wanted to call out to him, but she knew that doing so would be rash. She had no idea how many enemies were dispersed throughout the crowd. What Charlotte did know was that whoever had attacked saw her only as an obstacle.

But Grave was the target.

Someone crouched beside Grave's prone form—the skull-faced man. He covered Grave's head with a black hood embroidered with strange symbols in silver thread. Grave still hadn't moved.

Two more figures appeared, their faces also painted rather than masked. The three strangers lifted Grave's body and began to carry him away. Keeping low, Charlotte hurried after them.

Linnet's lesson about mesmers had proved invaluable, and now Charlotte was glad she'd had time to learn the skill of stalking from her friend, too. For reasons unknown, Grave was being spirited away—and Charlotte was certain that if she failed to track his abductors, she would never see him again.

15.

SIX OF THEM had come for Grave. Where they were taking him now, Charlotte couldn't divine; she could only follow. Tracking Grave's abductors meant crawling through a series of drainage pipes until she found herself outside the Iron Wall. She kept her focus on the cluster of skulking shadows ahead. The bayou east of New Orleans teemed with strange sounds and movements that threatened to overwhelm Charlotte with horrifying possibilities of what hidden threats surrounded her.

Despite its intimidating nature, the bizarre environs worked in Charlotte's favor as she stalked her adversaries by following the gleam of their lanterns. The swamp swallowed noise, lowering the chances she'd be discovered. Still, it was hard going. Not enough to make Charlotte despair, but the uneven ground and constant plunging in and out of waterways—some shallow, others dropping her into waist-deep pools of brackish water—sapped her strength.

When she reached the enormous trunk of a fallen tree, Charlotte paused to consider her best route. Grave's abductors had scrambled over the tree without hesitation, but Charlotte worried that doing the same would expose her too much, or that her swamp-slick boots and clothing would make the climb slower and more difficult, robbing her of time she couldn't spare.

Hunching over, Charlotte kept her body low as she quickly crept along the length of the tree. As soon as she'd rounded the end of the trunk, Charlotte peered ahead and her heart sank.

They were gone. All Charlotte could see was darkness. The beacons of lantern light upon which she'd relied had vanished. Panic welled up and her stomach gave a sickening lurch. She'd made the wrong choice. In attempting to stay hidden, she'd lost the trail.

It was difficult for Charlotte to stop herself from sinking to her knees and giving in to despair, but she made her feet take one step, then another. There was nothing to do now but continue with the hope that she could catch up with Grave's abductors. She kept walking.

The guiding lantern lights failed to reappear, but the ground beneath Charlotte's feet began to change. No longer squelching under her footfalls, it became firmer. The disappointment of losing the trail wore on Charlotte, as did the weight of her clothes. Her stockings and boots were sodden. Her skirts clung to her thighs, knees, and shins.

Charlotte moved quietly through the dark, waiting for any light or movement that could guide her. A short distance away, she made out dim lights that wavered in the air like drunken fairies. Beyond these hiccuping luminaries she caught the ruddy gleam of torchlight as it bounced off thick, column-like trunks of cypress trees and the tangles of moss that hung from twisting branches. These lights far outnumbered the lanterns she'd been following.

The fairy lights drew near, their whimsical dance stolen once Charlotte recognized delicate candle flame. Gentle footfalls approached with the candles, and Charlotte tucked herself behind the nearest tree. With luck she could escape notice until she had a better of sense of who had taken Grave—assuming that this new group of strangers were connected to the abductors.

But Charlotte's luck had run out. From amid the candlelight a man's deep voice called, "Don't dawdle hidin' yourself away. We'll be needin' to speak with you, now."

Charlotte couldn't see the speaker, but no menace accompanied his words, and her attempt at hiding had proven futile, so she left the cover of the tree trunk and walked toward the sound of the speaker's voice.

The candlelight grew brighter, forming a ring around Charlotte, closing until she could see faces illuminated by the subtle glow. There were at least a dozen candle bearers, both men and women and ranging in age from smooth-skinned youths to rheumy-eyed elders. Though Charlotte could have sworn the circle of light around her never broke, a man appeared within the ring. He leaned on a gnarled walking stick. The thick white tufts of his hair and beard spoke of the many years he'd seen. And though his dark skin was crinkled with age, his eyes were sharp and penetrating when they fell on Charlotte.

"I'm called Nicodemus."

Charlotte recognized his voice as the same that had spoken before. Nicodemus said nothing further, but watched her until she answered, uncertainly:

"My name is Charlotte."

Nicodemus offered her a gentle smile, but not a joyous one. "Charlotte. You've come a long way from home."

Charlotte decided against answering. She didn't know why she was here or who this Nicodemus and his compatriots were, but until she discerned their intentions, she had no desire to give them more information about herself than she had to.

"I am much given to wonder why you've come to us," Nicodemus said when Charlotte had stood silent for several heartbeats. "And if you know what you brought along when you came."

"I didn't want to come *here*," Charlotte said, "I'm looking for my friend."

Nicodemus chuckled. "He's your friend, is he?"

The line of bodies behind Nicodemus broke, parting to

allow two men through. They bore a pallet that they set at Nicodemus's feet. A prone figure lay on the pallet.

Grave!

Charlotte bit back her impulse to shout his name. Grave wasn't moving. Despite the time that had elapsed since his capture in the city, he remained unconscious.

What could they possibly have done to subdue him?

Studying Charlotte's face, Nicodemus said, "You're in fear that we've hurt him. Or that we yet will."

"Have you?" Charlotte asked.

Nicodemus shook his head. He crouched beside Grave, touching the tip of his twisted walking stick to the boy's sternum. The wood began to undulate. Charlotte gasped when she realized that what she'd taken for curving wood was a black snake coiled along the walking stick's length. The snake slithered away from Nicodemus and onto Grave's chest, where it coiled again, resting directly above his heart.

"We sent him to the Otherside for a spell," Nicodemus told Charlotte. "There he's gonna stay unless you have words to make us bring him back to you."

"What kind of words?" Charlotte's mouth was dry. The wrong answer, an unintended provocation, any misstep—and Grave might be lost to this mysterious otherworld forever.

"Truthful ones." Nicodemus leaned on his walking stick, peering into Charlotte's face. "Who is he?"

Charlotte had the unwavering sense that Nicodemus would know if she lied. She also suspected he already knew some things about Grave and that if she tried to hide them, it would make things much worse.

"He was lost in the woods, far from here, when I found him," Charlotte said. "He'd come from the Floating City."

Nicodemus nodded. "And you went to find out who he was."

"Yes," Charlotte replied. She didn't want to tell him more, but she doubted she had any other options.

"So I ask again." Nicodemus smiled at her. It was a kind, but sad, smile. "Who is he?"

Charlotte looked at Grave, wondering if she knew the real answer to Nicodemus's question.

Who is he?

The question didn't come from Nicodemus this time. It came from all around Charlotte; the wind moving in the trees, water rippling in the swamp.

Who is he?

"He's the son of an inventor in the Hive," Charlotte said. "His name is Timothy."

The snake coiled on Grave's chest raised its head and hissed.

"You gave me some truth," Nicodemus said to Charlotte, but his eyes were on the snake. "But not all of it. And not what matters most here."

Charlotte likewise stared at the snake, shaken by the suggestion that it not only listened and understood human words, but could also communicate with Nicodemus.

"I . . ." Charlotte's mouth was parched with fear. "I don't know who he is."

The wind rose, sighing through the trees in a way that made Charlotte feel as though it was disappointed in her.

"Tell me what you do know." With the tip of his walking stick, Nicodemus drew a spiral in the earth. "Tell me what you believe."

"Timothy died." Charlotte's heart jumped as the words left her mouth, and she realized that she never spoke of Grave's impossible origin. She didn't acknowledge his death. Now that she had been forced into a stark encounter with that truth, Charlotte understood that it truly frightened her. She kept it locked in the far recesses of her mind so she didn't have to face it, because she didn't know if she could.

Nicodemus nodded, still drawing in the dirt. He didn't speak, and Charlotte knew she was meant to.

"His father decided to take the sickly body and make it strong again," she said. "Make it devoid of weakness and suffering. He wanted his son back, but he wanted to keep him from ever being harmed again. He built a better body and then used the Book of the Dead to revive his son."

A murmur trickled through the crowd behind Nicodemus.

Nicodemus bowed his head. "Grief and madness. No good comes from that mixture, no matter the intent."

He lifted his face to meet Charlotte's gaze. "His son did not return."

"No," Charlotte whispered. "I don't know who he is . . . We call him Grave."

Nicodemus's laugh came so suddenly and was so loud that Charlotte startled, stumbling back and almost losing her balance.

"As true a name as any could be." The old man had a ferocious grin.

Resentful of Nicodemus's bizarre mirth, Charlotte said, "We started using the name before we knew about his past."

"Doesn't matter," Nicodemus replied. "Names find their way to the place they belong. The boy's name found him before you knew who he was."

"But I don't—" Charlotte began, then gritted her teeth.

"You do," Nicodemus said quietly. "You know who he is . . . in a way. What you lack is understandin'."

The murmuring became a hum, steady and full of warmth, a single note embellished by the high trills of insects and deep croaks of frogs.

Nicodemus closed his eyes and turned his face toward the night sky, silent, listening.

The coiled snake slithered off Grave's chest, returning to wind itself around the old man's walking stick once more. As Charlotte watched, the snake became still, and Nicodemus held a staff of twisted wood with no sign of a living creature.

Charlotte's heart beat so furiously her pulse sent tremors up and down her limbs. Impossible things were happening here. Things she couldn't understand.

The humming became quiet, still there but no longer

commanding all to listen. Nicodemus looked at Charlotte.

"You told us what you know," he said. "And as you spoke we heard your heart behind your words. You mean no evil. You are no enemy to us. We will not work to keep you and your friend apart, because you are his true friend."

He swept his walking stick toward Grave.

"We've seen where he comes from," Nicodemus told her. "Know what he is. These are things you must know as well. His life is tied to yours—that we have also seen."

Questions rushed into Charlotte's mind, crowding her thoughts.

With a knowing chuckle, Nicodemus said, "Easy, child. Let yourself take a few breaths and ask the question that's still waiting around when the others have gone."

Being patient enough to wait until the frenzy of questions calmed into order set Charlotte's teeth on edge, but after a few minutes a single question stood out from its fellows.

"How do you know what he is?"

"Because I can ask those that keep the great secrets," Nicodemus said. "Most people think those I ask have nothin' to tell. Most people are deaf to their voices, blind to their presence."

"Why?" Charlotte asked.

"Why is the world deaf and blind?" Nicodemus tilted his head, smiling as if he'd heard a joke he alone understood. "Because somewhere along the way it decided that everything on this earth should serve their iron god. They cut and burn and tear and bore so they can feed him. They worship by buildin' great cities that shun the land itself. They love all that is bright and hard and loud. All that noise drowns out the quiet, the murmurs, the hushed truths that only come when you're willin' to listen for a long, long time and then listen some more."

Charlotte had never heard such a bleak, harsh description of Hephaestus. Most hearers would label Nicodemus a blasphemer.

"You don't honor the Great Forge?" Charlotte was hesitant to pursue this thread of conversation. "Or marvel at the crafts of Athene?"

"The Imperial gods have no place here." Nicodemus spread his arms, and the sounds of the bayou became louder. "And what good are gods you can't welcome into your home?"

"But you came into the city," Charlotte countered. "You kidnapped him in New Orleans."

Nicodemus made a sour face. "Only because we had to." He turned so he could gaze down at Grave. "If we thought there was a chance that this one would come wandering into our bayou, we'd've waited. But he was behind the Iron Wall, and that's where we went."

"How could you even know about Grave?" Charlotte frowned, vexed by the nonsensical narrative Nicodemus offered. "If you've forsaken the French and British and live apart, why does the mishap of an inventor concern you?"

Charlotte regretted her choice of the word *mishap*, but

it was difficult to find a word that accurately conveyed the tormented relationship Hackett Bromley had with the boy who had once been his son.

"Because he is not some automaton built to do labor or serve human masters." Nicodemus's face clouded with anger. "When the inventor drew upon the power in the Book of the Dead, he invited a soul from the Otherside into this world. The earth under our feet shuddered when that soul came near unto us. There could be no ignoring his existence."

"You think he's dangerous." Charlotte was so weary of that assumption.

"No."

Nicodemus's reply took Charlotte by surprise.

"We didn't know how he'd come to be," Nicodemus explained. "Or why a new soul would manifest in our world. We needed to know whether his appearance brought with it good or evil. Wanderin' spirits in the Otherside got as many desires as the people on this Earth. Some want only the experience of life on our plane, some come seekin' a home, but others . . . they come full of spite and malice, bent on tearin' apart this world where they don't belong. Such spirits cannot be ignored or left to do as they will. Wicked spirits must be wrested from the body they've taken and sent back to the Otherside."

"But now you know he's good?" Charlotte glanced at Grave's peaceful face. He certainly didn't look evil, and he'd done nothing she would call malicious.

"He isn't good," Nicodemus said, but before Charlotte

could come to Grave's defense, he continued, "Neither is he evil. He simply is."

"And you'll leave him be?" Charlotte asked. "You aren't going to send him back."

"We will not undo what's been done." Nicodemus walked in a slow circle around Grave. "His soul is here now. He's part of the world as much as you or I. Killin' him isn't gonna right any wrong, or restore some sort of balance. That's a blind man shoutin' at a house cat, callin' it a lion for fear's sake alone. Fools' work, that is. And hateful. Hateful acts bring the spirits' fury. Them we won't affront."

Now convinced that Nicodemus meant neither her nor Grave harm, Charlotte asked, "And what about me? What should I do with him?"

"Do with him?" Nicodemus chuckled. "There's nothin' to be done, except to live. That's why the spirit crossed over. To live, to be. You can be with him however it is you like, but it's no matter of doin'."

Charlotte frowned at the conjurer. "But he's . . . different."

Nicodemus's double thatch of white brows lifted. "You afraid of him?"

"No," Charlotte said, but hesitated before speaking again. What was it that she was trying to ask? What did she want the old man to tell her?

"Grave is powerful." She turned her gaze upon the boy, who lay in quiet repose. "But so trusting. I don't want to ask him to do anything out of my own self-interest."

"That you choose to ask such a question is answer in it-self." Nicodemus leaned on his staff. "It proves your judgment will fall to the boy's well-being before anything else. You won't set him to tasks unworthy."

The conjurer's words filled Charlotte with profound comfort, despite his being a near stranger. Before she could thank him, Nicodemus abandoned his casual stance, stiffening into a tall, rigid pose.

He turned his walking stick so he held each end in one hand, and the length of wood was parallel to the earth. He closed his eyes. It was so quiet, Charlotte's shallow breaths sounded monstrously loud.

So quiet.

A cool prickling traveled down Charlotte's spine.

The entire bayou had gone silent. No creature stirred. A place teeming with life now mimicked a desolate tomb.

Then came a faint sound, the barest rustle in the tree-tops above.

Nicodemus's eyelids snapped open; his eyes went wide with alarm. He swept his walking stick in a great arc, shouting words unintelligible to Charlotte. Tiny flames leapt from the bearers' candles and rose into the sky. They grew larger and larger, chasing each other through the air until a blazing ring hovered over Nicodemus.

He shouted again. The flames roared and then snuffed out, leaving a thick cloud of smoke in their wake and casting a cloak of shadows over everything and everyone.

16.

NICODEMUS STALKED TOWARD Charlotte as his followers scattered, vanishing into the woods with nary a sound. Smoke still swirled high in the trees, but its cover had thinned to a mere veil that moonlight pierced easily. Where the glow of candle flames had been warm and golden, the moon poured cool, silver light into the bayou. Cypress trunks became bone-white pillars, and hanging moss floated on the wind like restless spirits.

Silence continued its oppressive reign and Charlotte felt as though she were shrinking into herself, attempting to hide from the lack of sound. In the New York Wildlands, a silent forest meant a predator was near. But what kind of hunter could make so many people flee at once?

Charlotte's gaze swung from the approaching conjurer

to the unseen threat among the trees. She stood firm when Nicodemus drew near, prepared to fight if his intentions were hostile.

He stretched a gnarled hand toward her, his voice a harsh whisper. "Come. We must defend the boy."

His glance fell to her waist where her dagger was sheathed. Charlotte took his hand with her left and drew her dagger with her right.

Though age made his skin like leather, Nicodemus had a remarkably strong grip. He led Charlotte to Grave's side and released her hand before stepping to the other side of his body.

Something cut through the moonlight, casting a shadow trail on the ground as it sailed over Charlotte's head. Whatever skulked in the treetops moved with incredible swiftness, yet created little sound. Charlotte brandished her dagger and crouched down, placing her left palm flat on the ground to anchor her body for now, but also to offer leverage should she need to propel herself away from that spot.

Another soft rustling came from above and was echoed in the treetops opposite the source of the first sound. Two shapes, moving in perfect synchronicity, spun out of the highest branches. They descended rapidly, like spiders traveling on silken thread from their webs to the earth, but when they touched the ground the figures rose to reveal their tall, human shape. Clothed in black from head to toe, their silhouettes were slender with gentle curves at their waists and hips. A pair of women, but who were they and what did they want?

Charlotte's curiosity dissolved into a mixture of anger and dread when she saw the glimmer of four long, silver blades extending from each one of their hands like wicked, curving claws.

The pair stalked forward, angling to either side of Charlotte and Nicodemus.

"Leave now and you will live," one of them said.

The sound of her voice breaking the long silence made Charlotte's heart lurch.

The second stranger added, "You are not our concern. Only the boy."

"This place is no domain of yours." Nicodemus extended his staff toward the woman to their left. He swept the staff through the air as if drawing an invisible line. "Begone and take your war goddess with you."

"The words of a heathen are empty to our Great Lady," the woman answered with disdain. "Stand against her and you will face her wrath."

"Summon your warriors, old man," the other woman added. "Drive us away if you can."

"We folk are no warriors," Nicodemus answered. "Leave us in peace."

"No quarter will be given as long as you harbor that." The first woman's silver talons flashed as they pointed at Grave.

"What do you want with him?" Charlotte asked, glad her voice came out strong despite her fear.

"It is not for you to know our purpose," the first woman

replied. They were on either side of Charlotte and Nicodemus now, making it impossible for her to watch both of them.

"Do not tether yourself to death," the second woman said. "We have given you leave to go. Should you refuse, know that you will not be offered mercy again."

They were closing on Charlotte and the Conjurer. The four bright blades that extended from each of their hands made Charlotte's dagger look as threatening as a butter knife by comparison, and Nicodemus's staff no more than a shepherd's crook. Their weapons would offer a much greater reach than Charlotte's. She couldn't land a blow without coming well within striking distance of their claws. Nicodemus's staff looked sturdy, but his age made it unlikely he'd be able to endure a long, arduous battle. Under other circumstances, Charlotte would have assessed these enemies and decided that flight, not fight, was her best chance of survival. But she couldn't run. Grave was still unconscious and defenseless.

"Your answer?" The first woman asked.

"I'm not leaving." Charlotte stayed low, waiting.

Nicodemus gripped his staff with both hands, adopting a defensive stance.

The second woman said, "As you will."

Charlotte tensed, waiting for the pair to rush her. But the first attack came from Nicodemus, who bellowed and lunged. His staff whipped through the air, powered by the long sinewy muscles of his arms. Charlotte's first thought was to follow and fight beside him, but she sensed movement to her right and whirled around just in time to jump out of the way. The second woman had leapt forward, claws extended and aiming for Charlotte's undefended side.

Unable to both track Nicodemus and fight the other assailant, Charlotte put her full focus on her attacker—but not quickly enough. The woman's foot shot out in a high, sharp kick, striking Charlotte's forearm with force that drove pain terribly deep, making her cry out as she lost her grip on the dagger. Charlotte's weapon hit the ground. She dove toward it, reaching for the hilt. Another searing pain flared through her left arm as the woman's steel claws sliced through her flesh.

Charlotte fell, tumbling along the ground as her arm throbbed and hot blood poured over her skin. She knew the woman must be following her and would strike again at any moment. Though the pain made spots manifest in Charlotte's vision, she rolled to her hands and knees. She would not simply submit to the next attack.

Ignoring the pain in her arm, Charlotte braced herself and gripped her dagger tight in both hands. Her attacker pounced. The woman's arms blurred as her claws cut through the air, ready to slice Charlotte once more. Charlotte shifted her weight forward and thrust her blade up. Her blow struck beneath the woman's sternum, cutting flesh but glancing off a rib bone.

The woman grunted with pain, briefly losing her focus

on the attack. Charlotte rolled back, flattening her spine against the ground while kicking up hard. Her feet hit the woman's stomach and used the assailant's momentum to propel her over Charlotte's head and onto the ground well beyond the place where Charlotte lay.

As Charlotte pushed herself into a crouch, she heard a horrible cry. From the corner of her eye, she saw Nicodemus fall. Rage surged through her, flooding her body with new strength. With a shriek of pure fury, Charlotte dove forward, arms outstretched with her dagger gripped between both hands. She'd kept low, and the unexpected move caught her enemy by surprise. The woman leaned over, swinging her claws downward. The blades ripped the fabric of Charlotte's dress but failed to reach her flesh.

Charlotte's trajectory sent her flying between the woman's calves. She hit the ground and immediately flipped over, bringing her dagger up with all the force she could muster. The wide blade sank deep into the woman's lower back.

The woman uttered a long groan of pain that became a guttural cry as Charlotte twisted the blade. Charlotte's feet came up kicking her enemy, forcing the woman to her knees while freeing Charlotte's dagger. Jumping up, Charlotte wrapped her left arm around the woman's head and jerked back. Charlotte set her jaw and, with a swift dagger stroke, opened the woman's throat.

With her enemy dispatched, Charlotte went to Nicodemus's aid. The conjurer was still on his feet, but his legs were streaked with blood and his movements had become slow and jerking. His opponent stood tall, watching Nicodemus with unconcealed contempt.

Fearing that an attempt at creeping up in surprise might be too slow, costing Nicodemus his life, Charlotte rushed at the remaining attacker. Sensing her approach, the woman pivoted and lashed out with her claws. Charlotte drew up short, nearly stumbling as she contorted her body to avoid the reach of the woman's blades. Regaining her balance, Charlotte adopted a defensive posture, deeming it wisest to gauge her adversary's attack style before devising a counter.

As she faced off with her enemy, Charlotte glanced at Nicodemus in the hopes he'd aid her. But the conjurer had fallen, and though his staff was still in his grip, he lay on his side, breathing heavily.

"You could still run," the woman facing Charlotte said in a coaxing voice. "I promise I'd let you go."

Charlotte glared at her. "I'm not running."

The woman's lips curled into a smile. "If you weren't such a fool in choosing your enemies, I'd be tempted to recruit you."

"Recruit me for what?"

Before the woman could answer, a shout came from the shadows along with a flurry of footsteps. Charlotte and her opponent looked toward the sounds, startled by the sudden interruption. When a figure appeared, Charlotte's heart lurched. She recognized a woman's silhouette garbed in dark colors like that of the other two warriors, but that semblance of uniformity was offset by startling flashes of gold and azure. She couldn't take on two opponents at once, at least not for long.

But instead of silver claws, the new arrival wielded two swords, and her charge aimed full tilt at Charlotte's opponent. Utterly taken aback by this unexpected ally, Charlotte stood transfixed as the two warriors crashed into each other, the force of their meeting sending both sprawling—though within a breath both were on their feet, facing one another again. The clawed fighter struck first. One arm slashed upward, demanding a block from one of the new-comer's blades. The woman's other arm thrust forward, aiming for the sword-wielder's abdomen.

The gold-and-blue-clad woman's right blade met the sweeping attack, and as her steel scraped against that of the claws she spun away from the second strike. Her opponent lurched forward and the sword-wielder continued to spin and then launched into the air, landing a kick in the center of the woman's back. She grunted and stumbled, but didn't fall.

When the swordswoman came at her again, she was ready for it. Her claws crossed over each other and steel screeched as two swords grated against eight claws. The warriors leapt apart and began to circle each other again. The ebony-clad woman darted forward, her claws raised as if to tear through her enemy's chest. The woman in blue lifted her blades to fend off the assault. At the last moment, the clawed woman dove at the swordswoman's legs, ready to rip into her thighs.

But the swordswoman shot upward, somersaulting over the slashing claws. The clawed woman hit the dirt and continued to slide forward. The woman in blue landed and whirled around, raising her blades once more. The claw-wielder had only begun to push herself up from the earth when two swords ran her through, pinning her body to the ground. She gave a horrible shudder, then went limp. The swordswoman jerked her weapons free. Her eyes remained intent on her dead opponent's body. Something grabbed her attention and one of her swords flashed out. Charlotte heard a metallic crunching sound. The warrior bent down and picked something up from the ground next to the dead woman.

Charlotte scrambled to Nicodemus's side. She bent over, searching for his wounds to assess their severity. Regret welled in her chest when she realized there was no need. Nicodemus's slumped form no longer drew breath. His eyes were open and glassy.

Despite feeling the swordswoman's eyes on her, Charlotte left the conjurer and went to Grave. She kept her dagger gripped tightly even though she worried that if she didn't drop the weapon and bind her wounded arm, she'd soon lose enough blood to faint.

Grave's prone body offered no sign that he'd regain consciousness any time soon. His stillness and the pale, near-translucence of his skin gave him the appearance of death—so much so that Charlotte's breath seized up. And yet she knew he could not be dead. Rendered helpless, yes, but dead . . . she'd witnessed nothing in the course of that harrowing night that could have killed Grave. At least she didn't think she had.

"He hasn't been harmed." The woman in blue's voice was low and slightly muffled, but familiar.

Nicodemus had assured Charlotte as much, but she replied, "How do you know?"

Three women warriors. Two had been enemies, but who was the third?

"The magicians and seers of wild places like this one rarely aim to do harm." The voice came again, but closer. Charlotte strained to see the speaker, but couldn't spy anything in the darkness. "The same cannot be said for the Order of Arachne, who live and die by their blades."

Charlotte's breath caught. She knew that voice. But how could it be possible?

"Meg?"

Soft footfalls sounded to Charlotte's left; she turned as a figure stepped into the moonlight, coming close enough that Charlotte could see the details of her clothing. Like the other two warriors, Meg was garbed in dark fabric and heavily armed, with calf-height boots featuring buckles that held slim daggers. Sleek, fitted trousers revealed the feminine curve of hips, accentuated by a deep blue sash. Gold cuffs guarded her arms from wrist to elbow, the metal etched with symbols unfamiliar to Charlotte. The swords with which she'd fended off their attackers were sheathed at her back. Their gilded hilts bore the same markings as her arm cuffs. Her face was almost entirely hidden by a veil of blue silk that wrapped around her skull and covered her nose and mouth, but her eyes were sharp as they held Charlotte's gaze.

The woman reached up and pulled back her veil so the gauzy fabric slipped off her head and away from her face. "Yes, Lottie."

Charlotte took in Meg's exotic garb, trying to piece together some explanation of what had just transpired. "But how—"

"I'll explain soon enough," Meg replied. "First we need to leave this place."

She drew a tiny flask from a pocket on her harness. "Drink this. I'll tend to your arm."

Charlotte obeyed. The liquid in the flask was bitter and scorched the back of her throat, but the fog creeping into her mind evaporated and the throbbing of her arm began to subside. Meg cut a length of cloth from her cowl and wrapped it around Charlotte's wound.

"I'll need to apply a poultice to this when we're back in New Orleans," Meg told her. "The Order of Arachne are fond of poison. The tonic I gave you works as a panacea against most of their formulations, but I won't know for sure if it's done all it needs to until I can make a closer examination of the damage."

"What is the Order of Arachne?" Charlotte asked. "Why did they attack us?"

Meg nodded toward Grave. "He's their target. You were simply an obstacle."

"But Grave doesn't know them," Charlotte said. She winced when Meg knotted the cloth tight against her torn flesh. "He couldn't. He still remembers almost nothing of his life before he met us and he's hardly more than a boy. How would he have enemies like that?"

"Who he is has nothing to do with their mission." Meg moved past Charlotte and knelt beside Grave. "What he is drives their purpose."

"What he is?" Charlotte looked at Grave. Unconscious, he seemed peaceful, entirely harmless.

"A wandering soul. Neither good nor evil. He simply is," Meg answered, repeating Nicodemus's words. "The echo of a person."

Drawing her gaze from Meg, Charlotte looked to the fallen conjurer. "He defended Grave. He didn't have to."

Meg nodded; her eyes held the same grief Charlotte felt. "His people will come for him. But they won't come until we're gone."

"Are you sure?" Charlotte couldn't tolerate the thought of abandoning the man who'd given his life for the sake of strangers.

"I am."

"Meg, I don't understand any of this," Charlotte said, her mind awash with the confusing scenes that had played out. "Where did you even come from?"

"I was tracking the assassins sent after you," Meg said,

her voice warm with sympathy at Charlotte's obvious weariness. "They encamped outside New Orleans, intending to take Grave in the city. His abduction caught them by surprise. They made quite a lot of noise about having to chase both of you down because of a meddling conjure man in the swamp. I'm sorry I didn't arrive in time to help. Perhaps then he wouldn't have lost his life."

"Why didn't you come to us right away?" Charlotte asked. "You knew we were in the city. You could have warned us."

"My warning would have meant nothing," Meg told her. "Arachne's assassins are the deadliest of warriors. I couldn't lose the advantage of surprise. Even so, I didn't know if I'd be a match for them. Thanks to you, I only had to fight the second. You have incredible courage, Lottie."

Charlotte rested her weight against the elbow of her good arm. "Who sent them?"

"The conjurer decreed Grave harmless," Meg said. "But not all agree with him. Some believe he is that which does not belong. That which must not be."

"How can you say that?" Charlotte snapped. "Who are you to know whether or not he belongs?"

"I don't claim that wisdom," Meg said, then sighed. "But the Sisters in the Temple of Athene have condemned him, and sent the Order to remove him from this world."

"You mean kill him," Charlotte said.

"More than that." She laid the back of her hand on Grave's forehead. "He's cold. He will never have the same warmth as you or I. The Sisters would say that is only one proof of many that the boy who was 'Timothy' is long dead. Grave is not the same. He is other. His soul does not belong. Yes, they will find a way to kill the body, but they will also banish the soul."

Charlotte felt the cool kiss of dread brush the back of her neck. Grave made the same argument about himself. He wasn't Hackett Bromley's son. He was something else. Someone who was learning his place in this world. Charlotte didn't know if she could deny that Grave was other, but she couldn't believe that meant he had to die. Grave might not be of this world, but he wasn't evil—the conjurer had proclaimed as much without any sign of doubt.

"When I learned of the Sisters' decree, I abandoned the Temple," Meg said quietly. "I knew I had to find you before the Order did. I almost failed."

"But you didn't." Charlotte pushed herself up and scooted close to Meg. "Where did you learn to fight like that? With the Sisters?"

Meg laughed. "You think I could learn those skills in a month?"

"I don't know. I've never seen you fight," Charlotte suddenly felt much younger than she had in weeks.

"You've never seen me fight. That doesn't mean I haven't been training for battle since I was very young, which I have. My mother was once a warrior. These clothes and weapons—they were hers. Your brother used to spar with me, and while I doubt he'd admit it, I usually won." Meg wrapped her arms around Charlotte, hugging her tightly. "Oh, Lottie. You have no idea how much I've missed all of you."

Charlotte's throat felt thick, as she held back tears. "We've missed you, Meg. Every day. So much happened and it's been . . . it's been hard. More than hard."

Meg nodded. "I know. I've learned some things. The Catacombs . . ." She closed her eyes. "I still find it difficult to believe they're gone."

Tears forced their way out of Charlotte's eyes and she let the wave of sorrow take her. While Meg rocked her, Charlotte cried in a way she'd needed to for so long. She cried for the Catacombs, for Jack's deception, for Rufus, for her mother's ruthlessness, for her father's death, for a Resistance she was no longer sure she believed in. Meg stayed quiet until the last of Charlotte's sniffles had subsided.

"I'm sorry I wasn't there to help you." Meg rested her cheek on the crown of Charlotte's head. "You had to bear so much, so suddenly. But, Lottie, you've done so well. You've been brave and unyielding. Ashley must be proud."

Charlotte didn't miss the catch in Meg's voice when she said Ash's name. "He'll be so happy to see you."

Meg pulled back and Charlotte turned, surprised to see a conflicted expression on Meg's face. "I don't know if seeing Ashley would be wise."

"But of course you'll see him," Charlotte said. "He's in the city. Do you mean to avoid him? Why would you do that?"

"You misunderstand my meaning, Lottie." Meg's eyes became distant and full of regret. "I don't have words to . . . when it comes to Ash . . ."

She shook her head and her wistful tone faded. When Meg's attention returned to Charlotte, her stare was hard as flint. "I won't see Ashley because we can't stay in New Orleans. We have to leave."

"Leave New Orleans?" Charlotte drew back and scrambled to her feet. "Why? And who do you mean by *we*?"

"You, Grave, and I."

Charlotte wanted to object, to cling to disbelief at Meg's pronouncement, but when Meg rose and stood face to face with Charlotte, Charlotte knew there was no question as to whether or not they would leave New Orleans. It was only a matter of when.

17.

TELL ME WHY we have to leave." Charlotte could see the resolve in Meg's steady gaze, but that didn't mean Charlotte had to acquiesce to Meg's plan without an explanation.

Meg's eyes shifted to the dead assassins sprawled on the ground. "They aren't reason enough?"

"Not when they're dead," Charlotte shot back.

"They were only two," Meg said. "There will be others."

"But not for a while." Charlotte's own feelings about New Orleans were mixed after overhearing her mother and the officers. Nonetheless, she didn't know where a better refuge could be. "The Sisters won't know these assassins failed. We have time to discuss the attack with the others. Then we can make a plan."

Meg reached into her pocket, then opened her hand to show Charlotte what she held. Though its body was crumpled, and its eight spindly legs twisted at strange angles, it was plainly a spider crafted of silver.

"I was able to catch this one before it fled." Meg examined the broken mechanical. "But the other is long gone."

"Is this what you stomped on?" Charlotte peered more closely at the spider. "What is it?"

"It's called a Web Minder." Meg returned the spider to her pocket. "When a woman is initiated into the Order of Arachne, a Web Minder is attached to the base of her neck. Its machinery is powered by the circulation of the blood, its gears wound with every beat of the assassin's heart. Should that heart stop beating, the Web Minder detaches from its host and returns to the Temple."

"Like a homing bird," Charlotte said. "But a bird flies. How fast can a scuttling spider get back to New York?"

Meg smiled, but her expression was one of tolerance, not happiness. "Web Minders don't have wings, but they travel through the air. The spider that left the assassin you killed immediately climbed to the top of the nearest tree and deployed a silk sail from its abdomen. Its legs spin like propellers. And it won't be going all the way to the Floating City. They're named Web Minders in reference to the network of informants the Order of Arachne controls. Our little spider is likely on its way to New Orleans, given that it's the nearest city."

That news quelled Charlotte's doubts about a Web

Minder's efficacy. She stayed quiet, disturbed by how quickly the Sisters could learn about the failed attempt to capture Grave and how soon more assassins would come to finish the task.

Leaving Charlotte to her thoughts, Meg crouched at Grave's side. She spent several minutes studying him and the pallet where he lay, before she drew a dagger and made a small cut in her left palm. When her blood welled, Meg swept the tip of her right index finger through it and reached over to draw a circle in the hollow of Grave's throat.

Hopes, fears, and confusion rattled about Charlotte's mind while Meg attended to Grave. Charlotte had worried that bringing Grave back from whatever or wherever the Otherside was could put him in danger, but Meg showed no hesitation as she worked. Peering down at them, Charlotte watched as Meg drew out a pouch hidden beneath Grave's shirt. Meg then unhooked a compact gadget that hung from her belt. About the length of a spoon, the device resembled an odd flower. The stem was made of two spiraling bronze pieces that partially obscured the tiny gears they wrapped around. The bloom featured concentric circles of curving metallic petals with tips that ended in sharp points.

Meg held the base of the bloom between two fingers while she gave several cranks on the stem. When she paused, the inner rings of the bloom whirred as they began to spin. With great care, Meg lifted the pouch, holding only the very edge of its fabric, and set the bloom against the pouch's base. The sharp petals ground into the small bag, shredding it and whatever it contained in a matter of seconds. Meg murmured steadily as the pouch was destroyed, though Charlotte could make no sense of the words she spoke.

Rather than dropping to the ground and lying there, the detritus of the pouch began to smoke and curl as it fell. By the time the flower's blades slowed and then stopped altogether, and only a tiny scrap of fabric remained between Meg's fingers, the pouch and its contents had been transformed into a pile of ash.

What had Meg learned in the Temple of Athene? Or was this yet another skill she had already had but kept secret? Charlotte marveled at, but also was unsettled by, these startling revelations about her friend. What else could Meg do?

Grave stirred and Charlotte shifted her attention to him.

"Are you all right?" she knelt at his side. "How do you feel?"

Propping himself up on his elbows, Grave squinted at his surroundings. "Where are we?"

"Deep in the Bayou," Meg answered. "On the eastern side of Lake Pontchartrain."

"But how did we get here?" Grave sat up, rubbing his eyes. "We were in the Market."

Charlotte swept her gaze over him, searching for any sign of damage, but found none. "You were kidnapped. I followed."

"Kidnapped?" Grave looked at Meg again, his brow

furrowing. "Meg? What are *you* doing here? I thought you stayed in the Floating City."

Meg offered him a tight smile. "I did. But circumstances changed rather quickly, and it became clear that rejoining you was more important than staying in the Temple."

Still frowning, Grave glanced at Charlotte, then asked Meg, "You knew I was kidnapped?"

Rather than answer, Meg leaned down and grabbed Grave's arm. "We need to get back to the city." She pulled him to his feet.

Charlotte groaned. Tramping back to New Orleans through the swamps at night would be perilous and exhausting, and she was already deeply weary from their ordeal.

Gauging Charlotte's expression, Meg said, "It won't take too long. I have a boat tied at the lakeshore."

"Thank Athene."

With a slight grimace, Meg added softly, "Don't thank her yet."

The shallow skiff glided along the still surface of Lake Pontchartrain, propelled by angled fins along the sides of the boat that fluttered through the water. Meg stood in the boat's stern, controlling the vessel's rudder to steer them toward New Orleans. From the time they'd boarded the skiff and tied on the masks that Meg had waiting for them, conversation had ceased and the whole of their journey passed in silence. Charlotte didn't know what Grave was thinking, and Meg's appearance and actions still puzzled her. Tired as she was, Charlotte didn't want to sleep. Remaining alert and observant felt imperative, though she wasn't certain what kept her more on edge: the threat of more assassins, or her lingering questions about Meg and the Temple of Athene.

Clouds rolled in to hide the moon, and it was very dark when they slipped through a small gate near the northeastern corner of the Iron Wall. A guard stood watch at the narrow portal, a tunnel that could only accommodate humble vessels like theirs. As they approached, Meg tossed the guard a bag that jingled of coins when he caught it. He let them pass without question. When they entered the tunnel, Charlotte turned back, wondering about the wordless exchange.

"A smuggler's gate," Meg said quietly. "There are several in the Iron Wall."

"Do the authorities know?" Charlotte asked. Given that New Orleans prided itself on defense and security, these breaches, however small, struck her as anomalous.

"Oh yes," Meg said. "Without smuggling, the city would be bankrupt. Of course, every so often they'll stage a raid or shut down most of the gates for a few weeks. But when they do, the most important smugglers receive notice well in advance so as not to disrupt the necessary flow of coin and commerce. Pull that lever to your right, Lottie."

When Charlotte did, the fins slowed their sweeps and

the skiff emerged from the tunnel to meander along a city canal. Thunder rumbled above them, quiet but menacing. The air was thick, pressing into Charlotte's skin until beads of sweat began to roll down her neck.

"We're staying at *Le Poisson Noir*." Charlotte wiped her brow.

Meg didn't answer, prompting her to ask, "Or are you taking us somewhere else?"

She couldn't see Meg's expression with a mask hiding her face, but she heard Meg sigh. "No. I'll take you to the Black Fish."

Why Meg sounded so reluctant, Charlotte couldn't fathom. Didn't she want to see the others? Hadn't she missed them? Even if Meg had to leave very soon, surely a reunion, however brief, could still be joyful for all of them.

They didn't speak again as Meg steered the skiff through the network of canals, following so many bends and turns that it left Charlotte completely disoriented. Meg kept their small craft in the center of the waterway, never coming close to shore. Beneath the city, sounds of life were present, but muffled. Occasionally Charlotte caught a furtive movement between the dusky silhouettes of buildings.

The Quay was below New Orleans, Linnet had said, so the indistinct shapes on either side of the canal must make up that foreboding part of the city. Meg's efforts to keep them away from the boat landings on either side of the canal indicated that Linnet and Lord Ott's warnings had been earnest.

At last Meg turned the skiff toward a dock.

"Charlotte, take the rudder."

Charlotte stood up and switched places with her.

"Keep us heading for the dock." Meg climbed to the front of the boat, putting the end of a rope in Grave's hands as she passed him. Just before the prow bumped against the wooden pilings, Meg jumped from the boat onto the dock.

"Toss me that line, Grave!"

Meg caught it and towed the skiff alongside the dock, tying the rope onto a squat bollard. "Come on, then."

Grave and Charlotte scrambled from the boat and hurried to catch Meg, who had already taken off down the dock. Meg moved swiftly and quietly, not even acknowledging the pair when they fell into place behind her. A drop of water hit Charlotte's shoulder, then another. She looked up, but the crisscross of metalwork that held the city above blocked out the sky. Charlotte turned and saw tiny circles blooming on the surface of the canal after each raindrop crashed into the water. Soon the circles overlapped and the canal resembled a roiling cauldron. Thunder boomed in the distance.

Meg took them to a ladder that blended so well with the brass, iron, and steel surrounding it that Charlotte didn't notice it was there until Meg began to climb. Charlotte gestured Grave past to follow Meg, then she climbed after him. At the top of the ladder Meg searched among the pipes, bars, and bolts until she found a lever. When she turned it, a hatch popped open and the storm from which they'd had some shelter came down unchecked. The rungs became slick and Charlotte's foot slipped several times, forcing her to catch herself and cling tightly to the ladder as she climbed the rest of the distance to the hatch. As soon as she was in his reach, Grave caught Charlotte beneath her shoulders and hauled her out.

Between the rain and the dim light, Charlotte couldn't discern their location. She was sitting atop a metal grating that ran a narrow length between two buildings. Grave helped Charlotte to her feet and Meg closed the hatch.

"Where are we?" Charlotte asked. The mask offered some protection from the rain, but not enough to stop rivulets of water from sneaking beneath the fabric to roll down her face.

"The Domicile," Meg said.

Charlotte glanced around, bothered that she didn't at all recognize her surroundings.

"We're in a corridor behind the Black Fish," Meg offered. "We can use the servants' entrance and stairs to get to your rooms. I'd like to avoid the foyer."

Meg's explanation took the edge off Charlotte's mood. The face that the Domicile offered the world had been crafted and embellished in ways that would please the senses. This hidden side was severely utilitarian; a place necessary and useful, but not meant to be seen. It was also a relief to know that since they'd emerged from the canals so close to the inn, they wouldn't have to be out long in the rain.

The servants' door opened into the scullery. They passed through to the kitchen and, given the lack of bustle and noise, Charlotte surmised it was still late into the night rather than the early morning hours when this part of the inn would be abuzz with preparations for breakfast. To reach the upper floor they ascended a steep and narrow staircase, and exited the spare passage to be welcomed by the finely appointed hall into which the guest rooms opened.

Charlotte unlocked the door to their suite as quietly as she could manage. The three of them stole inside and found the sitting room dark and empty. Charlotte sank onto a sofa and took off her mask, weary to her very bones. Grave sat beside her, but Meg leaned over to whisper in Charlotte's ear.

"I'm going back to the kitchen to make up a poultice for your wound. I won't be long."

When Meg had gone, Charlotte let her head loll back against the velvet upholstery. Grave remained upright, his hands resting on his knees.

"Grave." Charlotte looked at him. "Do you ever get tired?"

Grave considered her question, then said, "No. I don't think I do."

"But you sleep?"

He shook his head. "I close my eyes and wait when everyone else sleeps, but I'm always awake."

When Charlotte didn't say anything, Grave asked, "Does that trouble you?"

"I don't know," Charlotte answered honestly. "It's very strange, but there isn't any reason that you not needing to sleep should be bad."

He is neither good nor evil. He simply is.

Grave had been created through a heretofore unheard of mixture of mechanics and magic. It could be the machine, a system of perpetual motion at work within him, that rendered him tireless. Or it could be the magic that freed his body from the physical tolls life exacted. And there wasn't a way to know. At least, not one that Charlotte deemed feasible. Hackett Bromley could be questioned about his work, but he had been taken into custody. He couldn't be reached. Grave didn't know his own makeup, and opening up his flesh to see how he'd been put together was a horrifying proposition. It was even more horrifying because Charlotte was certain there were those in the Empire and in the Resistance who would rationalize that act.

The more entangled Charlotte became with Grave's strange existence, the more it became clear he needed to be kept safe. And not just from the Order of Arachne. That someone with inhuman strength and ceaseless energy required protection struck Charlotte as counterintuitive, but it was nonetheless true. Perhaps she wasn't the ideal person to take charge of Grave's well-being, but Charlotte believed the task was her responsibility.

The door opened and Meg slipped into the room. She carried a small bowl and a steaming towel, and fresh strips of cloth were tucked into her belt. Grave moved from the sofa to a chair so Meg could sit beside Charlotte. After she'd removed the temporary binding from Charlotte's arm, Meg pressed the towel against her wound. Charlotte drew a sharp breath. The towel was scalding hot.

"I'm sorry," Meg murmured. "It has to be cleansed before I apply the poultice."

Charlotte nodded. "It's fine."

When Meg was satisfied that Charlotte's torn flesh was sufficiently clean, she picked up the bowl. It was filled with a green paste with an acrid scent that made Charlotte's eyes water. With careful strokes, Meg applied the mixture to the four parallel gashes in Charlotte's arm. The paste was warm on her skin, and while even a light touch on her tender flesh was painful, the mixture itself didn't aggravate the wound. Charlotte remained still when Meg secured the poultice with bandages—at least until the suite door banged open and a rain-drenched man masked as a falcon stood framed by the doorway. Even with his face covered, Charlotte knew it was Jack who gazed at her, his eyes livid.

"Where in Hades did you go?" he demanded, tearing the mask from his face. "I've been looking for you for hours!"

Charlotte tried to jump up, but Meg caught her in a firm grip so she could finish binding Charlotte's wound.

"It's not your business where I choose to go," Charlotte told Jack, hating that she had to lift her face and look up at him from where she sat. "You had no reason to be looking for me."

"No reason?" Jack slammed his fist on the door frame. "The hell I didn't."

One of the bedroom doors opened and a bleary-eyed Pip peered out at them. "What's going on?"

"Go back to sleep, Pip," Charlotte said. "This is nothing you should worry about."

Pip nodded drowsily and closed the door.

While Meg had been focused on bandaging Charlotte's arm, she was angled away from Jack. She hadn't bothered to remove her mask when she returned to the suite, but she did now and turned to face him.

"There are better ways to tell Charlotte you were worried than to yell at her," Meg said.

Charlotte would never have guessed soft-spoken words could sound so menacing.

Jack took a few steps into the room, staring at Meg in disbelief. His brow knit when he assessed her clothing.

"What is . . . when did you . . . where . . . does Ash know?" Jack's anger had dissolved into bewilderment.

Meg laughed quietly. "All fair questions. I'll let Charlotte fill you in on the first few. As for Ash—"

She stopped because Ashley, the top of his face hidden by a mask of silver fish scales, had appeared in the doorway with Coe at his side. Ash stomped into the room, looking as hell-bent on scolding Charlotte as Jack had.

"I take it this ruckus means you found—" Ash jerked to a halt when he saw Meg. He fell silent for several seconds before he managed to whisper, "Athene's mercy, are you really here?"

Meg didn't reply. She didn't move, nor did she take her eyes off Ash.

Charlotte would have sworn that no one in the room was breathing. Even the deluge outside seemed muffled by the tension.

Without making a sound, Ashley was suddenly across the room gathering Meg in his arms. Meg started to say something, but Ash covered her mouth with a kiss.

Charlotte did jump up then, sidestepping quickly from the couple's embrace—which gave no indication of ending anytime soon. Of course Charlotte had known that her brother loved Meg, but it was quite another to witness Ash, always so reserved, utterly undone by passion.

Coe quietly stepped into the room and moved to Charlotte's side. "What happened to you? Was there trouble?"

It was all too much. Grave's abduction, the words of the conjurer, the assassins' attack, Meg's reappearance—the world was hurling shocks at Charlotte so often it felt as if she were dodging lightning strikes. She needed to breathe, to gather her thoughts. Ignoring Coe's expectant gaze, Charlotte retrieved her mask from the side table and went for the door without looking back.

18.

CHARLOTTE TIED ON her mask as she retraced her path down the servants' stair and out the back door. The storm had gone from sullen to furious. What had been pellets of rain now lashed through the air in sheets, accompanied by rumbles of thunder. Lightning webbed through the sky, flashing white against the impenetrable gray.

She didn't hesitate before plunging into the rainstorm. Within moments her already damp clothes were sodden. She hoped that her bandages could withstand this drenching. The excess of water poured off the roofs of buildings in spontaneous waterfalls before disappearing into the grates. Charlotte turned from the back corridor, rounding the side of the inn. She paused at the edge of the main walkway. Quite sensibly, no one shared Charlotte's proclivity for outings in a thunderstorm. The Domicile appeared deserted, its walkways empty.

Water sloshed in the corridor behind her at regular intervals, signaling footfalls of someone quickly approaching. Charlotte moved her hand to her dagger's hilt, flinching at the sharp pain caused by the movement. She cursed her luck for letting an injury befall her striking arm. She knew that spot would stay sore a long while.

When the heavy footsteps drew too close, Charlotte whirled around with her dagger held low and ready.

"I know you're cross with me, Charlotte." Jack had covered his face with the falcon mask, but Charlotte heard the smile in his voice. "But I'd rather you didn't stab me with that."

"I'm sure I can find something else to stab you with, then." Charlotte sheathed her dagger and turned away from Jack.

He came around to stand in front of her. "Where are you going?"

Charlotte didn't answer. She hoped that if she ignored him long enough, he'd get tired of standing in the rain and leave. And while she was ignoring him, she would also convince herself that she did in fact *want* him to give up.

"How badly are you hurt?" Jack reached for her arm, but she jerked back.

"Meg tended the wound," Charlotte said. "I'll be fine."

"Are you in pain?" he asked. He moved toward her again.

Charlotte backed up, but found herself pinned between Jack and the side of the building. "I'm fine, Jack."

"Charlotte, what happened to you?" Jack's piercing gaze was enhanced by the falcon, making her feel as if there was no way to escape it. "You and Grave were gone for hours. And now Meg is here? And what was she wearing? Did she *use* those swords?"

Dozens of answers crowded Charlotte's mind. Reproofs, explanations, apologies, dismissals, excuses, tirades all presented themselves, waiting to be selected. Charlotte didn't know what to say. Meg's arrival wasn't something to be happy about—Meg had made that clear enough. And Charlotte was certain all that Meg had told her about the Temple and the Order of Arachne was intended to be kept secret. Charlotte didn't know whether she could tell Jack the truth. She didn't know what she could tell him at all.

"You'll have to ask Meg."

Jack pulled off his mask and gave a low snarl of frustration. "Don't do this."

"Don't do what?" Charlotte began to edge along the building, toward the corridor at its rear. She was reassessing her decision to leave the suite. Meg wanted them to leave New Orleans.

Just the three of them.

As far as Charlotte knew, Ash and Jack had no role

in Meg's plan, and until Meg said explicitly otherwise, Charlotte wasn't going to give away any secrets.

"Don't try to push me away by pretending you're angry." Jack moved with Charlotte as she slid along the wall.

"I am angry!" Charlotte snapped, without even thinking about her reply.

"No you're not." Jack was infuriatingly calm.

Charlotte stopped her retreat, ready to offer Jack an elaborate description of all the ways she was furious with him. But she was already exhausted and refused to waste any more of her time bickering with him.

"Just leave me alone." Charlotte looked at her feet. "Leave me alone, Jack."

"That's not possible." Jack's voice had become quiet. Then his fingertips were under her chin, tilting her face up, forcing her to meet his eyes.

Charlotte heard footsteps coming up behind them. "I believe Charlotte asked you to leave."

Coe's face was soaked with rain and his eyes narrowed with fury.

"That's enough, Coe." Charlotte stepped between the two brothers. "I'm tired of enduring your petty spats."

"Petty?" Coe righteous anger dissolved.

"Spats?" Jack's expression was one of bewilderment.

"Yes on both counts," she continued. "Jack, I meant it when I told you to leave me alone. I shouldn't need Coe to threaten you for that to happen."

Jack blanched. He swiped rain from his face and cast a

furious look at Coe, but said to Charlotte, "Far be it from me to deny your wish."

He turned his back on her and walked into the rainstorm, disappearing behind the next building.

Coe chuckled. "Well done, Charlotte. I don't think I've ever seen that expression on his face. You taught him quite the lesson."

The rain on Coe's face amplified the sound when Charlotte's palm struck his cheek.

"You have no right to speak about Jack that way," she said, her voice shaking with rage. "You always talk as though you're superior to him, more noble, more worthy. But you're a manipulative liar!"

"What are you talking about?" Coe asked, startled, but beneath his surprise Charlotte could see outrage at the insults she'd thrown at him.

"I heard you speaking to my mother about Grave," Charlotte told him. "I know you're planning to mold all of my actions to your liking."

Coe's jaw twitched with anger, but he kept his voice steady. "You don't know what you're talking about, Charlotte. What's happening here is much bigger, and much more important, than you or Grave. This is about winning the war. This could change everything."

"For the war?" Charlotte snapped. "For the Resistance? Listening to you and my mother, I don't know what any of that means. You want to use Grave to make the perfect soldiers, but you have no idea what that truly entails. You won't be able to re-create Bromley's invention, and even if you could, you shouldn't. You'd be endangering us all."

"What do you mean we don't know what this truly entails?" Coe asked.

Charlotte silently cursed herself for saying too much.

"You know something," Coe continued. "Where were you? Who did you see?"

When she didn't answer, Coe said, "It would be unwise for you to keep secrets from me, Charlotte. Believe me when I say I have your best interests in mind."

"I have nothing else to say to you."

Coe leaned close, whispering in her ear. "You're a capable and talented girl; the Resistance needs you. I need you. Think carefully about what you want for your future, Charlotte; you want to give up everything you've been raised to fight for?"

She refused to acknowledge him.

Coe straightened and said, "We'll speak more of this tomorrow."

When he'd gone, Charlotte leaned against the wall, feeling as though the weight of Coe's chastisement and Jack's anger were crushing her chest.

"Isn't love wonderful?" Linnet's voice pierced the shadows, and a moment later the girl appeared, cloaked and hooded against the rain.

"How long have you been listening?" Charlotte asked. She didn't know whether to be relieved she could share the burden of her fights with the Winter brothers or if she was simply mortified that they'd been witnessed.

Linnet shrugged. "It doesn't matter. I'm here on official business."

"What sort of business?" Charlotte frowned at her.

Linnet nodded. "Lord Ott sent me. He's had some news and a bit of a fright. Did you know he abhors spiders?" Her glance flitted over Charlotte's bandaged arm.

"Spiders." Charlotte stepped toward Linnet, curious about how much she already knew regarding the Order of Arachne.

"I see from your expression you aren't fond of them either."

"Definitely not," Charlotte answered. When Linnet didn't say anything else, Charlotte said, "Aren't you taking me to meet him?"

"Of course I am," Linnet replied.

"Then why are we still standing here?"

"I'm waiting for you to be sensible and get a cloak," Linnet said. "You do know it's raining. Don't you?"

19.

LINNET NOT ONLY sent Charlotte back to the inn to get a cloak, but also suggested she take the time to trade her rain-soaked garb for dry clothes. While Linnet waited at the servants' entrance, Charlotte climbed the stairs and entered the suite.

Meg was alone in the sitting room, and when Charlotte drew near, she saw that Meg's eyes were red-rimmed, still bearing the sheen of tears.

Where is Ashley?

"Oh, Meg." Charlotte sat on the sofa and took Meg's hand.

Meg sighed and gave her a wan smile.

"What happened?"

"I hope that there will be a time when I can tell you

everything, Lottie." Meg withdrew her fingers from Charlotte's. "It would be such a gift to unburden my heart. But now is not that time."

"Where's Grave?" Charlotte asked, suffering a pang of guilt at having abandoned him when she'd fled the suite.

"Sleeping." Meg gestured to one of the closed bedroom doors.

He doesn't sleep. Charlotte held her tongue, still cautious with regard to how much she revealed about him. *But he's observant enough to go through the motions of seeking rest at the appropriate times.*

The thought of sleep reminded Charlotte of how hollow she felt for lack of it.

Reading her expression, Meg said, "You should get some rest, too. It's been a difficult night."

"It has," Charlotte replied, straightening and pushing her exhaustion aside. "But I can't sleep yet."

"What do you mean?" Meg frowned at her.

"I'm going to see Lord Ott," Charlotte said. "And you're coming with me."

A short while later, a much-drier Charlotte rejoined Linnet. Linnet's face registered surprise when Charlotte appeared with Meg at her side, but Linnet didn't object to or inquire about Meg's presence, and they left the inn without further delay. The storm had diminished, hard rain giving way to a misty veil. The city began to stir despite the absence of a morning sun to urge residents from their beds. They left the Domicile, crossing the bridge to the Market. A few merchants passed the three women, carts laden with canvas-covered wares, muttering complaints about the damp that clung to everything.

Linnet led them past the crossing where Charlotte's mother had taken her to the Sintians' Warehouse. Most of the stores on the main walkway were still shuttered, though a few buildings showed signs of people stirring within, and a handful of proprietors were taking their morning tea in their doorways or on their porches, while casting sour looks at the gloomy sky. A tall silhouette loomed up through the mist, an archway with curling sides that met at a high point to hold up a fleur-de-lis.

"Is that gold?" Charlotte asked, when the gilt shade of the archway became clear.

"Would the entryway to the Salon be sculpted of anything else?" Linnet replied with a snicker. "It's excessive. And that's just the bridge."

The golden trellis ran the length of the bridge between the Market and the Salon. On a clear day its gleam probably appeared to be in competition with the sun's rays. When they reached the other side of the bridge, Linnet's declaration that the Salon's design favored excess was brutally apparent. One of the most glaring differences between New Orleans' most exclusive district and the others was the space between the buildings. In the Domicile and Market quadrants, the structures were separated by narrow corridors, but broad swaths, each as wide as the main walkway, separated the grand habitations of the Salon.

Elegant porches wrapped around the ground floor of each building, and each porch was topped with a balcony. The *Poisson Noir* had its own balcony, of course, but any similarity ended there. The wrought-iron fish that decorated that inn's railing couldn't compete with the gold, silver, and copper sculptures that ringed balconies in the Salon. Neither were these railings static. Here, Charlotte thought, was the first place in New Orleans that she found reminiscent of the Floating City. Flocks of silver birds with copper wings fluttered from end to end of one balcony; automatons in the likeness of musketeers fenced at the center of another. One building's railing rose and fell in waves that crested and crashed down. For all its intricacy it actually made the Salon unpleasantly noisy, as if all the embellishments competed for attention.

Linnet looked Charlotte. "What do you think of it?"

Charlotte watched a dog chase a cat that chased a mouse around the corner of a balcony. "It's not as pleasant as I would have imagined."

"It's not without purpose," Linnet said, though she sounded as if she resented that admission. "The constant show of this place keeps people from noticing many of the important things that go on."

They walked among the grand homes with their gardens—some living, others mechanical—and fountains.

More activity, and not just that of the décor, was taking place here than there had been in the other two districts. Servants were tending the gardens, sweeping porches, running in and out of the rear entrances to complete whatever tasks needed doing before the lords and ladies of the houses left their velvet-draped beds.

Linnet led them to a building washed in pale blue. Flowers of hammered metal sprouted along the porch and roses bloomed and closed on the balcony's railing.

"*La Belle Fleur*," Linnet said.

"Is Lord Ott deigning to let us pass through the doors of his fine hotel?" Charlotte muttered.

She hadn't been looking for an answer, but Linnet replied, "He didn't want to go out in the rain."

"Lord Ott has never struck me as that delicate of a creature," Meg said. "Have I misjudged him?"

"No," Linnet told her. "I've seen him wade into a swamp with muck that rose to his chest, laughing the whole time. But he's in a foul mood this morning."

For the first time, Charlotte felt a pang of nerves in anticipation of meeting Lord Ott. He'd always been jovial and kind to her, but given his profession, he must have had more intimidating aspects to his person. Charlotte didn't know that she wanted to see them.

The lobby of the hotel offered a pleasant aural contrast to the tinny chorus outside. A harp stood amid overstuffed chairs and chaises, playing itself.

A man dressed in a peach silk waistcoat and pantaloons, wearing a black cat mask, met Linnet in the center of the room. "You're expected. He's having breakfast in the parlor."

Linnet nodded and continued through the lobby. Double glass doors gave them entrance to the parlor. When they were inside, Linnet closed the doors and locked them; then she pulled heavy violet drapes that cut off the view to the lobby.

Lord Ott sat at a small table carved of ivory. His breakfast covered most of its surface. The silver covers to his platters lay discarded on the floor, and steam rose from poached duck eggs, stewed tomatoes with herbs, fat sausages, and thick-cut bacon. Charlotte's stomach rumbled so loudly she clapped her hand to her abdomen.

"I'm not sharing." Ott didn't look up. He forked a tomato into his mouth. "Take off your masks so we can have an honest conversation."

They took off their masks, and Linnet brought chairs to the table. Ott grunted when they sat down.

"I am vexed, Miss Marshall," Ott said. He picked up a porcelain cup filled with coffee and looked at Charlotte. "Do you know how much I dislike being vexed?"

"Don't waste your time scolding her," Linnet said. "Whatever consequences you're dealing with now, you must know Charlotte didn't intend to cause them."

Charlotte decided it best to be forthcoming rather than wait for Ott to demand information.

"Linnet mentioned spiders," Charlotte told Ott. "So you know about the Order of Arachne."

Ott brushed crumbs from his beard. "Know about the Order? Yes. But knowing about them and having to deal with them are very different matters. I do not want to deal with the Order of Arachne, Charlotte. Do you know how often they're sent out on missions?"

Charlotte wondered how many things Ott planned to ask her about which he knew that she understood little, if not nothing.

"Never!" Ott traded his coffee for a slice of bacon. "Almost never. What have you been keeping from me? Because the Sisters don't release their black widows without serious provocation."

Meg had been silent up to that point, but she answered, "Charlotte, you should tell him about Grave."

Ott lifted his bushy eyebrows at her. "Your mother told me you'd be mixed up in this. She's holding me responsible for keeping you out of harm. If she knew that you're running around the bayous with swords, she might be a bit more reasonable about the limitations of my work."

"I can take care of myself," Meg said coolly.

"You know Madam Jedda?" Charlotte blurted.

"Don't you know that I know everyone?" Ott stabbed a sausage.

"You don't know about Grave," Meg told him. "And that's what matters."

"Grave," Ott spoke as he chewed, "the odd boy. The sick one."

"He isn't sick," Meg leaned forward, leveling a hard gaze at him. "He's dead."

Ott dropped his fork.

"Meg!" Charlotte snapped. "That's not—you know that he—"

"I was just getting Lord Ott's attention," Meg told her. "He needs to stop being cross and start listening."

"You have my attention." Ott pushed his chair back from the table.

"Charlotte?" Linnet was looking at her with a curious but puzzled expression. "What do you have to tell us?"

Charlotte folded her hands in her lap, took a breath, and told them everything.

When she'd finished, Charlotte was so tired she thought she might drop off to sleep in her chair. Reciting all that had taken place since she'd first found Grave in the forest had resurrected all the emotions she'd experienced along the way.

Lord Ott stood up. He went to an ebony cabinet and took out a crystal decanter. When he returned to the table he poured a healthy measure from the decanter into his coffee.

"Well." Ott slurped his drink, then set it down again. "That was not what I expected."

Charlotte glanced at Linnet, but her friend's expression was unreadable.

"I don't think Grave's existence is anything anyone expected," Meg said. "Ever."

"But now he's the most valuable commodity on the continent." Ott scratched his beard. "Possibly in the world."

"He is not a commodity," Charlotte said, but she couldn't muster any outrage. She was simply too tired.

Ott laughed. "My dear girl, everyone and everything is a commodity. That is the real world. My world."

Charlotte's mouth turned down in a sullen expression, but she didn't reply.

"We need to get Grave out of the city," Meg said. "He must be taken away. I'll find somewhere to keep him hidden until we can learn more about him."

Charlotte cast a sharp glance at Meg. She still didn't know what Meg thought Grave's fate should be. At times Meg seemed like she wanted to protect him, but there were moments, like this one, when Meg spoke about Grave as a threat.

"Hmmm." Ott folded his hands atop his generous belly. "I'm afraid I disagree with you there, Meg. And not just because I don't want to cross swords with your mother."

Meg's eyes narrowed.

"Caroline Marshall has the right of it," Ott continued. "If Grave is in the world, then the best place for him to be is here, with the Resistance. Any attempt to take him elsewhere could, and likely will, fail. It's too great a risk."

"The Resistance can't protect him from the Temple," Meg argued. "They have the ability to infiltrate any organization. They will get to Grave."

"I may not like the Order of Arachne," Ott shot back, "but I'm not afraid of them. No one—not even the black widows—will infiltrate the Resistance without my knowledge. The Resistance might not be able to protect Grave. But I can."

"Your hubris is foolish." Meg stood up, furious.

"Just because you've dressed up like a warrior doesn't mean you're capable of single-handedly taking the boy to some imagined sanctuary," Ott said.

Charlotte didn't think Ott would have maintained that opinion if he'd seen Meg in the bayou.

Meg laughed harshly. "You have no idea, old man. Leave us be."

"There will be no leaving." Ott's tone grew imperious. "None of you are permitted to exit New Orleans. The officers of the Resistance have issued that order. When I first learned of it I didn't understand why, but now that I do I tell you without reservation that I will help them to enforce it."

"You've made yourself clear, Lord Ott." Meg retrieved her mask and put it on. "We'll see ourselves out."

Ott didn't object, but when Charlotte stood, he said, "My dear Charlotte, don't be impetuous in this matter. Remember the danger you've already been put in. We still don't know who targeted you, but I'm certain that it is connected to this matter with Grave."

All Charlotte could do was nod.

She tied on her mask and went after Meg, finding her on the path outside the hotel.

"That was unfortunate," Meg told Charlotte. "I was hoping Lord Ott would be the way we gained passage from the city. It will take time to find another way. And I don't know if we have that time."

Charlotte was beyond tired, and Meg's words filled her with a sense of defeat.

Meg put her arm around Charlotte's shoulder. "No matter. We'll find a way."

They were halfway to the bridge when Linnet caught up with them.

"Does Ott have another warning for us?" Meg asked.

"I'm not here on Ott's behalf," Linnet said. "I want to help you. He's wrong about Grave."

Charlotte frowned behind her mask. "What do you mean?"

"I can get you out of the city," Linnet said. "As soon as you need, if you give me a day to make the arrangements."

"Your contacts are Ott's contacts." Meg's skepticism was apparent. "And your friendship with Charlotte makes you the most obvious means for tracking our movements."

"If you knew me the way Charlotte does," Linnet snapped, "you wouldn't suggest such a thing."

Meg looked at Charlotte.

"She's right," Charlotte said. "I trust Linnet. If she says she can help us, she can and she will."

"What about the Resistance?" Meg asked Linnet. "You have no qualms about working against them."

"I work for Ott, not the Resistance," Linnet answered.

"And most of the time I think the Resistance has worthy aims, but if they don't, I won't follow them blindly. And sometimes Ott gets it wrong. I choose my assignments, and I have contacts other than his."

"Very well," Meg said. "How are you going to get us out of the city?"

Linnet might have been wearing a mask, but Charlotte could tell she was smiling.

20.

HAVING ENDURED PROFUSE warnings from Lord Ott, Linnet, and Coe, Charlotte regarded her first true venture into the Quay with keen interest tempered by fear. She knew how to fight—she'd proven as much in the Iron Forest, when she and Coe were set upon by an unsavory lot of brigands. Charlotte had bested her attacker without any aid. But the confidence she drew from that victory had suffered due to the incident in the Garden of Mirrors and her poisoning on the *Calypso*. Charlotte knew that, had Linnet not played the savior that night—and both Linnet and Coe on the second occasion—her own life would likely have been forfeit.

Cloaked and bearing no lanterns, the pair of girls left behind the pleasant glitter of the city's faceted crystal street lamps. Darkness swallowed them more quickly than Charlotte expected. As they descended, the air thickened to the point that it seemed to cling to her skin and weigh heavy in her lungs. Fetid odors of sodden vegetation and brackish water welcomed them to the creaking planks of the Quay. Small fishing boats and flat-bottomed skiffs drifted alongside docks that jutted from the walkway. Fishermen on stools hunched over as they mended nets and sharpened hooks. Few bothered to spare a glance at Charlotte and Linnet as they passed the docks.

Weary-looking shacks that reeked of fish guts stood opposite the docks, but farther into the Quay those rickety structures retreated, replaced by storefronts—all shuttered at this late hour—mostly fishmongers, with a few purveyors of "oddities" speckled throughout. The shops brought with them some reprieve from the darkness, though the lamps of the Quay offered only murky yellow-green light that suggested the lamps had been shaded with translucent skins from an unlucky snake or alligator.

A short way ahead, Charlotte made out a different sort of light. Bright orange and jumping with the life of well-fed flames, whatever building featured this vivid beacon drew more attention than any other part of the Quay. The structure's dimensions emerged from the mist, revealing that, unlike its peers, this building rose to the height of two stories. When they neared the flames, Charlotte saw sconced torches framing a sign, giving name to the place, or rather identity. A single word had been carved into the wood square that hung above a narrow, iron-girded door: *Taverne.*

"Follow me," Linnet told Charlotte in a low tone. "And don't speak to anyone. Not even . . . no, especially if they call out to you."

Charlotte nodded. She tried to remain at ease though her heartbeat became uneven.

Linnet opened the door, startling Charlotte with a flood of light and sound. The tavern was clad in polished oak. Its furniture seemed to be in much better repair than Charlotte would have expected. A cheery fire danced in a large hearth; the flames sparked and crackled as fat dripped from a pig roasting on a spit.

Compared to the quiet of the night, the boisterous patrons who crowded around the tables filled the place with a clamor of shouts and laughter. To Charlotte's immediate left, a staircase gave access to a balcony that encircled the tavern's main room. Closed doors on the upper floor led Charlotte to conclude that rooms could be had in this place, as well as board.

A bar stood at the back of the room, barrels stacked behind it. A woman as stout as the kegs over which she held dominion passed to and from the bar as loud calls from the tables signaled new rounds of ale would be bought. A wiry boy scuttled between tables, collecting used tankards and taking armfuls through a swinging door largely hidden by the hulking stacks of barrels.

As discreetly as she could, Charlotte assessed the bustle of tavern-goers. Mostly men, they were more grizzled than the denizens of the city above. Their clothes reflected function, not fashion, with shirts sometimes threadbare and breeches often patched. Their masks kept faces hidden, but had little to no ornamentation. When they spoke, their words were laced with oaths of a fouler nature than Charlotte had ever heard. Her ears grew hot when several of those lewd shouts addressed the newly-arrived pair of ladies.

Linnet pushed her hood back. The ebony wings of her raven's mask wrapped from her cheeks to the nape of her neck. Charlotte wore a simple but sweet nightingale with soft brown feathers that reached from both sides of her nose to curve beneath her jaw. She could feel eyes following their progress from the front to the back of the tavern; even so, the carousing mood of the room did not wane.

The barmaid ignored Linnet and Charlotte when they passed her and continued through the swinging door. Their route brought them into a kitchen crowded into a too-tight room. A squinty-eyed, sweating cook wielded a large wooden spoon and shouted at the scrawny boy, who dropped tankards into a steaming vat. Neither paid the girls any mind. Rid of his burden, the boy bolted out of the kitchen, taking care to keep out of the swinging spoon's reach.

Linnet walked on, taking them down a set of stone steps and into a cellar. The cool subterranean air was a relief after the kitchen, and the cellar smelled of earth and root vegetables. When they reached a cupboard stocked with bottles of rum, Linnet ducked behind it with Charlotte at her heels. The cupboard hid a short passageway hewn from the stone, its path built of wooden planks. At the end of the passage there was a door.

To Charlotte it looked a quite plain door, wooden and sturdy but not out of place in a cellar—despite its being hidden. Looking more closely, she noticed something amiss. The door had no lock, nor did it have a handle. Charlotte stepped closer and lifted her hands to give the door a little push.

With a small cry, Linnet grabbed Charlotte around the waist and hauled her back with such force both girls toppled over.

"What was that?" Charlotte got to her feet, irked at Linnet's inexplicable attack.

Still sitting on the wood path, Linnet laid a cool gaze on Charlotte. "When we're in a place like this, you don't do anything unless I tell you to."

"Ugh," Charlotte replied. "I'm not—"

She never finished her complaint, because Linnet pulled a dagger out of her boot and hurled it at the door. The blade buried itself in the door with a solid thunk and what had appeared to be sturdy planks in front of the door dropped open. Charlotte stared, throat going dry, as the trapdoor hung open for another minute. The clack and whine of turning gears accompanied the planks' slow return to their original, deceptively benign, place.

"No unwelcome guests in the Cove." Linnet hopped up and went to the door while Charlotte tried to stop her hands from shaking.

Linnet turned to look at her. "Bravery is all well and good, but sometimes it's much better to be cautious."

She drew a large iron key from her coat pocket and fit it into a crevice in the stone to the right of the door.

Again the sound of gears moving, and the door swung inward. Linnet stepped through.

"Don't dawdle," she said to Charlotte, who was still having trouble convincing her legs to move.

Though she had to hold her breath while doing so, Charlotte hurried across the traitorous planks to join Linnet. When the raven-masked girl freed her dagger from the door, the planks dropped open again and Charlotte swore, pressing her back against the solid stone wall.

"Don't be too hard on yourself, kitten," Linnet said, coaxing Charlotte toward another set of stairs. "I should have thought to warn you, given your proclivity for daring deeds."

Charlotte laughed; it was a tight, nervous sound, but nonetheless it relieved some of her tension.

"Shall we?" Linnet offered her arm, and Charlotte was relieved to take it as they descended the stairs.

The stone walls went from cool to slick and damp. Moss crept through cracks in the molding and steady drips appeared here and there until they reached yet another door.

Linnet gave Charlotte's hand a squeeze before extricating herself from their linked arms. "Don't worry. This one isn't rigged with a trap."

"Welcome to the Cove," Linnet said, and opened the door.

As far as Charlotte could tell, candles offered the only light in this subterranean tavern. Small flames sprang from the tallow stubs, which flickered and swayed at the behest of drafts that seeped into the room. The close air smelled of tobacco and rum, and tasted of salt and brine.

Just beyond the door, a thick-bodied man sat on a barrel like a stool. He wasted no time sizing up Charlotte and Linnet. The doorman had a long, curving nose decorated with gold rings. When he opened his mouth to speak, Charlotte glimpsed a deep maw shielded by very few teeth.

"Masks." The man nodded at the wall behind him. It was covered with hooks, many obscured by the riot of masks that dangled from them.

Charlotte balked, but Linnet began to untie the ribbon at the back of her head with no sign of hesitation. Puzzled, Charlotte loosened the knot that kept her mask snug against her face. She placed her nightingale on the hook beside Linnet's raven.

From her vantage point, Charlotte could make out little more of the room. She saw only dark shapes within the play of light and shadow. Linnet put her hand on Charlotte's shoulder. "Let your eyes adjust to the shadows. We'll make our way into this hovel soon enough."

"Why don't they have proper lights?" Charlotte whispered through her teeth.

"Because the patrons of this establishment don't fancy being seen," Linnet answered. "Masks aren't allowed. Given the types of deals made here, you want to be sure you're meeting with the right person. But that doesn't mean these scalawags don't prefer to hide their faces in the shadows as much as possible."

As Charlotte's gaze slowly tracked the outline of the room, she noted it had the shape of a sphere halved, and the ceiling didn't appear to be man-made, but alike to a natural cave. What had been inky blobs and apparitions gained curves and angles. The hooded and cloaked figures seated at the handful of wooden tables had heads bent in hushed conversations, broken only by the occasional, startling, coarse laugh. The sweat beading at the nape of Charlotte's neck felt cold as she realized that despite the outward appearance of disinterest, they were being watched. Slitted eyes swept over the pair of girls, weighing the threat or worth of their arrival in a glance. Thinking it would intimate that she was not to be trifled with, Charlotte slid her hand from her waist toward the holster at her thigh.

Linnet's nails dug into Charlotte's skin, making her gasp.

"If you so much as touch a weapon, the entire room will draw on you before you can blink." Linnet's voice was a low growl in Charlotte's ear.

Taking care not to move too quickly, Charlotte let her

hand rest at her side. Noting a subtle shift in the room, a loosening of tension, Charlotte had no doubts Linnet spoke the truth.

"Sorry," Charlotte murmured.

"If you want to take on a room full of smugglers and assassins, kitten, far be it from me to stop you." Linnet laughed quietly. "But maybe you should wait until we don't need a favor from them. Come on, then. Try not to look any of these lot directly in the eye."

Charlotte kept her focus on Linnet's back as they moved forward. Linnet had to be searching the tavern for her contact, but Charlotte marveled at the way the other girl walked assuredly through the dim space, giving no sign that she was looking for someone.

Yet another trick she'll have to teach me.

Linnet changed direction, heading to a table tucked against the damp stone wall. Without hesitation, she slid into the chair opposite the table's lone occupant, leaving the chair nearest the stranger to Charlotte.

Charlotte risked sparing Linnet a reproachful glance before taking her seat. Linnet wore an unreadable expression as she stared across the table.

From the stranger's size, Charlotte guessed he was a man. His low voice confirmed her suspicion a moment later.

"You're wise to put a body between us, *ma chérie*," he said to Linnet. A hat with a broad, slouching brim shadowed most of his face; the sharp cut of his jaw and a crescent-shaped scar at the left corner of his mouth were the sole features Charlotte could make out. "After you lifted that cargo off me last spring, I owe you a knife in the belly."

"It's nice to see you, too." Linnet rested her hands on the table, presumably to show she wasn't bearing a weapon. Charlotte did the same, all the while wishing she could draw a gun and hold it in her lap.

The stranger smiled and his scar retreated like a dimple, softening the angles of his face. He lifted his chin toward Charlotte.

"Who's your friend?" he asked. "As I recall, you're not one for partners."

"This is Charlotte," Linnet replied, ignoring his other observation. "Charlotte, meet Jean-Baptiste Lachance. Though you're more likely to hear about his exploits as Captain *Sang d'Acier*."

Charlotte kept her voice low and steady. "Pleased to make your acquaintance."

In truth, Charlotte wasn't sure how she felt about someone known as Steel Blood. Especially when he'd just mentioned a desire to stab Linnet.

Lachance lifted his hand, extending three fingers. The barkeep nodded and soon enough, three stout cups arrived at their table.

"Your message intrigued me enough to show up," he said, lifting his glass in a toast before having a swallow. "Care to elaborate on the job?"

Linnet's fingers encircled her cup, but she didn't drink.

Charlotte eyed her own cup with indecision. She didn't want to appear rude—or even worse, weak-blooded—in this company, but she had no idea what the brimming liquid was. She did know that it was strong. Her nose was nowhere near the stuff and yet its fumes suffused her every breath. Charlotte looked at Linnet again, deciding that she needn't drink so long as Linnet did not.

Linnet kept a hard gaze on Lachance. "The job is transport, plain and simple. I didn't think it would pose a challenge to you, but then I could be wrong."

"Transport is never plain and simple," Lachance said. "At least not for someone reckless enough to want a place on my ship. Anyone wishing for such a journey will be more trouble than I'd like."

Ignoring Lachance's comment, Linnet said, "Four passengers. Myself, Charlotte, and two friends. All I ask is that you take us safely to the southerly capes of the Carolinas. We won't cause any trouble."

Lachance leaned back in his chair, tipping the brim of his hat just enough for Charlotte to catch the glint of his eyes in the candlelight. He didn't take his focus off Linnet.

"Because you never bring trouble."

"I can find another ship." Linnet lifted her cup and took a long swallow.

Charlotte eyed her drink, not convinced she should do the same.

That smile again, this time with teeth. "You will not find another ship. You want mine."

Linnet returned his smile, but hers gave nothing away.

They sat in silence, neither breaking their gaze. Charlotte forced herself to be still, despite how much the tension building at their table made her want to squirm.

At last, Lachance said, "And what will you give me in return for safe passage?"

"What do you want?" Linnet asked, then abruptly bit her lip. In the space of a breath she'd regained her dispassionate expression, but not before Lachance caught her misstep.

He laughed softly, leaning forward to rest one arm on the table. His other hand reached for Linnet's arm. He pulled her hand away from her cup, turning her wrist over and lightly running his fingers over the veins he found there. Charlotte watched with amazement, and then alarm, when Linnet didn't rebuff the pirate.

"You know better than to ask that, *ma sirène*," Lachance murmured.

Something he'd said triggered outrage in Linnet. She knocked his hand away.

"No. Don't you dare."

He straightened, then removed his hat. "As you wish."

Linnet stiffened, fury building in her expression.

Charlotte gripped her cup so tightly that her hands slipped, making some of her drink slosh onto the table. Neither Linnet nor Lachance took notice, as they were utterly fixated on each other.

Though few words had been exchanged, Charlotte suddenly had answers to a flurry of questions that spun in her mind. Something about Linnet had changed because of Lachance's presence. Whatever had shifted in her intensified when the pirate took off his hat, letting the candle's glow illuminate his face.

Charlotte thought of Jack and Coe Winter as handsome men; she still did. Jean-Baptiste Lachance was something else altogether. He'd emanated strength and confidence from the moment they'd joined him at the table, but now that she could truly see him, Charlotte could only describe the pirate's visage as unearthly.

He was much younger than Charlotte had expected from his tone; he couldn't have been more than five years older than she and Linnet. His hair was caught back in the common style, but it could well have been spun gold brushing the tops of his shoulder blades. Charlotte had taken note of Lachance's strong jawline, but the rest of his features proved no less striking. High cheekbones, a chiseled nose. Skin bronzed by the sun. His eyes were dark, but in brief flickers of the candlelight Charlotte saw irises blue as a storm-ridden sea.

Linnet's lips parted and she drew a sharp breath. Lachance tilted his head, watching her. When she didn't speak, he said, "Silence, Linnet? That's unlike you."

"Your terms," Linnet answered, voice stony.

With a wry smile, Lachance folded his arms across his chest, resuming his lazy pose in the chair. "Guaranteed purchase at market price, plus five percent from Ott, for all my goods through the next winter."

"You know he'd never make that deal." Linnet's hands disappeared beneath the table. Charlotte feared her friend was reaching for a dagger.

Lachance shrugged. "He's not here. You are."

"I'll do my best to convince him," Linnet said. She put a few coins on the table along with a scrap of paper. "For your next round. We'll bid you good night."

Lachance drained his cup and said, "I'm not finished."

Linnet's shoulders were set in such a way that Charlotte held her breath, waiting for the other girl to strike. Rather than a deadly thrust, Linnet offered a question.

"What else could there be?" Her words emerged as a whisper laced with poison, but Lachance continued to smile at her.

"You still have a debt to settle with me. Or have you forgotten?"

Linnet went very still, watching Lachance in silence.

When she finally spoke, it was in a whisper. "You're a scoundrel."

"I'm not called a pirate without reason," Lachance replied.

"This is when we need to leave," she told him, and slid the paper and coins across the table.

Lachance took the note, not bothering to read it before slipping it into his pocket. "Would you like to join me for another round? You've certainly just paid for more than one drink. And I've not been given the opportunity to converse with your friend."

For the first time since their conversation began, Lachance looked at Charlotte. She found it terribly difficult to meet his gaze.

Linnet didn't answer him, but rose from her seat, and with a glance indicated that Charlotte was to do the same.

"You know you must tell me that you agree to my terms." Lachance's words stopped Linnet from walking away, but she kept her face turned from him.

"I hate you."

Linnet spoke so softly, Charlotte couldn't believe her words reached him. But somehow they did.

"I know, *ma sirène*," he said quietly. "But you still must say it."

Looking over her shoulder, Linnet said, "We are agreed."

To Charlotte, it sounded as though Linnet had just made a deal with the devil himself.

21.

LINNET HADN'T SPOKEN since they parted ways with Jean-Baptiste Lachance. As they retraced their steps through the Quay, Charlotte threw darting glances at her friend, waiting for Linnet to say something. Anything.

Charlotte cleared her throat. "When are we leaving?"

"An hour before dawn," Linnet replied.

Silence built between them again until Charlotte couldn't bear it.

"Who is he, Linnet?" Charlotte asked.

"You know who he is." Linnet's voice was flat. "He's a pirate."

"No." Charlotte stopped and Linnet looked over her shoulder. "Who is he to you?"

"The Quay isn't a place to linger," Linnet said. She kept walking.

Charlotte didn't follow. She waited, listening to water lap against the docks. Linnet had almost reached the stairs when she stopped, pivoted, and stared at her. Charlotte stared back.

Linnet's hands balled into fists as she walked back to her. "Do you have to be so stubborn?"

"I think I do," Charlotte said. She was far more nervous than she sounded. Charlotte had come to value her friendship with Linnet deeply, and didn't want to put it at risk. At the same time she sensed that it was important for her to know what Linnet was withholding.

With a huff, Linnet said, "Fine. But we're walking to the Black Fish, not standing here like fools."

They set off again, and Charlotte stayed quiet.

"You saw him," Linnet said as they began to climb the stairs. "Tell me what you think."

"He's . . ." Charlotte cast a sidelong glance at her friend. "I . . . it's difficult . . . He has a rather . . . magnetic effect . . ."

"Exactly," Linnet growled. "Steel Blood isn't his only nickname."

Charlotte wasn't sure she wanted to know what other names the pirate captain had. "The other nickname is worse?"

"It depends on who you ask," Linnet replied. "They call him Lothario of the Sea."

Considering how attractive Lachance was, Charlotte

didn't find the name that surprising or unsettling. "I imagine he has many admirers."

Linnet laughed. "Admirers, yes. Companions, no. At least not anymore."

"I don't understand," Charlotte said.

They'd reached the Market district and turned in the direction of the Domicile. "A little less than a year ago Lachance made a sort of pronouncement. His days of Dionysian excess had come to an end."

"Why would he do that?"

Linnet paused beside the entrance to the bridge between the Market and the Domicile.

"According to Lachance, he met the woman he wants to marry," Linnet told her. "And until he won her hand, he foreswore all other lovers to prove his fidelity, which in Lachance's mind was an incredible sacrifice. He has a network of contacts that rivals Ott's, and he made certain his intentions and his suffering were known from the mouth of the Mississippi to the Amherst Province."

"Why was he so public about it?" Charlotte asked. "Couldn't he just tell the woman?"

Linnet's smile was like a knife in the dark. "She has a reputation for being difficult and disdainful of men's promises of love. He thought such a grand gesture would soften her heart."

"Did it?" Charlotte's interest had become fascination.

"No." Linnet started onto the bridge. "She has sworn she'll never marry, because marriage is a prison for women."

"So you know her?"

"Yes, kitten, I know her very well," Linnet said. "I am her."

"Linnet!" Charlotte grabbed the other girl's arm. "What do you mean you're her?"

Linnet shook Charlotte's hand off her wrist. "I mean Lachance claims he wants to marry me and he won't stop telling people about it. Spear of Athene, he's infuriating."

She set out at a faster clip.

"But . . ." Charlotte tried to catch Linnet and almost had to run to do it. "Linnet. Merciful Athene. The deal. What did you just agree to?"

Linnet walked even faster.

"Linnet, stop," Charlotte did run then, but only so she could cut Linnet off.

When they stood face to face, Charlotte glared at her. "You did not agree to marry him. Linnet, you can't do that to help me and Grave. It's too much."

Linnet gazed at her. Then she burst into laughter.

Charlotte crossed her arms over her chest, quite put out. "For someone who thinks marriage is a prison, you seem in rather good spirits."

"I'm not going to marry him, Charlotte," Linnet gasped through her laughing. "Of course I'm not."

"Then what are you so angry about?" Charlotte wasn't going to let Linnet avoid further explanation. "And don't try to tell me you're not upset with him. It was obvious that you are."

Linnet reached beneath her mask and wiped tears from the corner of her eyes. "Thank you, kitten. I needed that. And, yes, I'm furious with Lachance. He has a talent for making me furious."

"What did you agree to?" Charlotte asked.

Linnet sobered a bit. "When I first learned about Lachance's idiotic proclamation I tracked him down with the intention of sending him straight to Hades."

"You didn't truly want to kill him?" Charlotte frowned. As tense as their meeting with Lachance had been, Linnet and the pirate seemed to share an understanding of some kind.

"No." Linnet took Charlotte's arm and they walked on at a much gentler pace. "But I wanted him to know that I did not enjoy being wooed via gossip and exaggeration."

"What did he say?" Charlotte glanced at her.

"He said he'd be much happier to woo me privately."

Charlotte kept looking at her.

"Ugh." Linnet elbowed Charlotte in the ribs.

"Ow!"

"That's what you get for thinking I'd give him any sort of quarter," Linnet said. "When I rebuffed his advances he made another offer. He promised to end his pursuit of my hand in exchange for a kiss."

"One kiss?" Charlotte thought that hardly constituted a great demand. "That's all?"

Linnet walked more stiffly. "We're nearly at the inn. Tell Meg and Grave to ready themselves quickly. It's not as though Lachance's ship is docked in the canals. We have a long walk ahead of us."

Charlotte ignored Linnet's change of topic. "Why not just kiss him?"

"We're done talking about that, kitten."

"But—"

"We're done."

"A pirate ship, Linnet?" Meg asked, her voice sharp but quiet.

Charlotte, Meg, and Grave huddled with Linnet outside the servants' entrance to the *Poisson Noir*.

"You need to be smuggled, Meg," Linnet replied. "Pirates are the best smugglers. They'll take us to the Outer Banks. From there we'll travel to the Spanish. I have contacts on the coastal islands that can provide a hideout. The Empire pays little attention to the isles, and Ott doesn't know about my connection to the place."

"Very well," Meg said. "But first we have to leave the city. I don't believe Ott was making empty threats this morning. He'll have people following us."

"I'm certain he will," Linnet answered. "But Lachance is notoriously secretive about the locations he weighs anchor. We're the only ones who will be provided means to reach the ship."

Meg nodded her approval.

"If you're ready?" Linnet waited for any other concerns. When none came, she led them into the night.

Their escape route began in the Garden district. Moonlight gleamed pale off the broad leaves of hanging vines, and the air was redolent with jasmine. They passed gurgling fountains and sculpted hedges. A waterfall that tumbled over boulders until calming into a long reflecting pool had been constructed against the outer wall, and it was to this feature Linnet guided them. As they approached the tall stack of rough rock, two figures emerged from behind the waterfall. Linnet went to them, and after the exchange of a few hushed words, one of the men waved for them to follow him, while the other stood guard.

Charlotte stayed close to Grave as they squeezed through an opening in the rock. Since their return from the bayou, Grave had been calm, and when Charlotte told him all that had transpired and suggested that they leave New Orleans, he'd agreed without hesitation.

Does he have any fears or worries? Does he trust me so completely? Will he just as easily give his trust to someone else, someone who might use it for ill?

The gears, wheels, and pumps powering the waterfall banged around them as they skulked through the interior of the structure toward a large pipe. The pirate tossed his mask to the ground before he moved on, as did Linnet. Charlotte was happy enough to leave her mask behind. She'd grown weary of not being able to read expressions or gauge reactions. And sometimes the masks made her skin itch.

The tube was similar to that between the Sintians'

Warehouse and the Daedalus Tower, only much less accommodating. To fit meant crawling on all fours in complete darkness, which made it seem like they made no progress at all.

Charlotte felt like she'd been crawling for an hour when she saw firelight gleaming beyond the pipe. The pirate at the head of their group disappeared, then Linnet, who was just behind him. When Charlotte reached the end of the pipe, her heart stuttered. There was no more ground in front of her. Only a tangle of pipes and tubes suspended in a giant cavern.

"Charlotte!" Linnet's whisper drew Charlotte's gaze down.

Linnet and the pirate stood on a narrow platform below the pipe.

"Grab the rope." Linnet pointed to a thick rope that dangled to Charlotte's right.

Charlotte took hold of the rope and swung her body out of the pipe. Her weight caused the rope to lower until her feet hovered just above the platform. She released the rope, landing lightly. While Grave and Meg followed Linnet's instruction, Charlotte looked out from the platform.

Once again she was inside the Iron Wall, but unlike the repurposed Daedalus Tower, this was the true interior of the wall, filled with the pumps, filters, pipes, gears, and wheels that kept the city running. And unlike the Tower, the hollow space here wasn't limited to three stories. Charlotte peered down into dark waters a long, long way down.

As she searched for a safe means of descent, which she wasn't finding, Grave came to stand beside her.

"Is something wrong?"

Charlotte couldn't answer; she could only continue to seek a ladder or stair concealed in the metalworks while her heart pounded.

"I'm certain it's safe," Grave told Charlotte, who'd failed to answer his question.

Charlotte half turned to ask how he knew what she was looking for, when Linnet leapt from the platform. Charlotte almost screamed before she saw the harness buckled around Linnet's shoulders. Linnet sailed from pipe to pipe, belaying her way to the bottom of the wall. She disappeared from sight, but a minute later the harness came reeling up to the platform. Charlotte felt wooden when the pirate pushed the harness toward her.

"Wait a moment."

More than happy to let Meg go first, Charlotte took the harness and turned to hand it over.

But Meg was talking to Grave. "You see the way down."

Grave looked over the platform edge. He nodded.

"Does it pose a threat to you?" Meg asked him. "Does it make you afraid?"

Grave's brow furrowed, but he studied the drop and its web of metal before answering. "No."

Exasperated, Charlotte shook the harness at Meg. "I don't know what this is about, but we shouldn't keep Linnet waiting."

"Hush, Charlotte." The snap in Meg's voice silenced Charlotte at once, and stung more than a little.

But Meg's attention had already returned to the pale boy. "Then why are you waiting?"

Grave tilted his head, regarding Meg with curiosity. He nodded again. Then he turned and jumped off the platform. Charlotte shrieked, reaching out to catch him . . . as if such a thing were possible. He landed atop a pipe ten feet below without even a single quiver of his muscles. He leapt again. In two bounds, Grave was halfway down the wall.

"By the mighty forge," Charlotte breathed.

"I do not bear him ill will, Lottie."

Charlotte startled at Meg's words. Meg knelt at the edge of the platform, watching Grave's descent.

"I need you to trust me," Meg said. There was a kindness in her eyes that Charlotte found familiar. The soft expression, so rare since Meg had returned from the temple, made Charlotte's heart pinch. "I ask things of Grave only to understand him better. We must know who he is. Our ignorance will not keep him safe."

Though Charlotte's pride resisted it, she let go of her indignation. "I suppose we must."

Meg's answering smile was shadowed by sadness, and Charlotte saw for a moment that the sense of things lost, innocence, comfort, trust, cut her friend to the quick as much as it did herself.

A whoosh sounded nearby and Charlotte yelped in surprise when Grave landed on the balls of his feet, balancing easily as he stood above the girls.

"My apologies," he said to her. "That was very rude of me."

He dipped down and picked Charlotte up, before pivoting and jumping over the edge once more.

If Charlotte had been able to draw breath, she would have screamed until her lungs burst into flame. Instead she hung on to Grave's neck in silent terror as he carried her from pipe to pipe, his feet touching the metal cylinders so briefly it was as if he flew. Charlotte's limbs were trembling when he set her down on a ledge beside Linnet. A small boat was moored nearby, bobbing in the dark water.

Meg landed on the ledge soon after, having buckled herself into the harness to make the descent. She sent the harness back up to the pirate, and Charlotte wanted to knock her into the water. It didn't matter what she wanted, however, because she couldn't seem to move.

When Charlotte felt certain her legs wouldn't give out, she cast a worried glance at the descending pirate, who would soon join them. She garnered nothing from his expression when he landed, though Charlotte couldn't determine if that lack of response to Grave's unusual talents was due to the seaman's apathy, or the shaggy ginger-and-gray beard that hid most of his face. Apparently it would not be masks alone that kept Charlotte from reading a person's expression.

Linnet displayed a similar disinterest in Charlotte's unorthodox arrival at the bottom of the wall.

"Get aboard the boat, Grave," Linnet said. "We'll cast off soon enough."

Grave moved to the boat and Linnet grabbed Charlotte's elbow, drawing her aside.

"Did you know he could do that?" Linnet asked, her whisper sharp as a blade. "You should know that I do not like surprises."

"I didn't know." Charlotte was still too shaken to be aggravated by Linnet's harsh tone.

Linnet sighed, but the look she gave Charlotte showed sympathy. "I take that to mean there are likely other things he can do that you don't know about either."

"Likely, indeed." Charlotte didn't want to be this weary at the start of what was surely to be a long, arduous journey. But the ever-present reminder of Grave's latent abilities, any of which could be summoned up without warning, made her want to bend over from strain and exhaustion, like she would have when hauling around a sack of parts from the Heap.

Grave's skills and strengths, even if unexpected, should be assets to their cause. Yet the ever-increasing unknowns surrounding Grave chafed Charlotte, and clearly presented an obstacle to Linnet as well.

"Such sorrowful casts to such lovely faces," Meg said quietly. "Is not our imminent escape cause for rejoicing?"

"If I wasn't concerned with wasting time, I'd knock you senseless," Linnet snarled at her. "This is not the time for demonstrating your little pet's newest tricks."

Charlotte had to bite her tongue so she wouldn't laugh aloud. Where Charlotte, even when angry, felt twinges of guilt for harboring resentment toward Meg, Linnet's threat had given voice to all of Charlotte's building frustration.

Meg answered in a placid tone. "He's no one's pet. I know as little as you do, or anyone else for that matter. Yet I seem to be the only one who wants to find out more about Grave's true nature."

"Linnet has a point," Charlotte said, coming to Linnet's defense. "We're not alone. What if that pirate spreads news of what Grave just did?"

Meg didn't answer, but Linnet sighed.

"As much as I appreciate your support, kitten," Linnet said to Charlotte, "you needn't worry about *Sang d'Acier*'s men. Any waggling tongue is like to be cut out, and they all know it. Our payment is as much for silence as transport."

Linnet returned her hard gaze to Meg. "That truth doesn't excuse the foolhardiness of your game."

"It's not a game," Meg replied. "And the sooner the both of you realize that, the better off our cause will be. It pains me that I must remind you we're fighting for the same side."

Meg's words carried the weight of the exhaustion Charlotte had been feeling. Even so, that awareness didn't altogether reassure her that Meg brought only goodwill toward Grave.

When it became clear that neither Charlotte nor Linnet intended to respond to Meg's admonition, she shrugged and climbed aboard the boat to sit beside Grave.

Linnet uttered a tiny growl of disapproval, but gave Charlotte a gentle push toward the boat. "Let's go. And don't hesitate to nap on the way. You don't have to do any rowing. And, dear kitten, you look exhausted."

22.

AT FIRST, CHARLOTTE thought it was keening seagulls that woke her. But then she heard the bark of angry voices and scuffle of feet from somewhere not far off.

She sat up, blinking at the bright sunlight that spilled in through a porthole nearby. The seagulls' cries came in with the sun's rays and salt air.

Charlotte was sitting in a double bed, tucked into an alcove to the side of the room. The bedclothes were luxuriant, silky and as fine as any she'd seen.

"Ah, she wakes."

The rich male voice sent shivers down Charlotte's spine. The speaker was seated in a high-backed chair, his booted feet resting on a table. Charlotte relaxed when she saw Linnet sitting in another chair nearby.

"Welcome to my ship, the *Perseus*," Lachance said to Charlotte. He swung his feet down and strode to the bedside. Dropping to one knee, he lifted Charlotte's hand to his lips.

"When I saw you asleep I insisted that you must not be disturbed," Lachance told her. He was still holding her hand. "My cabin is far more comfortable than the quarters belowdeck."

Comfortable was a poor description of *Sang d'Acier*'s private quarters. The cabin walls were paneled in gleaming mahogany; one featured recessed bookshelves packed with leather-bound volumes, while another was home to an assortment of weapons—sabers, poignards, rapiers, longswords, muskets, pistols, and a few things Charlotte couldn't name. A simple but finely crafted writing desk sat in one corner, a jewel-encrusted globe in another. Lachance had an obvious talent for piracy.

"Leave her alone," Linnet muttered. "Don't you ever get tired of hearing yourself talk like that?"

"Talk like what?" Lachance dropped Charlotte's hand and flashed a smile at Linnet.

Linnet, however, appeared unaffected. She gave him a flat look and stood up.

"How are you, kitten?" she asked Charlotte. "I'm sorry if waking in a strange place gave you a fright, but it was obvious you needed the rest."

"No, I—" Charlotte scrambled from the bed, putting a fair distance between herself and the pirate captain. "I'm fine. Where are Meg and Grave?"

"They're sleeping belowdeck," Linnet replied with a pointed look at Lachance. "Where *we'll* be from now on."

"You wound me, *ma sirène*," Lachance sighed.

"Trust me," Linnet smiled at him. "When I actually wound you, you'll know."

Lachance laughed. "I have missed you."

"Give it time."

The shouts outside the cabin had grown louder, and Lachance began to frown.

"This sounds like more than bickering between sailors." He donned his hat. "Excuse my sudden absence, mesdemoiselles."

When he'd gone, Linnet pinched the bridge of her nose and groaned. "You might have to throw me overboard at some point."

"Linnet," Charlotte began, knowing she was about to cross into dangerous territory. "Do you really . . . does he not . . ."

Linnet's hands were on her hips. "Just spit it out."

"He's so . . . alluring. He could be Aphrodite's consort," Charlotte blurted. She could feel her cheeks reddening. "I have no interest in Lachance, but he's beguiling . . . by Athene, Linnet, don't make me keep talking about this!"

"You started it," Linnet replied.

"I just want to understand," Charlotte muttered.

Linnet didn't reply, and when Charlotte looked at her friend she was startled by what she saw. Linnet had turned her gaze toward the tall and broad windows that framed the rear of the cabin. Her eyes were soft, but her expression was strained, even fearful.

"I do feel it, Charlotte." Linnet's words were so soft, Charlotte wasn't even sure she'd truly spoken. "But—"

The cabin door banged open and Lachance strolled in. Two sailors came behind him, dragging a limp figure between them.

"My men would like to keelhaul this one." Lachance stepped aside, and the sailors dropped their captive on the floor. "I'm inclined to let them. Though I wouldn't give the order without some regret. He's managed what I believed impossible. I've never had a stowaway."

Charlotte stared at the unwelcome passenger with alarm. Was he one of Ott's men? Had he sent a message back to the city of their whereabouts before they'd set sail?

"It's not like you to hesitate, Lachance," Linnet said. "Why now?"

"He claims to know you." Lachance shrugged.

The stowaway coughed, wiping blood from his lip before he pushed himself onto his knees.

"Oh no." Linnet's face clouded with disbelief. "No. No. No."

Charlotte thought her heart had stopped. "Jack?"

Lachance watched them with interest. "You do know him, then? What a puzzle this is."

"What are you doing here?" Linnet snarled. "And how did you find us?"

"I can still put him on a hook and use him to fish, *ma sirène*," Lachance remarked. "He is your adversary?"

"He is my brother." Linnet made it sound like the latter was worse.

That admission startled even Lachance into silence.

Charlotte managed to recover from her shock and rushed to Jack's side. The sailors grumbled when she began to interrogate their prisoner without asking their leave.

"Athene's helm, Jack. What madness possessed you to board a pirate ship?"

"I could ask you the same." Jack turned his face to her. His lip was bleeding and swollen, but he'd managed to avoid a black eye.

"Jack." Linnet's voice lashed at him. "How did you find us?"

"I followed you to the Quay," Jack said. He pointed at Lachance. "I saw you meet with him, and then I followed him."

"You impersonated one of my sailors," Lachance said. "If you killed him when you took his clothes, your life belongs to me."

Charlotte waited for Linnet to object, but she didn't.

"I didn't kill him," Jack told Lachance. "I knocked him out. It was dark enough that I could keep my head down and go unnoticed by the others. When we got to the ship I hid for as long as I could."

"Why did you follow us?" Linnet asked. Some of the

edge had gone out of her voice, but she still looked unhappy.

"When you came looking for Charlotte. I knew something was wrong," Jack answered. "Then Coe told me that Charlotte had been confined to the city, but he wouldn't tell me what had led the officers to make that decision. I was going to ask Charlotte, but Coe kept stalling me in the Tower."

"He just wanted to keep you away from her," Linnet murmured.

Jack grimaced. "I know."

"But how did you follow us to the Quay?" Charlotte asked. "We were in masks."

"I got to the Black Fish and saw you leaving through the back." Jack cleared his throat, obviously a bit uncomfortable. "As far as the masks go . . . they didn't matter. I recognize the way you walk."

Lachance chuckled, and Linnet shot him a dark look.

"Did you tell anyone where you were going?" Linnet asked Jack. "Anyone at all?"

"No." Jack got to his feet. The sailors who'd brought him in moved to restrain him, but Lachance waved them off.

"Go back to your posts."

The two men obeyed their captain, but not before spewing French at Jack that couldn't have been complimentary.

Charlotte stood close to Jack, worried that he might be hiding some injury she hadn't been able to detect.

"You don't have to worry about anyone knowing where I'd gone," Jack said to Linnet. "When I saw you at the tavern, meeting with Lachance, I had no choice but to follow him if I wanted to find out where you were going. With his reputation, I knew your aim was to be secreted out of the city."

"Why didn't you just tell me you knew?" Charlotte asked. "You could have come back to the inn that night and asked to join us."

Jack smiled at his sister. "She never would have allowed it."

Linnet shrugged. "You're right."

"So you decided to stow away on a pirate ship?" Charlotte glared at him. "Why would you do something so foolish?"

"Why can't you understand that I'd sooner spend my life in the Crucible than let anything happen to you?"

It took Charlotte several breaths before she could ask. "You . . . why would you say that?"

"Because it's the truth."

"The mystery is solved, then. The true culprit here is but love." Lachance walked behind Linnet, resting his hands on her shoulders. "*Ma sirène, son frère* is now a guest on my ship. What would you have me do with him?"

"I'd still be happy to throw him overboard, but Charlotte is rather attached to Jack and I'm quite fond of Charlotte." Linnet's mouth curved with delight. "The only thing to do is put him to work. As long as you think your men won't kill him."

Jack's punishment exiled him from the main deck to the galley.

"He will never love a potato again," Lachance declared, and Linnet fell into gales of laughter.

Charlotte had thought to go with Jack, but Linnet forbade her. It would be no punishment, Linnet insisted, if Jack had Charlotte nearby to distract him.

Instead, Charlotte went to check on Meg and Grave, both of whom preferred to stay in the small cabin allotted to them. Meg, like Charlotte, was in dire need of sleep. Grave, however, surprised Charlotte with his reason for staying below.

"I don't like the sea."

"Does the rolling of the ship make you feel ill?" Charlotte asked him.

"The ship is fine. It is a fine ship." Grave climbed into the bunk above Meg's. "But the sea has no end and no beginning. I do not like it."

Charlotte gave up trying to make sense of Grave's aversion to the sea, but she chose not to remain in the cabin with them. Unlike Grave, Charlotte was captivated by the sea. She'd never seen so many varieties of blue. Not even on the clearest summer days of her memories had there been a shade to rival this vivid array of hues. With every swell the sea changed, turquoise to teal; waves shrugged indigo shoulders only to stretch wide arms of midnight. Charlotte sipped the air, which matched the sea's exotic character. The briny bite of the Atlantic had been subtled to a smooth saltiness kissed by a sweet green flavor that Charlotte couldn't place.

Linnet joined Charlotte at the rail. "I adore being at sea."

"It's beautiful." The waves rocked the ship like a cradle, lulling Charlotte into a peaceful mood.

Linnet turned around, resting her elbows atop the rail. "Mind you, today is a fine day to sail. When the sea is angry, she's cruel. I've seen ships torn to pieces by storms."

"You've seen that without being shipwrecked yourself?" Charlotte asked.

"Lachance is an exceptional captain." Linnet glanced toward the captain's cabin. "But don't ever tell him I said that."

Charlotte returned Linnet's broad smile.

High above the billowing sails, a bell began to clang. Its shrill peals carried on without pause.

Linnet pushed off the rail. "That's an alarm. Another ship's been sighted."

"What kind of ship?" Charlotte chased after Linnet, who darted toward the prow.

Lachance stood at the center of the prow in his full regalia: a long, deep blue coat with silver buttons over his white shirt and hat atop his head. Just shy of the bowsprit a sailor turned a large crank, raising an enormous brass contraption. Its bulbous shape tapered toward the ship, ending in a narrow slot that the sailor peered through. He flipped switches and pulled levers that sprouted from the device.

"What is that?" Charlotte asked Linnet.

"It's called a Fortune Teller," Linnet answered. "Meg's mother would not approve."

The sailor began to shout. Lachance called back to him and when the sailor answered, the captain drew a brass tube from the base of the ship's wheel.

Lachance's voice boomed in the air and his crew exploded into action. The pirates raced to various stations along the ship; some scaled the masts, others disappeared belowdeck. After giving further orders to the sailor operating the Fortune Teller, Lachance came to Linnet. His face was terribly grim.

"Tell me," Linnet said.

"A Titan," Lachance told her. "And two Hermes frigates."

"A Cerberus patrol?" Linnet spat and began to swear.

"We can outrun the Titan," Lachance said. "But the frigates we'll have to fight, at least long enough to hobble them."

Linnet nodded, her jaw tightening. Lachance bent and brushed his lips across her forehead. When Linnet didn't object, Charlotte began to be truly frightened.

"Come on." Linnet took Charlotte's hand, drawing her

away from the prow to the midship rail.

The ship shuddered, making Charlotte stumble, and there was a deafening boom.

"Did something hit us?" Charlotte asked.

"No. We fired at them." Linnet looked out from the rail. She pointed starboard of the prow. "Look there."

A trail of smoke floated in the air between the ship and three shapes in the distance. Charlotte saw a bright flash, but nothing else.

"They're still too far out," Linnet murmured.

The three shapes were quickly drawing closer, becoming more distinct. One of the three was twice the size of the other two.

"I know the ships," Charlotte said to Linnet. "But you called them something else."

"A Cerberus patrol," Linnet replied. "A three-ship configuration the Empire favors. One for power, two for speed."

The *Perseus* shuddered again. This time Charlotte covered her ears before the boom.

Linnet followed the arc of the shot, but Charlotte kept her eyes on the enemy ships. She could see their features now. The frigates were lean vessels with sharply cut sails. The Titan lumbered through the sea, its sides pocked with broadside guns. There was another flash, but this time a second flash followed the first, then a third. A joyful roar went up from the crew.

"We hit one of the frigates," Linnet said with relief.

One of the smaller ships began to lag behind; wide columns of smoke rose above it. The Titan and the second frigate continued to bear down on the *Perseus*.

"Be sure to always hang on to the rail," Linnet told Charlotte. "Lachance tends to be unpredictable in these situations."

"What do you mean?" Charlotte asked.

She got her answer a moment later when the *Perseus* lurched violently to port and she lost her footing and fell to the deck. Charlotte climbed to her feet and hugged the rail.

The Titan had turned as well, mirroring the *Perseus* so the two ships knifed through the waves on parallel courses. The frigate continued its pursuit, driving straight at them.

Charlotte's eyes flew from the massive warship to the nimble attacker. She was afraid to look away from either of them, as if her gaze could ward off any harm they might do. As she watched the frigate gain on the *Perseus*, a strange whistling pierced the air.

Beside Charlotte, Linnet whispered, "No."

Charlotte tracked her friend's focus to a cannonball hurtling into the air above the Titan.

The projectile soared, arcing high, but heading toward the waves rather than the *Perseus*. Sunlight illuminated the metal of the falling object, flashing copper, gold, and silver. Just before it hit the sea, the sphere began to break apart; what appeared to be its casing fell into the waves in pieces, and then the strange cannonball disappeared beneath the surface.

The gun must have misfired, Charlotte thought. *What else could have resulted in such a terrible shot?*

She was about to say as much to Linnet. Linnet, however, drew a hissing breath, then began to swear.

"What's wrong?" Charlotte asked.

Linnet pounded her fist on the rail and shouted toward the stern. "Jean!"

The captain ceased shouting orders, turning to Linnet.

"The starboard side!" Linnet pointed at the spot where the cannonball had sunk. "The Titan just launched a Charybdis globe!"

"What?!" Lachance abandoned his post, leaping over the rail from the deck above to land beside her. "You must be mistaken."

"I'm not." Linnet shoved him toward the rail. "Look!"

Charlotte looked to the sea between their ship and the approaching frigate; within the deep blue swells, something stirred. From below came a great bubble that pooled onto the surface in a smooth, still circle between the waves. The stillness only lasted a moment before the ocean seemed to turn against itself, giving birth to new swells and currents that clashed, creating strange and violent patterns. The sea frothed and surged until a great spout of water shot toward the sky.

"They're mad." Lachance glared at the churning

waters. "That frigate is lost. They've sacrificed her and all aboard—their own sailors. Why?"

"And what about us?" Linnet asked. "Are we lost as well?"

Lachance touched Linnet's cheek, then pushed away from the rail. "Perhaps not. You should get below."

"I *am not* going below," Linnet snarled. "You should know better than to suggest that I would."

"At least stay away from the mast," Lachance shot back at her. "And by Athene, put a harness on."

Lachance shoved off the railing and ran up the deck, barking orders at his crew.

"Come on!" Linnet grabbed Charlotte, tugging her toward the ship's stern.

"What about the others?" Charlotte asked. "They're still in the cabin. And Jack's in the galley."

"They're likely safest if they stay put." Linnet stopped and crouched down, opening a compartment in the deck. "If you want, you can go to them."

"No." She didn't want to be in the bowels of the ship, blind to what took place above.

"I thought as much." Linnet drew a bundle from the compartment. She handed one to Charlotte and shook the other out. What Charlotte held in her hands resembled a web of leather. She wasn't certain what to do with it until she watched Linnet slide her arms through the largest openings and buckle three straps at her waist. Two long, braided leather cords trailed after Linnet as she walked away, headed back to the railings at the prow. Charlotte hurried after her, shrugging on the harness as she ran. Linnet stopped and fastened the brass clips at the end of the braided cords to metal rings that protruded from the deck near the railing, and gestured to Charlotte to do the same.

When she'd secured herself to the ship, Charlotte's gaze swept the length of the deck, taking in the mad rush of activity around her. Lachance's shouts to his sailors miraculously won out over the roaring wind and pounding waves. The crew had also donned harnesses, though the cords that tethered them to the deck were twice as long, if not more, than those at Charlotte's back. That extra length freed them to cross the deck and climb to the sails. One sailor scrambled up the mainmast, appearing smaller and smaller as he scaled the great column. From what Charlotte could see, it appeared all the men were rapidly altering the rigging on the sails. They tossed lines to one another, installed levers, and turned cranks—all the while wearing faces taut with fear.

Something terrible was about to happen. Something even a crew of hardened sailors thought they might not survive.

Charlotte's thoughts flashed to her friends below. Meg. Grave. Jack.

If the ship goes down, should I be here? Or with them?

A moment later Charlotte knew it was too late for her to do anything but pray for Athene's mercy.

The roaring wind was joined by a new sound, deep and

hollow; its relentless drone pulled her attention from the sailors to the sea.

Linnet was already staring at the sound's source. Her hands gripped the rail, knuckles bloodless and face whiter than the sails, while the wind tore at her hair. She focused on a shadow that lay across the span of water from which the spout had erupted. The dark spot shifted restlessly, expanding outward. A pattern formed within its bounds, currents chasing each other in concentric circles, growing ever wider at its outer rim and ever tighter at its center. Tighter. Tighter. Until the center of the shadow disappeared, swallowed by the sea itself, only to leave a gaping maw in its place. The drone became a howl and Charlotte fell to her knees at the sight of the ravenous maelstrom.

"Charybdis." Linnet knelt beside her and reached for her hand. They laced their fingers together.

Charlotte now understood what Lachance had meant when he said the British had sacrificed their own ship. The Imperial frigate had been bearing straight and hard at the *Perseus*. A swift, small ship, it had been closer to the site where the globe had landed, and now it barreled toward its doom. The crew made a desperate attempt to escape the vortex. The ship swung hard to starboard, turning from the whirlpool. Their efforts were futile. The ship skirted the outer currents of the maelstrom as it fled. At first, the frigate slowed until it ceased to move altogether. Then it began the horrible, inexorable drift backward.

Charybdis claimed the ship, casting it into ever-swifter revolutions. The frigate pitched and rocked. Its mainmast broke first, snapping like a splinter to be swallowed by the dark abyss. The frigate's prow lifted, rising from the whirlpool like a rearing steed. And then Charybdis broke the ship in half. The two halves cracked, splitting into ever-smaller pieces.

Charlotte saw other things amid the wreckage, and she knew some of those things were people. She couldn't discern British sailors from the milieu of destruction, but all was lost. Within seconds the maelstrom had swallowed every part of the ship. No evidence of the frigate remained. Charybdis churned on, howling to be fed again.

Such disregard for human life left Charlotte speechless. Was Grave the sole reason for that vicious act? Did the Empire believe that having lost the living design for the perfect weapon, his destruction was their only course? Would the Resistance reach the same conclusion when they discovered they no longer had Grave in their grasp? Were such drastic, final solutions the logic of war? Could anything good emerge from a society shaped by violence?

"Charlotte!" Jack had emerged from belowdeck. He dashed toward her, faltering when he saw what lay beyond the ship's prow.

Like Charlotte and Linnet, he dropped to his knees. When he spoke, it was Linnet he addressed, though his eyes remained on the whirlpool.

"I heard the sound," Jack said. "But I couldn't believe it."

"It just took an Imperial frigate," Linnet said in a frighteningly empty voice. "You shouldn't be here. Get back below."

"I'd sooner jump into Hephaestus's forge," Jack said, his gaze shifting to Charlotte. "I'm not leaving you."

Linnet made a sound of disgust. "You fool. Lachance will do everything he can to save us, but none of that will matter when you go flying off the deck."

"Here." Charlotte unfastened one of her harness cords from the deck. "Tie this around your waist."

Jack took the cord and glanced at Linnet.

"It *might* hold both of you," Linnet grimaced. "How would I know?"

"It'll do." Jack knotted the leather tight around his torso. "Now how is your pirate going to save us?"

"He is not my pirate," Linnet snapped, though her eyes drifted to the ship's wheel, where Lachance stood. "And you'll thank me for not telling you what I suspect he'll do. You might decide you'd rather try your luck by jumping overboard."

"That's a lovely sentiment." Jack shifted his body toward Charlotte, but he didn't put his arms around her until she leaned into him.

The *Perseus* began to swing to starboard.

Jack's eyes narrowed, then went wide. He stared in horror at Lachance.

"He's steering us *into* the maelstrom!"

"I told you you wouldn't want to know." Linnet's stare had fixed on Lachance as well.

The captain's focus was unwavering as he drove the *Perseus* toward its doom. His jaw clenched from wrestling with the wheel; the ship itself wanted to retreat when its captain forced it ahead.

"Linnet." Jack's arms tightened around Charlotte. "What in Hades is he doing? He's going to kill us."

Linnet didn't answer. She would not look away from Lachance.

Charybdis roared and the *Perseus* bucked as it traversed the outer rim of the whirlpool. Lachance bore down on the wheel, fighting to keep the ship on course. The *Perseus* heaved and rolled to port. Charybdis grasped the ship, flinging it forward. Faster and faster they flew. The wind ripped tears from Charlotte's eyes and the maelstrom whipped the *Perseus* till it ran over the waters at an impossible pace.

A shout rose over the wind's screams and Charybdis's howls. A single word, thrown into the sky by the ship's captain.

"VOLONS!"

The ship's masts split down the center with a mighty groan. The sails divided with the masts. Silver darts shot out from the fallen masts, carrying trails of twisted wire. The darts buried themselves in the far ends of the sails and the sails became stiff, ribbed by the rows of thick ropes of silver.

"Helm of Athene," Jack breathed, his voice full of amazement.

Charlotte, too, was enthralled by the metamorphosis. She gasped as her stomach dropped, not from dread, but because the *Perseus* rose. Charlotte watched as the prow lifted up, pointing at the sun. Wind rushed beneath the sails and the *Perseus* abandoned the sea, soaring into the sky.

ACKNOWLEDGMENTS

THE WRITING OF this book took place during one of the most trying, frightening years of my life. For several months I couldn't write at all and feared I might never be healthy enough to write again. The compassion, encouragement, and tireless support of colleagues, friends, and family carried me through that storm and brought me safely to shore. I'm particularly indebted to the wonderful souls at Penguin Young Readers Group who made such gracious accommodations as I fought a long illness. Thank you especially to the incredible team at Philomel Books, for having faith in me and always offering a deep well of care and kindness. Jill Santopolo deserves all the chocolate on the planet for enduring the unpredictable creation of this book. My wonderful team of agents at

InkWell Management provided counsel and much-needed reassurance. Thank you especially to Charlie Olsen, who helped me take the long view in the face of a difficult present. Friends literally and figuratively stood by me and held my hand when I most needed them. My deepest thanks to Casey Jarrin, David Levithan, Sandy London, Michelle Hodkin, Beth Revis, Jessica Spotswood, Marie Lu, Rachel Noggle, Conor Anderson and Brian Anderson. Eric Otremba helped me understand, endure, and eventually thrive in face of uncertainty. My parents gave love and shelter, shouldering burdens I could not. My brother Garth and his wife, Sharon, are sources of inspiration and great joy. The year of writing this novel was one of the most difficult I've experienced, but suffering is part of life's journey. Two of my greatest supporters lost beloved family members this year and this novel is dedicated to the memory of Richard Pine's mother, Harriette Pine, and Charlie Olsen's father, Charles J. Olsen III.